# A WEE CHRISTMAS HOMICIDE

Books by Kaitlyn Dunnett

KILT DEAD

SCONE COLD DEAD

A WEE CHRISTMAS HOMICIDE

Published by Kensington Publishing Corporation

# A WEE CHRISTMAS HOMICIDE

## KAITLYN DUNNETT

KENSINGTON BOOKS
www.kensingtonbooks.com

KENSINGTON BOOKS are published by

Kensington Publishing Corp.
119 West 40th Street
New York, NY 10018

Copyright © 2009 by Kathy Lynn Emerson

All rights reserved. No part of this book may be reproduced in any form or by any means without the prior written consent of the Publisher, excepting brief quotes used in reviews.

All Kensington titles, imprints and distributed lines are available at special quantity discounts for bulk purchases for sales promotion, premiums, fund-raising, educational or institutional use.

Special book excerpts or customized printings can also be created to fit specific needs. For details, write or phone the office of the Kensington Special Sales Manager: Kensington Publishing Corp., 119 West 40th Street., New York, NY, 10018. Attn. Special Sales Department. Phone: 1-800-221-2647.

Kensington and the K logo Reg. U.S. Pat. & TM Off.

Library of Congress Card Catalog Number: 2009930441

ISBN-13: 978-0-7582-1647-2
ISBN-10: 0-7582-1647-5

First Hardcover Printing: October 2009
10  9  8  7  6  5  4  3  2  1

Printed in the United States of America

# A WEE CHRISTMAS
# HOMICIDE

# Chapter One

anners reading HAVE A JOYOUS YULETIDE, MERRY NOLLAIG BEAG, and HAPPY HOGMANAY decorated the interior of Moosetookalook Scottish Emporium. A box of Yule candles sat next to Liss MacCrimmon's day-by-day calendar on the sales counter. It was open to the current page—Tuesday, the ninth of December.

As Liss wielded a feather duster and rearranged stock, a snippet of an old Christmas carol lodged in her mind and stuck there. *Christmas was coming. The geese were getting fat.* Or at least Liss supposed they were, not being acquainted with any personally. But with sales virtually nonexistent, she had a scant supply of pennies to put in *the poor man's hat.*

Or was it the *old* man's hat?

Liss never could remember the exact lyrics. She wasn't much of a singer, either. Alone in the shop, she contented herself with humming the melody aloud. Even that small musical effort was off-key, but not far enough to silence her.

A glance through the plate-glass display window at the front of the store revealed the same bare, unappealing landscape she'd seen every other time she'd looked. Skeletal branches reached up into an impossibly blue sky, starkly silhouetted against that cloudless backdrop. On the ground, patches of dead, yellow-brown grass alternated with piles of rotting leaves, pummeled by hard rains into shapeless, colorless lumps of vegetation. The vivid hues that had brought tourists flocking to Maine in the fall were only a distant memory.

Bright morning sun made the scene even more depressing. Still no snow. How could it *not* snow in Maine in December?

"Think snow," Liss muttered to herself. "I ought to put *that* on a banner."

People had a right to see the white stuff on the ground by now. Skiers expected to be able to take their first outing of the season during Christmas vacation, if not before. Even more important, the residents of Carrabassett County needed tourists to show up and spend money on lift tickets, lodging, food, and gifts. Without that regular influx of business, everybody suffered, especially the tiny town of Moosetookalook.

With a sigh, Liss turned away from the window. Wishing wouldn't make it snow, not even if she had Aladdin's lamp and a genie at her beck and call. What a pity that neither magic nor science could accurately predict the weather, let alone control it.

After retying the bright red scarf holding her long, dark brown hair away from her face, Liss busied herself straightening the display next to a sign that read KILT-HOSE STUFFERS. To Liss's mind kilt hose—or knee socks, as those not into Scottish-American heritage in a big way would call them—made ideal Christmas stockings. She'd gathered together an eclectic assortment of items that might be tucked into the toe or made to cascade enticingly over the top. There were pennywhistles and small figurines of pipers, refrigerator magnets, and campaign buttons bearing pseudo-Scottish sayings and puns, and the cutest little stuffed bears Liss had ever seen, all dressed up in kilts and plaids and wearing minuscule Balmoral caps. Liss had dubbed the four-inch high toys "Wee Scottish Bears" in the online catalogue she'd set up for the store.

The display table in order, Liss turned next to the tall shelves that held a variety of Scottish imports, everything from tins of Black Bun, the traditional Twelfth Night cake made with fruit, almonds, spices, and whiskey—*lots* of whiskey—to canned haggis. She had no trouble dusting the upper reaches. She stood five-foot-nine in her stocking feet.

Fourteen shopping days till Christmas, Liss thought as she worked. There was time yet to make a profit. If she started opening on Sundays, then it would be sixteen shopping days. She already planned to extend the shop's hours by adding the two Mondays before Christmas. The rest of the year she took that day off to compensate for working Saturdays. Would it be worth the effort, and the expense, to staff the store *seven* days a week?

The loss of her part-time sales clerk, Sherri Willett, had made scheduling more difficult. At the moment, Liss was not only half owner of the Emporium, but the store's only employee. To leave the shop for any reason, she had to lock up and put the CLOSED sign in the window.

Still, the extra hours might pay off. There was always the chance of a stray shopper wandering in. Liss sighed again. She should give it a shot. After all, she'd already calculated expenses down to the last decimal point. It wouldn't cost all that much more to keep the heat at sixty-eight degrees for those extra days.

The raucous jangle of the sleigh bells she'd attached to the door had Liss smiling in anticipation. A customer at last!

Her spirits plummeted when she recognized Gavin Thorne. Like Liss, he owned a store that faced Moosetookalook's town square. Several months earlier he'd bought the building that had once housed Alden's Small Appliance Repair and opened The Toy Box.

"Don't you look the fine Scottish lassie!" Thorne had a

big, booming voice and a smile that showed a great many large white teeth. Both were in marked contrast to a milquetoast appearance.

Liss glanced down at the white peasant blouse and tartan miniskirt she'd selected from the store's stock that morning and was suddenly glad she'd put on wooly dancer's tights beneath the skirt. She did not know Gavin Thorne well, but the last thing she needed was for *another* man to take an interest in her. Juggling the two she already had was hard enough!

"You know the store policy," she quipped. "Model what we sell."

"When am I finally going to meet this aunt of yours?" he asked as he made his way slowly through the shop. He paused to look at several of the displays, including the one of kilt-hose stuffers.

"She's arriving on the nineteenth."

A sudden thought had Liss taking a closer look at Thorne. She saw a lumpy individual with hair the color of dry grass and eyes hidden behind small, round-framed glasses. Liss wasn't sure how old the toy store owner was, but he was surely closer to Aunt Margaret's age—fifty-nine—than her own twenty-eight years. Could Thorne have a *personal* reason for asking about her aunt?

He approached the sales counter with one of the "Wee Scottish Bears" in hand. "These selling well for you?"

"They do okay," Liss fibbed.

She'd sold only one, to Sherri as a present for her young son. She'd expected to sell another to Angie Hogencamp, who owned the bookstore on the other side of the town square and had a small collection of designer teddy bears that her children were not allowed to touch, but Angie had taken one look at the stuffed toys and given a disdainful sniff.

"Maybe they'd do better at my place." Thorne's watery

blue eyes looked straight at Liss, but only for an instant. The speed with which his gaze skittered away from hers set off an alarm of air-raid-siren intensity. "I could take them off your hands if you're willing to sell them to me at dealer discount."

Liss's suspicion that he was trying to pull a fast one hardened into a certainty. The standard discount businesses gave one another didn't leave much room for resale profit. The little bears were cute, but their suggested retail price was only $9.99.

"I don't want to mess up the display." Liss waited, curious to hear what he'd say next.

Thorne fiddled with the bear, smoothing one broad thumb over its tiny kilt and tugging at the itty-bitty hat to make sure it was securely attached. He inspected the minuscule manufacturer's tag, which identified the company that had produced and distributed the toy.

"I don't suppose you have any more of these in your stockroom?" He glanced toward the closed door to the area where Liss processed mail orders and unpacked deliveries. "Some you haven't put out yet."

"A few." In fact, Liss had been so taken with their Scottish regalia that she'd bought an entire case—an even hundred of the little bears.

"Well. Well, that's good then." All sorts of nervous twitches suddenly manifested themselves, from the traditional shuffling of feet and playing with rings to an odd little gesture unique to Thorne—he rubbed his knuckles back and forth over the underside of his chin. "I don't suppose—?"

"No." Liss injected every bit of firmness she could manage into her voice. "The way I see it, you hardly need one more toy in a store that already offers hundreds of selections, whereas these little guys fit in perfectly with the other items the Emporium sells." Liss leaned across the sales counter until she was almost nose to nose with the shorter man. She plucked the stuffed bear out of Thorne's hand and tried to recapture his gaze. "What's this *really* about?"

"Nothing. Not a thing. Just making conversation. Well, gotta go now. Bye." Backpedaling, literally and figuratively, the toy seller beat a hasty retreat.

Something landed on the Emporium's hardwood floor with a soft plop just as the door slammed behind Gavin Thorne. As soon as the sleigh bells had stopped their racket, Liss came out from behind the counter to investigate.

He had dropped a folded section of a newspaper. It had been sticking out of the pocket of his jacket, Liss realized, and had been knocked free when he bumped into the door frame in his rush to get away. She picked it up, glancing at the date. When she saw it was from the previous weekend's Boston paper, she started to toss it into the trash. A headline caught her eye as it fell, and she quickly snatched it out again.

TINY TEDDIES IN SHORT SUPPLY.

Heart rate speeding up as she read, Liss skimmed the article. Then she took a good hard look at the small bear she still held in her other hand.

Liss carried the newspaper to the section of the store her aunt had dubbed the cozy corner. It was furnished with two easy chairs and a coffee table. She settled into the more comfortable of the chairs, curling her legs beneath her. Then she slowly reread every word of the story. There was no mistake. "Tiny Teddies," the proper name for her "Wee Scottish Bears," were the hot gift item this Christmas . . . and they were sold out in much of the U.S. The reporter who'd written the article believed there were no longer any to be had in the six New England states.

"Holy cow," Liss whispered. If this was for real, she was sitting on a gold mine.

*   *   *

Across the town square from Moosetookalook Scottish
Emporium, an imposing red brick building housed the town
office, the public library, the fire department, and the police
station. Sherri Willett, wearing a stiffly starched blue uniform
that sported a shiny new badge above the breast pocket,
was the sole occupant of the three small rooms that com-
prised the latter.

Once she'd caught up on all the outstanding paperwork,
she had nothing in particular to do. In fact, she'd been ordered to do nothing unless someone actually asked her for
help. Jeff Thibodeau, who'd been promoted to chief of police just before Sherri was hired, had explained that the town
budget didn't extend to extra gas money. They were not to
use their one patrol car to go out looking for trouble.

Never good at twiddling her thumbs, Sherri wandered
into the reception area. The police department had never
employed a receptionist. Three full-time officers and a handful of part-timers handled everything. The door straight ahead
of her led, by way of a short hall, to the town office and the
bays for the fire trucks. Another, to her right, opened directly
onto the parking lot at the rear of the building.

Sherri straightened a row of uncomfortable-looking plas-
tic chairs, then wondered why she'd bothered. There was
no other furniture in this outer room. No plants. No magazines. Just a scuffed-up tile floor and a cobweb hanging
undisturbed in one corner of the ceiling.

Retreating back into the office, recognizable as such only
because it contained two battered army-surplus-style desks
and an equally antiquated metal file cabinet, Sherri headed
for the coffeepot. The glass was so streaked and spotted that
it was difficult to tell what color the contents were, but what
landed in Sherri's cup had the consistency of sludge. She
shuddered when she inspected the grounds.

Carrying the whole mess to the communal kitchen down

the hall, she scrubbed the coffeepot and basket, then returned to the P.D. to collect all the mugs and cups scattered about and toss them into the suds. She hoped she wasn't setting a bad precedent. She might be Moosetookalook's only female police officer, but neither making coffee nor cleaning house was part of her job description.

She'd made that very clear to her coworkers when she'd started her last job and there had never been any trouble. Until recently, she'd been a corrections officer, dispatcher, and deputy—the three jobs were all one in rural Carrabassett County. She'd worked at the county jail, appointed by and responsible to the sheriff.

Sometimes she regretted leaving the sheriff's office for the police department, but not when she opened her pay envelope. The town fathers of Moosetookalook might be frugal, but they were nowhere near as miserly as the county commissioners.

While a fresh pot of coffee brewed, Sherri resumed rambling. She stopped on the brink of entering the tiny holding cell in the P.D.'s closet-size third room. It probably *had* been a closet at one time, since it could only be reached through the office.

"What were you planning to do?" she muttered to herself. "Dust?"

Reversing course, she flung herself into the oversize chair behind one of the two desks in the larger room. The seat, which bore the permanent imprint of Jeff Thibodeau's posterior, seemed to swallow her whole.

This was not what she'd expected. Oh, sure, she'd always known police work was 99 percent boredom and 1 percent sheer panic, but—

The shrill ring of the phone at her elbow startled her so badly that she let out a small squeak of alarm. Embarrassed, she cleared her throat as she reached for the receiver and put all the authority she could muster into her voice.

"Moosetookalook Police Department. Officer Willett speaking."

Ten minutes later, Sherri strolled into Moosetookalook Scottish Emporium. Although Liss hadn't made a lick of sense on the phone, Sherri was relatively certain there was no crime in progress at the shop. Curiosity, rather than concern for her friend's safety, had convinced her to forward all incoming calls to the P.D. to her cell phone and venture out on "foot patrol."

It took another ten minutes for Liss to bring Sherri up to speed. She recounted Gavin Thorne's visit and its outcome, stopping now and again to answer Sherri's questions.

"So you *do* have more of these Tiny Teddies?"

"Almost a hundred of them. And Marcia bought some too."

"Why?"

"I liked the little kilts. I figured I'd corner the market on kilted teddy bears. I never expected—"

"No, I mean why does Marcia have Tiny Teddies? She runs a consignment shop. Second Time Around stocks mostly clothing."

"She bought hers for decoration. They're dressed like Santa's elves. From what I can gather—I did some checking on the Internet—the company that makes Tiny Teddies only manufactures a limited number wearing any particular costume. That makes all the varieties more collectible."

Sherri nodded. Now that she thought about it, she'd noticed that the Tiny Teddies in the display window of The Toy Box, Gavin Thorne's store, all wore different outfits. "So Tiny Teddies come in many varieties, in all sorts of get-ups. They're considered collectible by adults as well as being toys for kids. And if you really have cornered the market on teddies in kilts, you can name your own price. But if this is such a hot item, why haven't buyers already found your supply? You put the bears in the online catalog at the Emporium's Web site, right?"

"Yes, but I didn't call them Tiny Teddies."

"So update the description."

"I've had a better idea." Liss's changeable blue-green eyes gleamed with barely suppressed excitement. "We make the buyers come here. This could be just what Moosetookalook needs. There isn't much time, but we do still have more than two weeks until Christmas. I've been making lists."

"Of course you have." Liss always made lists.

"First I have to talk to Marcia. Then to Gavin Thorne. And then we need to bring the whole town in on this." Liss turned the OPEN sign to CLOSED, grabbed her bright green coat off the rack by the door and led the way back outside.

A blast of cold air hit Sherri as soon as they left the Emporium. She looked hopefully at the sky, but there wasn't a cloud in sight.

They hurried past Stu's Ski Shop with its life-size skier on the roof of the porch and dashed across the intersection of Pine and Birch Streets. Marcia and her husband had bought the corner house a few years back. In common with most of the old Victorians that surrounded the town square, the downstairs portion had been converted for use as a business while the upstairs rooms had been turned into an apartment. Marcia lived there alone now. Almost a year ago, apparently in the throes of a midlife crisis, Cabot Katz had decamped. Sherri had no idea where he'd gone, but several months later, Marcia had dropped the name Katz and gone back to being Marcia Milliken.

A small bell above the door tinkled merrily and more melodiously than the one at the Emporium. Once inside the consignment shop, Liss waited a moment, then called out a greeting: "Anybody home?"

"Hang on a sec!" The sound of a disembodied voice was

followed by a flush. Sherri and Liss exchanged a rueful grin. When you owned a small shop there was rarely anyone available to cover for you when you needed to use the facilities.

Marcia emerged through a door behind the small desk she used as a sales counter. She was a tall, angular woman in her forties with a pale complexion and wheat-colored hair. Unlike Liss, she did not wear her store's stock. She was comfortably dressed in well-worn jeans and a cable-knit sweater. She needed the latter. Marcia kept the temperature in her building at a frugal sixty-two degrees.

"Liss. Sherri. Hi. What brings you out on this nippy morning?"

"Have you seen this?" Liss thrust the newspaper at her.

Marcia's eyes widened as she read. "Those dumb little bears? Get out of here!"

"How many do you have?"

"Two dozen. I didn't buy them to sell. I'm using them for Christmas decorations."

Liss started to explain her plan but Marcia didn't let her get very far.

"eBay."

"What?"

"Online auction. That's the best way to sell them. Put the bears up one at a time. Set a nice high minimum bid for each one."

If this were a cartoon, Sherri thought, the artist would draw dollar signs in place of Marcia's eyes.

Liss looked horrified. "You can't do that!"

"Why not?"

"Because we have a chance to do something good for this whole town. Gavin Thorne has some of these Tiny Teddies, too. We need to go talk to him. If we work together, I know we can pull this off."

Marcia looked doubtful. "Are you sure you want to

deal with Thorne? I can't say as I like him much. I stopped by to welcome him to town when he first opened The Toy Box and he gave me such a chilly reception that I haven't been back since."

"He's recently divorced," Sherri put in. "That tends to make folks sour." She gave herself a mental kick when she realized Marcia might take that comment personally, but the consignment shop owner simply nodded in agreement.

"He and his wife had a toy store in Fallstown," Marcia said. "The wife got the building. Thorne got the contents."

Sherri tried to think if she'd heard anything else about Gavin Thorne, but the local grapevine had been remarkably quiet on the subject.

"He did join the Moosetookalook Small Business Association," Liss said, "but he hasn't been to any meetings." Quickly and concisely, she filled Marcia in on Thorne's visit to the Emporium.

"He tried to con you and you still want to work with him?" Marcia's outrage showed plainly on her long, thin face.

The show of temper surprised Sherri. Until now, Marcia had never struck her as one of those people with a short fuse. Then again, she didn't know the woman well. Marcia was a relative newcomer to Moosetookalook. She hadn't grown up in the village, as Sherri and Liss had.

"It couldn't hurt to talk to Thorne," Liss insisted. "For one thing, he's the closest thing we have to a local expert on toys."

A short time later, Marcia in tow, Sherri and Liss retraced their steps past Stu's Ski shop and the Emporium. They passed Liss's house—one of only two surrounding the square that was still used exclusively as a residence—and turned onto Ash Street. The Toy Box was located in the center of that short block, between the post office and Preston's Mortuary.

Thorne's shop had no bell over the entrance. The door closed, however, with a resounding thunk that echoed in every corner of the small store.

"With you in a minute," Thorne bellowed from behind a sales counter built so high that a child would have to reach above his head to pay for a purchase. It was also an awkward height for Sherri, whose friends universally described her as a petite blonde. It hit the taller Liss squarely at bosom-level.

The minute stretched into several. Sherri and Marcia wandered off to inspect the shop's offerings, leaving Liss to inch closer to its surly proprietor.

Keeping her six-year old son's belief in Santa Claus in mind, Sherri browsed. Thorne had a great selection of action figures and shelves filled with board games and jigsaw puzzles, but the store seemed a trifle thin on miniature trucks and cars. Video games took up another significant section of shelving. So did toys for very young children. In a far corner she came upon two Tiny Teddies, one dressed as a ballerina, the other as a clown.

Marcia joined her there. "There are ten more on a table on the other side of the shop. All different."

As one, they headed for the front of the store, arriving just in time to see Liss go up on her toes to prop her elbows on the polished wooden surface of the sales counter in order to thrust her face into Thorne's peripheral vision. He gave a start and looked up from his computer screen with a glower.

"We need to talk," Liss said. When he stood, she stepped back and held out the newspaper.

Thorne leaned over the sales counter, his expression still thunderous. The floor on his side was a good foot higher than the area where Liss stood, so that he loomed over her. Nobody, not Liss or Marcia and Sherri, who had formed ranks behind Liss, was impressed.

Thorne did a double take at the sight of Sherri's uniform. "You planning to arrest me?"

His sneer faded when she just stared at him, her gaze level and no hint of a smile on her face. Holding her head at that awkward angle was giving her a kink in her neck— another black mark against the surly toy seller.

"Come out of there!" Liss snapped the command in a no-nonsense voice.

Thorne blinked hard behind his Harry Potter glasses and obeyed, descending the two little steps from the office area. He led them to a small seating area at the back corner of the store. Small was the operative word, since the chairs were designed for children. While Thorne leaned against the wall, Marcia dropped into a beanbag chair, joking that she'd probably need a forklift to get her up again. Sherri was small enough to ease into one of the child-size rockers but she still had to stretch her legs out in front of her to avoid a collision between knees and chest. Following Thorne's example, Liss opted to remain on her feet.

"How many Tiny Teddies you have?" she asked him.

"Two crates. Mixed."

"Two *hundred*?"

Sherri felt a slow grin spread across her face.

"It looks as though the three of us may have the only supply of Tiny Teddies in New England. There are people everywhere who want them. If we work together, we all increase our profits." Liss rubbed her fingers together in the universal gesture for money.

"What do you have in mind?" Thorne's aggression had vanished. He looked harmless again, even amiable, a short, middle-aged man with a sagging midsection and weak eyesight.

"We make the customers come to us. That way the whole town benefits."

Thorne looked skeptical, but he kept listening.

Liss took out the lists she'd tucked into her coat pocket and ticked off each point in turn. "One: get hold of the rest of the members of the Moosetookalook Small Business Association and tell them what's going on. Two: attend the board of selectmen's next meeting, which just happens to be scheduled for tonight. Both groups are a potential source of seed money. The selectmen know business has been slow, even with the boost Moosetookalook got when the hotel reopened last summer. So, when we ask for assistance to get the word out about our supply of Tiny Teddies—the financial wherewithal to run ads—I think they'll go along with our request."

"Newspaper, television, or radio?" Thorne asked.

"All three if we can swing it. The thing is, we want to do more than just attract customers to our own stores. We want to encourage shoppers to stick around long enough to spend money at all the local businesses. It's short notice, but I think I can pull together a Christmas pageant—I've been thinking of it as The Twelve Shopping Days of Christmas." She gave a self-conscious little laugh. "Maybe we could be a tad more subtle than that, so any suggestions for alternate names are welcome."

Sherri repressed a snort of laughter. Subtlety was not Liss's strong suit, but Sherri had to give her friend credit for ingenuity. As Liss expanded on her idea—twelve days of special ceremonies, one for each stanza in the Christmas carol, culminating in a pageant on the last day that included them all—she could see how the events might encourage tourists to come to town.

"I can find the ten ladies to dance and the eleven pipers," Liss said, "but I may need some help recruiting leaping lords and milkmaids. And drummers. We'll need twelve of them."

"Try the high school," Sherri suggested. "Convince one of the teachers to offer extra credit to those who participate."

"When will you hold the final pageant?" Thorne asked. Whatever his earlier reservations, he sounded as if he'd now come around to Liss's way of thinking. Although he still propped up the back wall of his shop, his stance had changed from studied indifference to rapt attention.

"If we call Saturday the first day of Christmas, then the twelfth day will fall on Christmas Eve." Liss frowned. "That's wrong, of course. Twelfth Night is actually *after* Christmas, but since celebrations in the U.S. center on the twenty-fifth of December, we'll just have to take a little poetic license. I—"

"Christmas Eve is too late," Thorne cut in. "You need to schedule things so that the final pageant falls on the weekend *before* Christmas."

Liss's face fell as she mentally subtracted days. "That would mean we'd have to have to hold the first day's ceremony tomorrow!"

"Partridge in a pear tree, right?" Marcia asked.

At Liss's nod, Marcia gave a dismissive shrug.

"No big deal if people miss that one. Or the next six, either." She ticked them off on her fingers. "Two doves, three hens, four calling birds, five gold rings, six swans, and seven geese. All poultry except for the rings, Liss—and boring! Until you start counting people, there won't be anything interesting to see."

"Okay. Okay, you're right. But on the twelfth day we can make a terrific spectacle out of all of them." Her enthusiasm only momentarily dimmed, she rummaged in another pocket for a pencil and started making notes on the back of one of her lists. "We'll put a pear tree up in the town square next to the municipal Christmas tree. I know a taxidermist who can supply a stuffed partridge. Jump ahead to—"

"Jump ahead to customers arriving in droves to spend money," Thorne interrupted, "and to the prices we're going to charge. People will pay a heck of a lot more than ten bucks for these babies now."

Liss looked as if she wanted to object, but held her tongue when she saw Marcia's eyes light up.

After Thorne and Marcia had agreed to attend the selectmen's meeting that evening with Liss, Liss and Sherri left the two of them engrossed in a discussion of the best wording for their ads.

"Time to get back to the P.D.," Sherri said. "You won't need my help dealing with the MSBA. You've already got an in with the top man." Dan Ruskin, newly elected as president by the other small businesspeople in town, was one of the two men Liss had been dating since she'd returned to Moosetookalook seventeen months earlier.

Sherri started to cross the square, then paused to look back over her shoulder. "By the way—thanks, Liss."

"For?"

"Salvaging my morning. I was bored to tears." She grinned. "And if this plan of yours actually works, it will also be thanks for all the overtime I'm going to earn working crowd control."

# Chapter Two

Liss's mouth kept moving but Dan Ruskin couldn't hear a single word she said. So much for squeezing in an hour or two of woodworking between helping out at The Spruces, the hotel his father owned, and his regular job with Ruskin Construction. Resigned, he turned off the scroll saw and removed his safety glasses and ear protectors.

"Say again," he instructed.

As the story tumbled out, Dan collected the blanks he'd just cut in various shapes and sizes and carried them to his worktable. Everything was a "blank" until it was finished. With a little work these would become small boxes, each one unique. They sold reasonably well at Angie's Books, as did his small battery operated clocks. Like the boxes, no two were exactly the same. Sometimes he also supplied Angie Hogencamp with cherrywood walking sticks and wooden back-scratchers to sell in her shop.

He didn't usually have so much trouble finding time to turn out these small projects. He used scrap lumber, so they didn't cost him anything to make. If he figured by the time involved—a couple of hours for each box—he wasn't making much profit, but every little bit helped. Besides, it all went to building his reputation as a custom woodworker. One day, with luck before he was too old and gray to appreciate it, he'd be able to strike out on his own and make things from wood full time.

Liss was still talking. As some of what she had already said sank in, Dan sent an incredulous look in her direction. That single glance was enough to tell him she was completely serious.

He went back to loosening the clamps on a box he'd glued together the day before. He didn't say anything. He didn't know what *to* say. Liss appeared to have everything worked out already. As usual. He wondered when he'd started to resent that quality.

"They call them the Daft Days in Scotland," Liss concluded, "instead of the twelve days of Christmas, but I think we'd better stick with what most Americans will find familiar."

"Whatever works," he mumbled, and crossed back to the scroll saw. His workshop was almost the way he wanted it. He'd acquired a table saw, a miter saw, and a band saw. Next time he had a little extra saved, it was going for a drill press. "Liss, I'm sorry to give you the bum's rush, but I need to finish cutting these before my lunch break is over."

He flipped a switch. Immediately, the workshop was filled with a loud hum that drowned out every other sound. He'd just dropped his ear protectors back into place when Liss jabbed him in the ribs. She kept her fingernails cut short but put enough force behind the poke to make it hurt like blazes.

"Not while I'm cutting!" he yelled.

"You're not cutting yet!" she shouted back. "Turn off the saw! This is important!"

Swallowing his irritation, he obeyed. "Okay. You've got my attention." He turned to her with arms folded across his chest and a look of annoyance on his face. He'd give her five more minutes.

"Did you hear a single word I said?" He heard frustration in her voice, but what he saw in her expressive blue-green eyes was disappointment.

Dan suddenly felt ashamed of himself. So they hadn't progressed to the point he'd thought they would in their personal relationship. They were still friends. They had been since they were kids. It was a given that if Liss needed him, he would be there for her.

With a sigh, he raked his fingers through his hair. Sending her a sheepish, apologetic look, he asked her to explain the situation to him again.

The second time around it still didn't make a lot of sense, but Dan was willing to take Liss's word for it that a rare opportunity had just fallen into their laps. She had a better head for business than he did.

"So, can we tap into funds from the Moosetookalook Small Business Association for this?" she asked.

"Not without calling an MSBA meeting and taking a vote, but I think they'll go for it."

His father was certainly desperate enough.

Five months earlier, on Fourth of July weekend, Moosetookalook's venerable old grand hotel, The Spruces, had reopened. Joe Ruskin had poured heart, soul, and every penny he had to spare—and some he didn't—into renovating the place. He was convinced getting the hotel up and running was the key to putting Moosetookalook back on the map.

Dan had to admit that things had started off well. Most of the rooms had been full during the summer and the hotel had held its own during leaf-peeper season. But ever since the trees went bare, they'd struggled to fill even half the rooms, and heating the place cost a small fortune. With no snow on the ground to support winter sports, they'd started to accumulate canceled reservations. With each passing day, the hotel sank deeper into debt.

"That it?" Dan asked when they'd settled on a time for the members of the MSBA to gather at Liss's house.

"I'd appreciate it if you'd attend the selectmen's meeting with me tonight," Liss said. "Lend support to the cause. It starts at seven."

"No problem, but I'm not sure how much help I'll be."

"You know the selectmen better than I do. They may take some persuading to support us, especially since it involves spending money." She gave a small, humorless laugh. "I expect the whole scheme will sound crazy to them at first."

"No more than some of your Scottish heritage stuff." Dan quickly threw both arms up to shield his face as Liss raised her fists. "Kidding, Liss. Just kidding!"

A wicked grin overspread her face. "You'd better be." Eyes sparkling with mischief, she added: "'Daft Days' is also the title of a poem by Robert Fergusson."

"Who?"

"He was a Scot born in 1750. He inspired Robert Burns to become a poet."

The snicker that escaped her warned Dan she was up to no good. Besides, he recognized Burns's name as the guy who wrote "Auld Lang Syne." "I assume you're using the word 'poet' in its broadest sense?"

Liss struck a pose more in keeping with a nineteenth-century actor declaiming Shakespeare than a twenty-first century businesswoman. *"Now mirk December's dowie face/ Glowrs owre the rigs wi' sour grimace,"* she recited in a faux-Scots accent.

When she made "grimace" rhyme with "face," Dan rolled his eyes. The rest of the poem was just so much gobbledygook as far as he was concerned. Still, he didn't say a word until she was finished and even then refused to be goaded into making any more snide remarks.

"Let's go inside," he suggested instead. "I haven't had

lunch yet." His workshop was a converted carriage house only a dozen yards from his back porch.

"I'll make sandwiches," Liss offered.

She knew where everything was. This was the house she'd grown up in. Dan had bought it after Liss's parents moved to Arizona. Back then, she'd been long gone, earning her living performing with a professional Scottish dance troupe. He'd never expected to see her again.

While Liss foraged in his refrigerator, Dan pondered the best way to help her with the board of selectmen. "You do know one of them," he said when she handed him a can of soda. "Jason Graye."

She made a face before proceeding to slather mayonnaise on white bread and slap lettuce, bologna, and cheese together between the slices. When she had three sandwiches ready—two for him and one for herself—she unearthed a bag of sour cream-and-onion-flavored potato chips to go with them.

"Graye doesn't like me." She bit into her sandwich with enough force to remind him that she didn't much like Jason Graye, either.

A local real estate agent and self-proclaimed entrepreneur, Graye had walked precariously close to the boundary between ethical and unethical business practices in the not-so-distant past. That he seemed to be making an attempt to clean up his act, mostly because people were on to him, did not inspire either Liss or Dan to trust him.

"Who else is on the board?" Liss asked.

"Doug Preston and Thea Campbell." Doug was the local mortician and somewhat staid. All the selectmen were frugal.

"Pete's mother?" Liss brightened when she recognized the second name. "There's a piece of luck."

"Not necessarily. She's pretty conservative in her views and she's gotten more so since her husband died."

"But she'll go for the Scottish angle."

"I know Pete competes in athletic events at Scottish festivals, but—"

"The whole clan used to be very active. I can't imagine she's completely lost interest."

"She might have, if it was Pete's father who was the fan of all things Scottish. If I'm remembering right, and I'm pretty sure I am, Thea Campbell was born a Briscetti."

"Then I'll just have to get Pete to work on her. Or rather, I'll get Sherri to work on Pete to work on his mother."

He wasn't quick enough to hide his reaction.

"What?"

"Nothing."

"Dan."

Shaking his head, rolling his eyes heavenward, he gave in. "I just don't think you should put any additional pressure on Pete and Sherri right now."

"What are you talking about? They're engaged to be married. They—"

"They don't exactly see eye to eye about Sherri's current career path."

Liss blinked at him in surprise. He swore he could hear the gears whirring as she ran that concept through her mental computer. Apparently she'd been clueless about the conflict between their two friends.

"Sherri said she'd had a difference of opinion with Pete," Liss said slowly, "but she dismissed it as a minor problem. Said he'd come around."

"Well, he hasn't."

"I knew he was unhappy when she went to the police academy. Sixteen weeks is a long time to be separated, even if she did come home on weekends."

"Most of those she spent with her son, not her fiancé. But that wasn't the real problem. Pete's worried about Sherri's safety."

"Dan, she's working for the Moosetookalook Police Department. How much safer could she be?"

"She could be back in the sheriff's office, working dispatch."

"Oh, for heaven's sake. Will you listen to yourself? It's okay for Pete to be a patrol deputy, out there all alone with a whole county full of bad guys, but it's too much of a risk for Sherri to walk around the square and check the locks on the shops?"

"That's just it. He's seen firsthand the kind of nasty situations a cop can get into. Domestic disputes, for one thing. Not to mention the—"

"Of all the male chauvinist pig mentality! Pete's a Neanderthal."

"Probably, but—"

"I'll just have to convince Mrs. Campbell to support us without her son's help. So, we'll make our appeal, and then, as soon as there's money to pay for them, we launch the ads." Liss glanced at her watch. "I've got to call Rich Smalley. See if he's got a partridge. Do you have any idea where I could find a pear tree?"

Liss breathed a sigh of relief. She didn't know what she'd been so worried about. The board of selectmen had given their approval with barely a moment's hesitation. Even Jason Graye had supported her proposal. Doug Preston, whose mortuary was hardly likely to profit from the festivities, thought her plan was a stroke of genius. Thea Campbell had been slightly less enthusiastic, but she'd gone along with the wishes of her two colleagues.

The amount of money they'd been able to free up for the campaign was disappointing, but Liss still had hopes that the MSBA would make up the difference. Heck, she'd max out her own credit cards if she had to. This was too good an opportunity to miss.

Everyone agreed that whatever was to be done needed to be done fast, to take advantage of their windfall. Having dealt with all old and scheduled business—whether or not to grant a building permit to add a storage room at the grocery store; whether or not to close a little-used road, so the town wouldn't have to plow it if and when they finally got snow; whether or not to repair the municipal parking lot now or wait until spring—the selectmen adjourned their meeting.

"We'll take a break," Graye declared, "then talk informally with you folks." He indicated Liss, Gavin, and Marcia before he drifted off, cell phone in hand, in search of privacy and a signal.

"If you don't need me anymore," Dan said, "I should head over to The Spruces." In spite of the scarcity of guests, they were always shorthanded. The renovations, even with the help of historic preservation grants and other funding, had taken a huge bite out of available funds. Dan's father intended to hire trained professionals to handle management-level positions eventually, but just now he couldn't afford expert help. He was making do with family.

Liss wanted to ask him to stay, but she bit back the request. Was it her imagination, or did Dan seem unenthusiastic about the Tiny Teddies? She told herself he was just exhausted. Who wouldn't be, working what amounted to three jobs? Still, she hated the way they'd drifted apart since the previous spring.

"Walk me out?" he asked, and stepped into the hallway.

Liss followed. Directly across from the entrance to the town office was the door leading to the fire department. The main entrance to the municipal building was to their left. To the right, just beyond the doors to the staff kitchen, public restrooms, police department, and the stairs that led up to the public library, was a drinking fountain that boasted the coldest, best-tasting water in the world. Automatically, they headed straight for it.

In long swallows, chilled liquid ambrosia slid down Liss's parched throat. "Still number one."

She backed off to give Dan a turn, absently tucking a strand of wet hair behind one ear. She'd substituted a jaunty little black beret for her scarf and changed into a sleek black velour pantsuit for her presentation. A hand-painted pendant broke the unrelieved expanse between turtleneck and hem. On it, the artist had depicted a mythical creature that was half cat, half dragon.

"Wicked good." Dan wiped a drop of water off his chin as he lifted his head from the fountain.

Some things never change, Liss thought. On impulse, she grabbed his hand and pulled him with her to the stairs. How many times had they sat on the third step when they were kids? Sometimes they'd been with friends and sometimes it had just been the two of them, talking about nothing and everything.

"I've missed you lately," she whispered as she settled on the hard wooden surface with its bumpy rubber matting. The stairs dipped slightly in the middle, worn down by generations of feet tromping up and down.

"I've been busy." He looked away, then back. "Missed you, too."

A moment of breathless silence descended. Then he crossed the requisite few inches to kiss her.

It was a splendid effort. For a few moments, the rest of the world went away. Liss forgot all about Daft Days and Christmas pageants and Tiny Teddies. She even forgot about Gordon Tandy, the other man in her life. Her hands went to Dan's collar, smoothing the soft cotton between her fingers as she kissed him back.

A harsh whisper intruded on the moment.

"Sure took you long enough to get here," Jason Graye hissed.

Liss froze. Slowly, Dan released her.

It took a moment for Liss to realize that Graye was not talking to them. Shielded by the banister, Liss and Dan were well hidden. She lifted one finger to her lips, warning Dan not to speak. Careful to make no sound, she turned her head until she could see that two men stood in the shadow of the stairwell.

"Came as soon as you called," the newcomer said irritably.

Graye clapped a hand on the other man's shoulder and leaned in. He spoke too softly for Liss to catch a single word. She started to shift closer, but Dan caught her arm and shook his head. Reluctantly, she subsided. Graye's demeanor piqued her curiosity, especially when she saw him pass an envelope to his companion, but she had no desire to be caught eavesdropping.

The whispering continued for several more minutes before the two men broke apart. Graye headed back into the town office. The other fellow left through the fire station. No one would challenge him. Moosetookalook had a volunteer fire department. Both the garage doors and the exit on the far side of the municipal building were left unlocked for their convenience.

"Who was that?" Liss kept her voice low even though there was no longer anyone around to overhear.

"Eric Moss, I think."

Liss knew Moss slightly. He was a former delivery service driver who'd had a hard time making ends meet after he retired. Since he was already acquainted with all the local businesspeople and familiar with the products they sold, he'd been able to develop a reasonably profitable sideline as a picker. He located odd lots and interesting single items and resold them to shopkeepers who handled similar merchandise.

"What business would Moss have with Graye? Graye sells land, not goods."

"No idea." Dan tugged at her hand until she rose from the stairs.

His grip was firm, his skin warm against hers but Liss ignored the sensual tingle his touch produced. Wrong time. Wrong place. And she was distracted by an almost overwhelming desire to discover what Graye and Moss had been discussing.

"They looked furtive to me, sneaking around like that. Didn't they look like they were up to no good to you?"

She justified her curiosity by rationalizing that any nefarious plotting on Graye's part just now might have a negative effect on her own plans. She wasn't about to let a slimy toad like Jason Graye mess with her pageant or the successful sale of Tiny Teddies.

"Graye always looks as if he's up to *something*. It's part of his charm."

The sarcasm in Dan's tone told Liss he didn't really care what was going on, but she didn't trust Graye as far as she could throw him. She hesitated outside the door to the town office, groping for the words to express her concern. She hadn't come up with anything more specific than a gut feeling before Dan bent to give her a light kiss on the cheek.

"I gotta go, Liss."

As quick as that, she banished Jason Graye to the back burner. Priority one was the welfare of the town, but number two was a more personal issue. She caught up with Dan at the coatrack as he shrugged into his L. L. Bean Maine Guide's jacket. "I appreciate your support this evening."

"No problem." His expression somber, he wished her good luck. "You've got a lot of hard work ahead of you."

"It will bring in business for all of us, Dan. I know it will."

"So would a nice northeaster." They had reached the entrance, which gave them a clear view of the expanse of bare ground that was Moosetookalook's town square.

"We'll get snow eventually. We always do."

"It can't be soon enough to suit me. I gotta tell you, Liss, the sight of all those tarp-covered snowmobiles sitting in garages and on the dead grass of side lawns is really starting to depress me."

On that less-than-cheerful remark, Dan left for the hotel.

Liss sighed as she headed back to the Town Office. She'd see him at the MSBA meeting in the morning, but there had been a time not so long ago when he'd have suggested stopping by at her house after he finished whatever job he had to do at The Spruces tonight.

The lack of snow was depressing, but it was nothing compared to the lack of romance in her life!

# Chapter Three

By eight o'clock on Wednesday morning, twenty people had crowded into Liss's living room. She had plenty of coffee ready, thanks to her own eight-cup pot, the large coffeemaker she'd brought home from the shop, and her aunt's old-fashioned percolator, but she could have kissed Patsy of Patsy's Coffee House when she turned up carrying two boxes of assorted homemade pastries—everything from doughnuts to scones to blueberry muffins. The smell of fresh baked goods had Liss's mouth watering even before she lifted the lid of the first box to peek inside at the goodies.

"For this," Liss told the pale, cadaverously thin genius-in-the-kitchen, "you get to sit in the place of honor." A few minutes later, Patsy was installed the overstuffed easy chair, Liss's favorite spot to curl up in and read.

Liss cleared her throat and waited for everyone to quiet down. "I'm speaking for myself, Gavin, and Marcia," she began.

The two of them shared the sofa with Stuart Burroughs, owner of Stu's Ski Shop. Marcia, considerably taller than either of them when they were seated, looked like a beanpole between two pumpkins. Liss had to work to dislodge that image from her head. It didn't help that Stu, who had always been chunky but had recently put on quite a bit of weight, was wearing a blaze-orange fleece sweat suit.

"Okay," Liss said, starting again when she had the urge to giggle under control. "Here's the deal."

A quarter of an hour later she concluded her pitch: "This will make Moosetookalook a destination shopping venue. People will come for the toy, stay over at The Spruces because they've had to travel so far, and spend money at all the shops in town."

Liss stopped, feeling like a toy that had wound down. No, she decided, more like someone caught in an endless loop, repeating the same refrain over and over again. Fortunately, her words seemed to be having the desired effect. The board of selectmen had fallen in line and she had the expense check to prove it. Yesterday, even before the board of selectmen met, she'd won the support of the principal at the regional high school in Fallstown. She had been promised her nine lords a-leaping and her twelve drummers drumming, as well as some necessary props. She was still working on the milkmaids, the dancing ladies and the pipers, but she expected no problems finding them, especially now that the folks in her living room were talking to each other and nodding.

Stu Burroughs was the first to speak up. "I'm in, but only if I get a couple of these teddy bears to sell in my ski shop. I don't suppose you've got any that are wearing parkas and carrying little skis?"

"Oh, I like that idea," Betsy Twining chimed in from her perch on one of Liss's kitchen chairs. "I want some teddy bears to sell in my place, too."

Betsy owned the Clip and Curl, a combination beauty parlor and barber shop, located in the back half of the building that also housed the post office. Stu could have used her services, Liss thought. His hair was the flat black of a do-it-yourself dye job.

"Are you talking about selling on consignment?" Thorne asked.

"I'm saying you should sell me a couple for resale. Call it a good-will gesture among local businessmen."

"If you wanted to sell teddy bears, Burroughs, you should have bought your own supply in the first place. Mine are staying right where they are."

"What do you think, Joe?" Stu appealed to Joe Ruskin, Dan's father, who had appropriated the Canadian rocker in Liss's bay window. "Share the wealth, right?"

Liss had only to study the older Ruskin's features to know what his son would look like in twenty years. Dan's sandy brown hair would have a bit of gray at the temples—very distinguished. There would be more lines around his molasses-brown eyes. But he wouldn't stoop, for all that he was over six feet tall, and he'd still have the muscular build that came from working in construction and owed nothing to exercise machines in a gym.

"Thorne has a point," Joe said. "He was the one with the foresight to buy the bears."

"Or his ex wife was." Marcia's mutter was just loud enough for everyone in the room to hear.

Liss sent her a repressive look, thinking that Marcia should be the last person in the world to look down on the idea of consignment sales. Marcia ignored the warning glance. Apparently she considered these extraordinary circumstances.

"I want at least ten teddy bears in my store." Deliberately rude, Stu leaned in front of Marcia to glare at Gavin Thorne.

"You're not getting them." Thorne folded his arms across his chest but ended up looking sulky rather than resolute.

"Oh, for heaven's sake! *Nobody* has teddy bears!"

At the aggrieved outburst, everyone turned to look at Angie Hogencamp, owner of Angie's Books and secretary of the Moosetookalook Small Business Association. Seated beside the small telephone table on which her notebook rested, Angie ignored the startled silence in the room. She fished in her tote until she came up with a small pencil sharpener. In her agitation, she'd broken the point of the pencil she'd been using to take minutes of the meeting.

Joe Ruskin cleared his throat. "You want to explain yourself, Angie?"

She finished sharpening her pencil before she answered him. "Do you have any idea how annoying it is to have to keep writing the words 'teddy bears' when those . . . those *toys* are clearly *not* teddy bears. Teddy bears are a very specific sort of stuffed bear. They have beads for eyes and stitched noses and arms and legs that move . . . oh, what do any of you care!"

Angie collected *designer* teddy bears, Liss remembered. She'd never bothered to ask the bookseller exactly what that meant, but apparently those who engaged in the hobby were particular about nomenclature.

She got that. No one could nitpick better than a person passionate about an activity pursued for pleasure. She saw the same thing all the time among those who had chosen to celebrate their Scottish heritage. Debates on the proper way to wear the kilt—and who could or could not wear one—had been known to go on for hours!

"Can we agree to call these bears Tiny Teddies," she suggested, "and move on?"

Angie gave a curt nod and returned the pencil sharpener to her tote bag.

"Whatever you call them," Thorne said in a loud, belligerent tone of voice, "the idea is to make it easy for shoppers to find them. Spread them out and you create confusion. Nobody wants that."

"On the other hand, we do want to keep people moving from store to store," Liss interjected. "The Twelve Shopping Days of Christmas promotion, with a ceremony every evening, will help with that. Then the pageant will draw everyone to the town square on the final day."

She'd spent hours last night—who needed sleep?—working on the logistics. Each evening they'd add a new "day" to the festivities. The twelfth would now fall on the twenty-first of December, the beginning of winter. That seemed appropriate.

"How does the shopping days thing get them to stop in at *every* business?" Betsy asked.

"They probably won't need my services," Jim Locke of Locke Insurance commented, "and I hope there won't be any call for Doug's." He and Doug Preston of Preston's Mortuary sat side by side on two more of Liss's kitchen chairs.

Laughter helped ease the tension but Stu wasn't about to give up. While he continued to lobby for a consignment of bears and others tried to talk him out of his stand, Liss kept mum. Her gaze roamed over the rest of the gathered businesspeople. Her eyes locked momentarily with Patsy's and the coffee shop owner sent a sympathetic look and a shrug her way, then mouthed, "Some people could find things to argue about till doomsday."

At least they were discussing the twelve days proposal, Liss told herself. That was good, right? She resolved to let them have at it for a few more minutes before attempting to restore order and take a vote.

She jumped when something heavy bumped against the back of her calf. Liss looked down into the malevolent gaze of the big yellow Maine coon cat she'd inherited along with her house. Lumpkin glared back at her, obviously displeased by the presence of all these noisy people in his domain.

"Go back into hiding," she advised.

She couldn't blame the cat for disapproving of all this noise and confusion. Truthfully, She hadn't expected to see him again until everyone had left. At the first sight of strangers approaching, he'd taken shelter under the kitchen sink.

When Lumpkin stayed put beside Liss's chair, she reached down to scratch behind his ear. A deep, rumbling purr made his entire body vibrate.

Meanwhile, Stu had progressed to waving his arms in the air as he expostulated. With one particularly emphatic gesture, his hand came within an inch of the end of Marcia's nose. She sent a withering glance in his direction, but he didn't seem to notice.

"My toy store should be the only place to sell Tiny Teddies," Thorne declared in a loud voice.

"You just want to jack up the price!" Betsy snapped at him.

"You say that like price gouging is a bad thing." The wounded look on Thorne's face was far too theatrical for anyone to take seriously.

Marcia cut short that incipient debate by rising abruptly to her feet. "If you idiots can't agree, then I'll just go ahead and sell *my* Tiny Teddies in an online auction." She reached behind her for the coat she'd been sitting on.

Stu bounced up, ready to square off with her. "I thought you were in favor of this one-for-all and all-for-one deal?" Since Stu Burroughs was only an inch or two over five feet tall, going nose-to-nose with Marcia was a physical impossibility. He only succeeded in making himself look foolish.

Liss took a deep breath. This was going nowhere. Someone had to step in before the meeting dissolved into total chaos. "Enough!"

Startled by the volume she'd managed—all those years onstage had included more than dancing—everyone shut up. Lumpkin streaked back into the kitchen.

"I'm calling for a vote," Liss said. "Yea or nay—will the

Moosetookalook Small Business Association support this project or not?"

Dan Ruskin had taken pains to stay out of the fray, but as soon as Liss made her demand, he put it into the form demanded by *Robert's Rules of Order* and asked for a show of hands. Liss had already told everyone how much money she needed. No one questioned her math, and the vote to authorize funding a group ad and a pageant was unanimous. In spite of their differences, Moosetookalook's businesses were all desperate for customers.

A second vote, much closer than the first, left the matter of displaying and pricing Tiny Teddies entirely in the hands of the three individuals who actually had supplies of the toy.

That settled, everyone was in a hurry to leave. They all had businesses to run or jobs to go to. Even Dan did a rapid disappearing act, escaping before Liss had the opportunity to thank him for his help.

"Marcia, wait," Liss called as the other woman made a beeline for the front door. She caught the sleeve of Marcia's coat, drawing her back inside until everyone else had gone. "Are you still set on online auctions?"

"Why not? Good money there."

"Also a lot of hassle. You've got to make sure the buyers' credit is solid. Then you have to ship and insure the merchandise. There's always a chance of something getting lost in transit."

Marcia's frown told Liss that her arguments were getting through. Who hadn't heard at least one horror story about an online auction gone wrong?

"You can always auction off your Tiny Teddies at the last minute if they don't sell here."

"True."

"And you're free to price them as you see fit."

"Also true. Okay. I'll wait." That said, she took off at a fast clip.

Liss wondered what her hurry was. Second Time Around was open only "by chance or appointment," although Marcia usually hung out the OPEN sign around ten.

Lumpkin sauntered into the living room as soon as he was sure Liss was alone. "Why do I have the feeling," she asked him, "that Marcia's bears are not going to be sold for $9.99?"

Liss spent a few minutes clearing away coffee mugs and paper plates. She stuck the two remaining doughnuts into a ziplock bag and put it in the refrigerator so that Lumpkin wouldn't eat them. He was an expert at opening cabinets, louvered doors, even the old-fashioned bread box on the counter.

Instead of leaving by the back door and crossing the driveway and a narrow strip of lawn to enter the Emporium through the stockroom as she usually did, Liss left her house by the front entrance so that she could dash across the intersection of Pine and Ash and pick up the mail before she opened the shop for the day. Moosetookalook was too small to have a postman who went door-to-door. Both Liss's home address and the Emporium's mailing address were P.O. box numbers.

She was just leaving the post office with a handful of bills and advertisements and a letter from a friend in her old dance troupe, *Strathspey*, when she heard raised voices coming from the house next door. Since the combatants were standing on the porch of The Toy Box, it was impossible not to overhear.

"We're not married anymore, Felicity!" Gavin Thorne shouted. "You can't just barge in here like you own the place."

"You bastard!" shrieked the woman squared off against

him. "You greedy son of a bitch! I'm the one who ordered those bears. You thought they were stupid."

Thorne didn't have to say a word. His attitude alone was apparently enough to infuriate his ex wife. Felicity Thorne stood facing the post office, giving Liss a clear view of her expression. Rage was not a good look for her.

Judging by the crow's-feet around her eyes and mouth, Felicity Thorne was about the same age as her ex husband. She was carrying thirty or forty extra pounds but looked healthy as a horse. She had an air of energy and athleticism about her that made Liss think she could probably lift crates full of toys without breaking a sweat. An inch or so shorter than Thorne, Felicity had a wild mane of black hair just starting to go gray and dark eyes that were slightly tilted at the corners. Catching sight of Liss, those eyes narrowed in suspicion.

"What do you think you're looking at?" she snarled.

Before Liss could reply—not that she intended to—Thorne's ex turned away. She gave him a shove that propelled him back into the toy store and strode through the door after him. It slammed behind them with such a resounding crash that Liss was surprised the glass didn't break.

Shaking her head, she retreated to the sanctuary of Moosetookalook Scottish Emporium. She had too much work of her own to spend time worrying about domestic discord at the toy shop.

Liss awoke on Saturday morning to find herself nose to nose with Lumpkin. His was cold and wet. "We've had this discussion before," she told the big cat. "You're not supposed to sleep on the bed."

He stretched out an oversized paw and patted her cheek with it.

"Think you're cute, don't you?" But she ran her palm

over his furry head and back in a long, loving stroke before she swung her legs off the side of the bed and got up.

The movement was fluid, causing only the faintest twinge and accompanied by a little early morning stiffness—both reminders that she'd had major knee surgery less than two years earlier. Liss did a few stretches to limber up, but nothing close to the routine she'd once gone through to start every day.

Her career as a professional Scottish dancer had ended abruptly with an injury that, while it did not prevent her from leading a normal life, had put an end to doing high-impact jigs and reels as a way of making a living. Liss still missed being part of *Strathspey*, a touring company intended to be to Scottish-Americans what *Riverdance* was to those of Irish descent. Gradually, however, she had come to appreciate what she was doing now. These days, the occasional ache in her knee and the stiffness that sometimes set in when she went too long without moving were petty annoyances rather than emotionally painful reminders of what she had lost.

A quick glance through the corner window as she dressed was enough to tell Liss there was still no snow on the ground. In fact, it looked to be another clear, cloudless day. There were, however, two strange cars parked on the street in front of Moosetookalook Scottish Emporium. A pickup truck she didn't recognize sat idling outside The Toy Box.

The number of vehicles had increased to seven by the time Liss slipped across the back way to the shop in preparation for opening at eight. A hopeful sign, she thought, and pretty much right on schedule.

Word of a cache of Tiny Teddies in Maine had hit the Internet even before the first newspaper and television ads appeared on Thursday, along with a brief news item on the partridge-in-the-pear-tree ceremony. That was how Felicity Thorne had discovered what her ex was up to.

By Friday morning, Liss had received several dozen e-mail inquiries. She'd sent the same reply to everyone: "Come to Moosetookalook, Maine, to shop. No mail orders will be filled."

As she'd expected, there had not been an immediate upsurge in business. Friday had been almost as slow as it usually was. Liss had been prepared for that. After all, most people had jobs. If they were going to drive to central Maine, a solid four hours northwest of Boston, they had to have the time to do it. That meant the weekend . . . and here were the first of them.

She loaded the change from the safe into the cash register, turned on the lights, made one last check of the displays, pasted a smile on her face, and opened the door. That was the last moment she had to take a deep breath for the rest of the day.

Within an hour, at least in terms of what was usual for a small, rural Maine town, hordes of shoppers had descended upon Moosetookalook. Liss was down to sixty Tiny Teddies in kilts by the end of the day. She'd done pretty well selling other items, too, and been kept so busy by the steady stream of customers that she'd barely had time to scarf down a couple of power bars and a soda for lunch and take a bathroom break. She had no idea what might be happening beyond the Emporium's front door.

She had seen the last customer out and was about to lock up when a bright red Lexus with Massachusetts plates screeched to a halt at the curb in front of The Toy Box. The woman who barreled out of the driver's side, barely taking time to slam the door behind her, was swathed in layers of vivid electric blue. The garment appeared to be a cross between a Victorian greatcoat and a cloak—lots of capes attached.

Shaking her head, Liss watched the woman race up the steps to the porch of the toy store and into Gavin Thorne's shop. She didn't look particularly young, which meant it was probably collecting fervor that put wings on her feet. Either that or she was an extremely dedicated grandma.

Liss turned the dead bolt on her own door, lowered the shade over the glass, and headed for the half bath next to the stockroom. By the time she came out, someone was knocking with enough force to make the panes in the door rattle. Liss sighed. She had a pretty good idea who was on the other side. One glimpse of the woman in blue had been enough to tell her that she wasn't the type who went away before she got what she wanted.

"Just a minute!" Resigned to another delay before she could fix supper and put her feet up, Liss trudged through the shop to unlock the door.

"Well, finally," said the caped customer on the other side.

She pushed past Liss into the shop, craning her neck and swinging her head from side to side, her beaklike nose all but sniffing the air. She was older than Liss had thought, with wattle showing above the neckline of her incredible coat. Liss couldn't help but imagine her as a giant bird turning beady-eyed curiosity onto new territory.

Just lately, birds had been much on Liss's mind. This was the third day in a row she'd had poultry on the premises. The "first day of Christmas" had featured a partridge provided by the local taxidermist, but on Thursday she'd taken custody of two turtle doves—actually carrier pigeons—and yesterday she'd added a crate containing the chickens who had played the roles of "three French hens" in last night's festivities. After a while she'd gotten used to the continual scratching sounds, but the truly incredible smell was something else entirely. Today, this evening's "calling birds" had been delivered, one by one, during the height of the shopping frenzy. All four now resided in the stockroom with the rest of the livestock.

"This is it?" The woman in blue was holding up one of Liss's wee teddy bears. "You don't have any other costumes?"

"Sorry. We didn't know they were going to become so collectible."

"No, I suppose you didn't." But the woman's look said she *should* have. "Is this price right? $9.99?" She carried her prize to the sales counter where Liss was waiting.

"That's right, and you also receive a free Yule candle." She opened the box next to the cash register. "The Yule candle is a symbol of good will, given to you along with our wish for a fire to warm you by and a light to guide you."

The woman looked suspicious of this largesse, but dug a credit card out of an oversized shoulder bag and handed it over. The name embossed on it was Lovey FitzPatrick.

"Here you go, Ms. FitzPatrick," Liss said a few minutes later, handing over one of the bright red bags with Moosetookalook Scottish Emporium emblazoned on the side. "I hope you'll be staying for the festivities this evening. We'll have carolers out singing. Santa Claus will visit the gazebo in the town square. And since this is the fourth day of Christmas, according to the old song, we will be introducing our four calling birds."

"Unless you have more of these bears, I've got what I came for."

"You've already been to The Toy Box, I take it?"

She snorted. "Oh, yes. Talk about overpriced!"

"But he does have a dozen different bears, and—"

Lovey FitzPatrick's face turned bright red. "A *dozen!* That rotten liar!" Clutching the bag with the kilted bear and the candle, she stormed out of the Emporium.

Through the plate glass of the display window, Liss watched her sail back across the street and into Gavin Thorne's store. "Good luck to you both," she murmured.

This time when Liss locked up, she also turned out the

lights. She wasn't done for the day. Not by a long shot. She still had the next stage of the pageant to run. But she was through dealing with crazed customers until tomorrow.

A raucous shout of "Bring me my tea!" from the stockroom made her jump. Her hand to her heart, she fought the urge to reply. Yelling "Get your own damn tea!" would have no effect, not when the one demanding service was a parrot.

Liss entered the stockroom, her nose wrinkling at the smell of chicken manure. If she'd realized before she started this that she'd have to clean crates and cages, she'd have . . . done the same thing. With a sigh, she set to work cleaning, feeding, and watering. Chicken mash, she'd discovered, also had its own distinctive odor. It wasn't unpleasant exactly, but she wouldn't forget what it smelled like anytime soon.

The doves came with their own individual carrying cages. The chickens were in an oversized wooden crate that took up the rest of the space on top of the Emporium's worktable. The cages of the four "calling birds"—played by pet parrots borrowed from all over the county—hung from every convenient hook.

"Okay, boys and girls," Liss told them when she'd finished with the chickens. "Your turn."

Parrots seemed to be somewhat cleaner in their habits, and they were certainly prettier to look at. Still, they came with their own set of problems. For one thing, they had to be kept warm, a tricky proposition with a pageant that was being held outdoors.

They also talked.

It had been the blue and yellow parrot who'd wanted tea. Winston. She gave old Winston some seeds and refilled his water dish. The mostly yellow one—Claudine—appeared to be sleeping. Liss hoped she was sleeping. Visions of reliving parts of the dead parrot sketch from *Monty Python's Flying Circus* danced in her head. The third parrot, Augustus, was mostly red. He gave her an evil leer as he sidled back and forth on his perch.

The fourth parrot was named Polly. She was green. She watched with ill-disguised mistrust as Liss put out food and water. Liss latched the door to Polly's cage when she'd finished, but didn't cover it. She planned to leave the lights on for the birds, too. She'd come back to collect them in an hour or so for the ceremony, after which they'd go back to their owners until the pageant a week from Sunday.

"Polly want a cracker," Polly said in decidedly cranky tone of voice.

"That is so clichéd!" About to leave the stockroom, Liss turned to look back at the bird. "Besides, I don't have any crackers."

"Polly hungry," the parrot screeched, sounding even more irritable than before. "Gimme the f_ _ _ ing cracker!"

# Chapter Four

*B*e *careful what you wish for,* Sherri Willett thought on Sunday evening as she directed yet another out-of-state car toward the parking lot behind the grocery store. Shoppers had come to Moosetookalook, all right, and they'd brought their bad manners with them.

The town selectmen, Jason Graye in particular, were up in arms. The invaders were so desperate to lay hands on the one toy every child must find under the tree this year, or to score collectibles for themselves, that they had wrecked lawns by parking on them, created traffic jams, and even engaged in fistfights.

Things became quieter once darkness fell—thankfully early at this time of year—but the need for a visible police presence had everyone in the department working overtime. Sherri had barely seen her son all weekend. It wasn't that she didn't appreciate the extra income, but she was not looking forward to working twelve-hour shifts from now until Christmas. According to the newly posted schedule, she'd get off at midnight, have a whole twenty-four hours to catch up on sleep and play with Adam, and then work midnight to noon for the next week. Both her feet and her head ached just thinking about it.

During a break in traffic, a team from one of the Portland television stations approached Sherri. A microphone was thrust into her face and she could see the red light indicating that the camera was running.

"Any trouble with the crowds, officer?"

Sherri had no great desire to see her own image on the small screen, bigger than life and in high definition that showed every wrinkle and blemish, but it didn't look as if she had a choice. Repressing a shudder, she managed a stilted smile. "Everything's going very smoothly. We have plenty of parking available for anyone who wants to come to Moosetookalook."

She wasn't about to reveal the selectmen's gripes or describe the disgruntled customer who'd stomped down the porch steps of The Toy Box empty-handed and cussing a blue streak because Thorne's markup was too steep for his wallet. Nor was she going to mention the shouting match she'd witnessed earlier that day between Stu Burroughs and Gavin Thorne.

In Sherri's opinion, Stu was beating a dead horse. No way was Thorne going to share the goodies. Stu would do better to think of some novel way of his own to attract passing customers into his shop. A sale, maybe, though she could understand why cutting his prices might not appeal to him when Thorne kept raising his.

Sherri was vaguely aware of the reporter blathering on for the camera while she continued to direct traffic, but she was startled when the woman suddenly thrust the microphone in front of her again.

"Is that true, officer?"

"I couldn't say." Sherri kept smiling and hoped she hadn't just made a fool of herself. She couldn't say because she had no idea what the question had been.

A spattering of applause heralded Liss's introduction of the symbol of the fifth day of Christmas—five huge, interlocking rings made of cardboard and covered with sparkly gilt paint.

Sherri jerked her head toward the town square behind her. "You might want to head over there before you miss this evening's ceremony."

"Five golden rings," the reporter murmured.

"Looks like a poor man's version of the Olympic symbol," her cameraman muttered, but he dutifully aimed his equipment away from Sherri and toward the gazebo-style bandstand.

A small crowd of locals and tourists had gathered around it. The children playing on the jungle gym, merry-go-round, and swings in the playground area ignored the podium and the P.A. system that squealed when Liss tested it, but the grown-ups filling the space between the flagpole and the monument to the Civil War dead quieted down enough to listen. Feeling cynical, Sherri decided that was probably because there was a camera rolling. Or else they were hoping for another embarrassing incident. One of the previous night's featured performers had proved to have an . . . interesting vocabulary.

Assisted by chief of police Jeff Thibodeau, dressed as Santa Claus, Liss hoisted the rings into the air. She said a few words about the twelve days of Christmas shopping in Moosetookalook, and encouraged everyone to take advantage of the opportunity to visit all of the community's shops. Then she turned the gazebo over to the carolers.

They sang standing next to the "pear tree" from the first night of the pageant. It was actually a young apple tree in a large pot. Wax pears and a stuffed partridge had been wired to otherwise bare branches. Sherri was glad Liss had reconsidered asking the art teacher at the high school to make her something out of papier mâché. Precipitation of some sort was likely during the twelve days it would have to sit outdoors, even if that precipitation didn't fall in the form of snow.

Sherri hummed along with the Christmas carols while

she continued to direct traffic. Things were slowing down a bit, but The Toy Box was still open. With the other stores around the town square closed for the night, Gavin Thorne's shop windows shone like a beacon. He'd strung Christmas bulbs around every frame and across the porch. A flashing light highlighted a sign announcing the current price for Tiny Teddies. It seemed to go up every time Sherri turned around.

The cost of a Tiny Teddy from Gavin Thorne's shop was now a hundred and fifty dollars. He'd jacked the price up yet again just as soon as Liss sold the last of her supply. Sherri wasn't sure, but she thought Marcia might still have one or two left. Then again, Marcia had started out pricing her bears at a hundred dollars apiece.

*Crazy*, Sherri thought. *People who'd pay that much for a stuffed toy have got to be nuts.*

But like moths to a flame, shoppers couldn't seem to stay away. Almost everyone who entered Thorne's store came out carrying a small Toy Box bag in a manner that suggested it contained treasure more precious than gold.

"I haven't seen anything like this since the Beanie Baby craze back in the late '90s," the cameraman said as he and the reporter passed Sherri again on their way out of the town square.

Sherri had a vague memory of what he was talking about, but only that there had been a shortage of the toys, not that prices had gone sky high. Back then, she'd been a rebellious teenager living on her own after she'd dropped out of high school and run away from Moosetookalook.

How things had changed!

On Monday morning, Liss was in no hurry to reopen the Emporium. A sign in the window told shoppers she was sold out of Tiny Teddies. She did not expect anywhere near as many customers as she'd had over the weekend, although she did hope there would still be some overflow from The Toy Box. After all, she had other items in stock that would make wonderful Christmas gifts.

She took her time feeding and cleaning up after the assorted poultry living in her stockroom and only when that was done did she unlock the shop. During the morning and the first part of the afternoon, business was steady, if not exactly stellar. Then it fell off entirely. The sleigh bells on the door hadn't jangled for over an hour when Eric Moss turned up with a delivery—six geese for that evening's ceremony.

"Are they getting fat?" she asked, remembering again the song about Christmas, pennies, and hats.

"Why?" Moss asked. "You planning on eating them after the ceremony?"

Taken aback, Liss just stared at him. She honestly hadn't made the connection. Her family usually had a nice turkey and maybe a ham at Christmas. She peered into the huge crate. Two of the geese stared back at her. One stuck its head through the slats and tried to peck her.

"You'll have to watch out. Geese have nasty temperaments. Do best if they weren't so confined, too."

"They are *not* getting the run of the stockroom."

"You got a garage, don't you? Use that as a coop."

"Isn't it too cold out there? And I have chickens and pigeons, too."

Moss shook his head in disbelief as he wheeled the dolly with the crate toward the stockroom. "Used to be kids who grew up in the country knew something about farm life. You do know eggs come from chickens and milk comes from cows, right?"

"There's no need for sarcasm," she muttered, following him.

"My folks raised chickens. Had a few goats and a couple of cows, too, and our own apple trees. Planted vegetables every year."

"The good old days?" Liss wrinkled her nose as one of the geese made a deposit in the straw in the crate. It was *not* an egg, golden or otherwise.

Moss snorted. "Not so good. Folks around here barely got by even back then. Anyway, what I was going to say is that our chicken coop was a wooden building with no heat or insulation except for the straw in the nests. Never seemed to bother the birds none to be cold. They got them nice feather coats." He grinned, showing a mouthful of store-bought teeth.

The retired delivery service driver was a lean man of medium height, although age had given him a slight stoop. When he'd unloaded the crate, he wheeled the dolly back into the shop. "I hear you're all out of Tiny Teddies."

"I'm afraid so." Liss retreated behind the sales counter.

"You sold 'em too cheap."

"Probably, but I didn't feel comfortable putting the price up higher." Her profit had been healthy enough and her customers had gone away happy. Many of them had spent time browsing in the Emporium and made other purchases before they left. Others had promised to check out her Web site next time they needed a unique gift.

"Would you charge more if you had to do over again?" Propping an elbow next to the cash register, Moss leaned close enough for Liss to catch a whiff of the Ben Gay he used to keep his arthritic fingers limber.

She considered the question for only a moment before she replied. "I doubt it."

He frowned at her answer and seemed to be pondering its significance as he left the counter to wander around the shop. It took him a good ten minutes to finally came to the point. "I can get you more."

Liss felt her eyes widen in disbelief. "More Tiny Teddies?"

"Yep. And 'cuz I like you, Liss, I'll sell 'em to you for only fifty bucks apiece."

"How . . . generous of you."

"Interested?"

"No."

He looked at her as if she'd lost her marbles. "Why not?"

"These bears of yours aren't wearing kilts, are they?"

"No."

"There you have it, then. Besides, you want too much for them."

"I could come down a bit."

Liss sighed. She really didn't want to ask. "Where did you get them, Mr. Moss?"

"I've got my sources."

"Yes, well, I've got a source, too—for information. It's called the Internet, and this last week I've been reading up on Tiny Teddies. Seems there are some unscrupulous people who are trying to pass off counterfeit bears as the real thing."

"I don't know nothin' about that," Moss mumbled.

"No? Seems these bears are cheaply made in China. The collectors don't want anything to do with them. They aren't, well, collectible. One report I read said they weren't particularly safe for toddlers to play with, either."

Moss looked offended. "I wouldn't try to pull a fast one on you, Liss. These are the real deal."

"Then you'll have to tell me how you got hold of them. Otherwise I can't risk buying them."

"You saying they might be stolen? No such thing! I'll have you know I'm an honest businessman!"

He acted as if she'd insulted him, but Liss remembered his clandestine meeting with Jason Graye. Something had been "off" about it. "Can you prove your bears were made in the U.S.?"

Aside from the counterfeiting issue, Liss's research had revealed that the toys were legitimately manufactured on both sides of the border. There was a limit, however, on the number of Canadian-made toys that could legally be brought into the U.S. Taking a trip to Quebec Province and filling the trunk of your car with bears, intending to resell them back home, was a big no-no. There had been several recent arrests at border crossings around the country, although none so far in Maine.

His eyes narrowed. He edged toward the exit. "I don't have to prove nothin'!"

"Did Jason Graye set this up?"

Moss made a sound of disgust but he kept inching away from her.

"Come on, Mr. Moss. I need answers." She slipped out from behind the sales counter, trying not to look as if she wanted to stop him from leaving. "I don't do business with anyone who isn't up front with me."

"Man's got to have some secrets." Moss tugged nervously at a frayed section at the hem of his coat. "I stand to lose big time if someone else discovers my sources."

"I'm not your competition."

"So you say." He hesitated at the door, looking uncertain whether he wanted to go or stay.

"Is Jason Graye? Or is he your partner?"

"I work alone!" Indignant, he left in a huff.

Liss peered through the display window, curious to see what Moss would do next. To her surprise, he was standing stock still on the sidewalk out front, staring at The Toy Box.

Her gaze followed his to Gavin Thorne's display. The flashing light revealed a single Tiny Teddy, one of the ones dressed in a chef's hat and apron. Next to it was a new sign, the black letters so huge that Liss could read them easily even though she was two houses over and half a block away.

LAST TINY TEDDY IN NEW ENGLAND—$750

Eric Moss took off across the town square. Liss found it odd that he didn't approach Thorne or stop in at Marcia's consignment shop but she told herself it was none of her business. She went back behind the counter, intending to look at spring catalogues and plan her stock orders.

Instead she found herself staring into space, elbows on the counter, chin propped on her fists. After a moment, her fingers moved to toy with the small silver pin of a Scottish dancer that she'd used to hold the lacy white jabot at the neckline of her blouse in place. As usual when at work, she wore an outfit from the Emporium. Her floor-length skirt was made of wool woven in the Royal Stewart tartan.

Double duty, her Aunt Margaret called the habit of dressing up for work and modeling what they sold at the same time. Sales staff automatically became walking advertisements for the merchandise.

And this year, the merchandise had included bears. Until she'd run out. They were *all* sold out of Tiny Teddies, or all but. Some fool would undoubtedly pay Thorne's asking price for the last one. The trouble was, today was only the fifteenth of December.

People who arrived in Moosetookalook expecting to find Tiny Teddies for sale would be sorely disappointed. The Spruces was fully booked, but those guests wouldn't stay if their reason for coming to the area was gone. Word would spread. There would be cancellations. Too many of those would be an unmitigated disaster. Joe Ruskin had gone to considerable expense to bring in extra food and supplies and hire more staff. He couldn't afford a hit of this magnitude.

Groaning, Liss let her head fall forward until it hit the

hard wooden surface with a thump. She conquered the urge to bang it a few more times in frustration. She wasn't into self-inflicted pain, physical or mental. Still, this *was* all her fault. She'd counted on an influx of happy shoppers that would continue through the entire week and into next weekend. The sale of the last bear was supposed to coincide with the twelfth day of the pageant on Sunday afternoon.

"Idiot!" she muttered as she straightened. She should have allowed for this, should have seen it coming. She'd known how eager people were to buy this particular toy.

She should have charged more, if only to make her Tiny Teddies last longer. Well, that ship had sailed. Her only recourse now was to contact Eric Moss. She'd told him the truth. She couldn't afford to pay fifty dollars a bear and she didn't trust the provenance of the toys he'd offered her. But she wasn't the only business in town.

Her expression grim, Liss reached for the phone. Marcia owned a *consignment* shop. Maybe she and Moss could work something out.

Sherri had just started her shift at midnight when a call came in from Gavin Thorne. She could barely make out what he was saying.

"Slow down," she told him. "Are you hurt?" She listened a moment, shaking her head in disbelief as the story tumbled out. "Okay. I'm on my way."

She kept her hand on her holster as she trotted across the town square. Lights blazed inside The Toy Box. She wished she'd told him to turn them off. Then again, she didn't suppose Thorne himself was a target.

As she took the porch steps in one bound, she got a good look at the damage to the display window. The glass hadn't shattered. There was just a neat, round hole surrounded by a spiderweb of cracks to show where the bullet had gone through. Thorne would still have to replace the glass, but at least there wasn't a huge mess for him to clean up.

Inside she found the remains of the victim. Tufts of stuffing clung to every nearby surface. Sherri couldn't believe there had been so much cotton—or whatever it was—inside such a small bear.

"Thorne?"

She located him behind the high sales counter, slumped in his expensive office chair, his head in his hands and a hand gun dangling from his fingers. Sherri did a double take at the sight of the weapon.

"Whoa! Is that thing loaded?"

Thorne looked up, a dazed and stricken expression on his paste-colored face. It took him a moment to process her question. Then he nodded. "I thought the villain might still be in the store, but I was too late."

"Why don't you put that away, then, and tell me what happened?" She wanted to yell at him for being an idiot, but instead kept her voice as low and soothing as she could. It was the same tone she used to calm her son Adam when he was out of sorts.

His movements erratic, Thorne complied. Once the gun was out of sight in a drawer, Sherri breathed easier. Civilians and firearms were a bad mix, especially when the civilians didn't show proper respect for a deadly weapon.

"I take it you didn't shoot out your own window?"

"Don't be absurd!"

That was better. Nothing like a little righteous indignation to snap someone out of a pity party. Now maybe she could get some straight answers. "Any idea who did?"

"No. An intruder, I thought. But I didn't see any sign of one." He shook himself like a dog shedding water and managed a glum smile. "Lucky for him, whoever he was."

"Sit tight," Sherri advised. "Let me take a quick look around. Then we'll talk."

It didn't take long to confirm that no one else was in the shop. The back door was still secure. The lock on the front door didn't look as if it had been tampered with. "Was this open?" she called to Thorne.

"No. I unlocked it right after I called you."

A closer inspection of the bullet hole in the window convinced Sherri that the shot had been fired from outside. Whoever had been responsible for the damage was long gone, and since no one had come out of any of the nearby houses or called her to report anything out of the ordinary, it was a good bet there had been no witnesses.

She paused to study what was left of the Tiny Teddy, then eyed the window again. The bullet had passed right through the toy. After a short search, she found what she was looking for embedded in the back wall of the shop. Very carefully, she pried the bullet loose and popped it directly into a small ziplock bag. Only then did she take a closer look at it.

The police academy didn't spend a lot of time on forensics, so Sherri wasn't an expert on firearms. For major crimes, officers called in the state police. Sherri could see that the bullet had been only slightly squashed by its impact with the wall. It was a small caliber, but she couldn't be certain if it had been fired by a handgun or a rifle.

Frowning, Sherri tucked the bag into the inner pocket of her uniform coat and focused her full attention on Gavin Thorne. He was not a pretty sight—bed hair, no shirt, sagging sweatpants that undoubtedly revealed a butt crack when seen from the back, and bare feet. He had a painful-looking bunion on one of them.

"I take it you were upstairs asleep when this happened?"

He nodded. "Something woke me. I didn't realize it was a shot until I came down here and saw the bear."

"What made you think you should check on things?"

"I don't know. Just an uneasy feeling, I guess. I came down, saw the bear, got my gun out, and checked the shop. Then I called you."

"Ever think keeping a loaded firearm in a toy store might not be such a great idea?" She had nightmares about her own son, Adam, finding her gun and thinking it was something to play with, and she kept hers unloaded, secured with a trigger guard, and well hidden when she was off duty.

"Man's got a right to protect his property," Thorne insisted.

"You're missing the point. What if one of your customers got hold of it. We have gun locks available at the police station if—"

"What the hell does me owning a gun have to do with a vandal shooting my bear?" Agitated, he rose from his chair to tower over her. "It wasn't this gun he used!"

Sherri didn't back up, but she did drop the gun safety lecture . . . for the moment. "Did you see anyone?"

"No."

"Hear anything else suspicious?"

"No. Well, maybe a car."

Sherri continued to question him, making him repeat everything twice, until she was satisfied he had nothing left to tell her. Then she gave the chief of police a call. It would be up to Jeff to decide how to proceed.

He heard her out in thick silence broken only by the occasional yawn. "Question the neighbors," he instructed when she wound down.

"Now?"

He chuckled. "Not unless you want people calling the town office to complain about police brutality. Start making the rounds once it's reasonable to expect folks to be awake."

# Chapter Five

Sherri waited until seven. She didn't bother with the buildings on either side of The Toy Box. Preston's Mortuary had no occupants at the moment and was not yet open for the day. The structure that housed the post office in the front and the Clip and Curl in the back had an apartment upstairs, but it had been vacant since September.

The nearest inhabited residences were Angie's Books—the Hogencamp apartment was above the store—and Liss MacCrimmon's house adjacent to Moosetookalook Scottish Emporium. Sherri decided to leave Angie in peace until after she'd sent her kids off to school.

"Have you taken a look at The Toy Box's window this morning?" she asked as she breezed into Liss's kitchen.

"What's the price up to today?" Liss looked a bit bleary-eyed, peering over the rim of a mug of coffee. The heavenly aroma of a freshly brewed pot of the stuff filled the room.

Sherri helped herself to a muffin and slathered it with the cholesterol-improving spread Liss had recently started using. "No price. No value." She took a bite, chewed, and swallowed.

"Sherri, you'll have to spell it out for me. I'm too tired to think straight until I've had at least two more cups of coffee."

"It's dead," Sherri said. "Shot through the heart."

"I beg your pardon."

"During the night someone took a potshot through Thorne's window and nailed the Tiny Teddy." The grin she'd been trying to contain slipped free. "Sad, sad case. Stuffing everywhere. Poor wee bear never had a chance."

"Right through the heart?" Liss stared at Sherri, incredulous.

"Bull's-eye." Sherri mimed firing a pistol. "Bang."

In spite of Liss's best efforts, a giggle escaped her. "It's not funny."

"Vandalism of the worst kind." Sherri gave up trying to stifle her own laughter. "Thorne was almost incoherent when he called the P.D. and requested an officer."

"Angry?"

"Upset. And at one point I thought he might burst into tears. He really expected someone to pay $750 for that bear."

Liss got control of herself first. "It's *not* funny. The thought of someone shooting out store windows . . . *my* store window, for example—who on earth would do such a thing?"

Sherri had spent the last few hours trying to make sense of the crime. There *was* no rhyme or reason to it, which was probably why she felt so punchy. *Get a grip*, she told herself. She wasn't here for the baked goods. Well, not *only* for that. "Did you hear anything strange last night around midnight?"

"A car backfiring?" Liss threw out the cliché, then abruptly sobered. "You know, *something* must have awakened me in the wee hours. I don't remember hearing anything specific, but once I was awake, I wasn't able to get back to sleep for ages."

"I don't suppose you looked at a clock?"

"Sorry. I just tossed and turned a lot and finally put the pillow over my head. I know I fell asleep at some point, but only because I jumped a foot when my alarm clock went off."

"I'm surprised the hammering didn't wake you."

"What hammering?"

"Thorne nailed plywood over what's left of his window."

Liss inhaled the rest of the coffee in her mug and got up to refill it. "So, you've got no idea at all who did it?"

"Nope. Any suggestions? I'd dearly like to solve this one. It's my first real case since coming on the job." The scene, however, had been sadly lacking in clues.

"I suppose it could have been someone ticked off at the prices Thorne was charging." Unasked, Liss brought Sherri a cup of coffee, already doctored just the way she liked it.

"Maybe, but if it was a collector, why not break the window and steal the bear?"

"Nothing else was damaged?"

"Nope. Just one shot by someone with a pretty good aim." Sherri sipped cautiously at the hot liquid and decided it was cool enough to drink without scalding her tongue.

"Could it have been personal? Vindictiveness toward Thorne himself? Get back at him by destroying the most valuable item in his store?"

"Who'd hate him that much?"

"His ex?"

"Too obvious." Sherri would check it out, of course, and very often the simple answer was the right one, but it didn't *feel* right to her. "I'm still inclined toward random violence as the answer."

"I don't much care for that explanation." Liss shivered.

"Most likely it was just a prank." She put more reassurance than she felt into her voice. She suspected she'd be doing a lot of that today as she talked to other neighbors. "A *stupid* prank, but then most pranks are pretty dumb."

"Teenagers?"

"Could be. Jeff wants me to ask around to find out if anyone heard or saw anything out of the ordinary last night."

"Man I wish I'd decided to get up and look out the window." Liss shook her head. "What woke me probably *was* your gunshot."

Sherri nodded and took another sip of coffee. "Don't feel bad. Thorne's bedroom is upstairs over his shop. Granted, it's at the back, but after he heard the noise, he still waited several minutes before he decided to go check on things."

"Why on earth didn't he take the bear out of the window when he closed for the night? Put it in a safe or something?"

"What? Miss catching a potential customer's eye? He had a light shining on the darned thing." A thought occurred to her. "I wonder . . . is it possible Thorne could have shot out his own window? He has insurance on the stuff he sells, right?"

Liss's laugh was short and humorless.

"What?" Sherri *liked* Thorne for the villain.

"He'll get his window replaced, but no insurance company is going to pay him his asking price for that bear. At best, he'll be reimbursed what he paid for it—less than five bucks wholesale. No wonder he's upset!"

*Damn*, Sherri thought. *I knew that. I must be more tired than I thought.*

She'd worked part-time at the Emporium for years. She'd even had her name on the store's checking account for a while. Margaret MacCrimmon Boyd, Liss's aunt and business partner, formerly the sole proprietor, had made sure Sherri was familiar with everything about the store, from order forms to their insurance policy.

"Someone *shot* it." Liss shook her head. "That doesn't make a lick of sense. *Steal* it, maybe. But destroy it?"

"One for the books, that's for sure. I wonder if the news crew will come back."

"Oh, that's all we need! The idea was to get *good* publicity for the town."

Sherri polished off a second muffin, one of Patsy's, she assumed, since the breads and pastries Liss baked tended to have the consistency of rocks. "Isn't there some old saw about any publicity being good publicity?"

"A vicious lie." Liss buttered a second muffin for herself. "Is Jeff calling anyone in to help investigate?"

"I doubt it. Vandalism isn't that serious a crime. There was no threatening note tossed through the window or anything. Jeff will probably let Sheriff Lassiter know what happened, but there's no reason to bring in the state police." She sent Liss a sudden impish grin. "Why? Were you hoping to see Gordon again?"

"I don't know *what* you mean." Liss tried to feign innocence, but after a moment she smiled, a dreamy look in her eyes. As Sherri well knew, Gordon Tandy, the state police detective assigned to Carrabassett County, was the *other* man in Liss MacCrimmon's life.

After Sherri left, Liss opened the Emporium, took delivery of seven swans, and for the next five hours waited on a steady stream of customers, all complaining about the lack of Tiny Teddies. Some of them, however, bought things.

At two in the afternoon, she heard a cheer go up outside. It didn't take long for word to spread. Gavin Thorne had a new supply of Tiny Teddies. The Emporium promptly emptied out.

Liss stepped onto her porch to have a look. The plywood Thorne had used to board up his display window was now plastered with flyers. She couldn't read them at this distance, but it was pretty obvious what they were advertising. She spared a glance for Marcia's consignment shop, wondering if the other woman had ever contacted Eric Moss. Liss had left a message on Marcia's machine about Moss's Tiny Teddies, but maybe Marcia, too, had thought fifty dollars a bear too steep a price.

A car horn sounded, jerking her attention back to the crowd mobbing the toy store. She spotted Lovey FitzPatrick among them, and a few other faces that looked vaguely familiar.

Thorne had probably struck a deal with Moss, Liss decided. She told herself that if the toys were counterfeits or had been brought into the country illegally, she didn't want to know. As long as she wasn't selling them, it was no business of hers. The only real question was how high the toy shop owner would jack up his prices this time around. She expected that someone would stop by the Emporium sooner or later and tell her.

In the meantime, the chill in the air made her shiver. On the way out the door, she'd wrapped a shawl in the predominantly yellow MacMillan tartan around her shoulders, but it wasn't sufficient protection from the cold, not even when worn over a knit sweater imported from Scotland and a pair of slacks in the Black Watch pattern. She ducked back inside, grateful for the warmth of the shop.

The deserted store, however, had a depressing effect on Liss. It was quiet. Too quiet. Normally, neither solitude nor silence bothered her, not for brief stretches anyway. Sometimes she played Celtic music in the background when the Emporium was open. At others she opted for the local radio station or for no noise at all. She was about to reach under the sales counter for a CD of one of her favorite bagpipe bands when she heard an odd little squeak at floor level.

Something slithered across her shoe.

Liss froze.

*There are no poisonous snakes in the state of Maine.*

Almost as soon as the thought slashed through her mind, she knew she was being foolish. It was too cold for snakes, even if that explanation for what she'd just felt made sense. It didn't. Neither did thinking the shop had rats.

At worst, they had mice. Or one of the chickens had gotten loose. Liss braced herself and looked down.

A small, furry black face stared back at her with big, green eyes. The creature clambered onto the toe of her shoe once more, opened its mouth, and meowed.

"Oh, for Heaven's—!" Liss scooped up the tiny kitten, cuddling it against her chest for a moment before she set it down on the sales counter. "Aren't you the cutest thing!"

It was only a few months old, barely weaned. Its head seemed too big for the rest of its body. On closer examination, Liss discovered a few specks of white in the long, black fur, but not enough to make much difference.

"Where did you come from?" She didn't expect an answer. Besides, she could make an educated guess.

At this time of year, the end of the semester at the Fallstown branch of the University of Maine, the number of abandoned pets in the area always underwent a dramatic increase. Departing students didn't usually dump cats and dogs this far north, but for all Liss knew, one of them could have been in town looking for a Christmas present for dear old mom and dad.

That the kitten could have strayed from a litter and have a family that loved it and was even now frantically searching for it seemed much less likely. Just in case, Liss made a sign and stuck it in her window: FOUND—BLACK KITTEN, INQUIRE WITHIN. She also phoned the local animal shelter, located in Fallstown, in case someone went looking there for the little feline.

After a dash next door to her house, Liss returned toting a spare litter box, a box of clumping cat litter, a can of cat food, and two bowls, all of which she set up in the tiny bathroom next to the stockroom. Putting a cat among the pigeons and the other poultry did not strike Liss as a good idea.

The kitten was already chowing down on tuna treat by the time Liss filled the second bowl with water from the tap. She watched, enjoying the little animal's antics, until she heard the jangle of sleigh bells.

"Okay, Junior. I'm going to have to leave you here. Try to be good." She stepped out into the shop, then turned and pulled one of the soft, fluffy towels off the rack, folded it, and placed it on the floor. "Take a nap," she suggested, and closed the door. She left the light on.

Lovey FitzPatrick and another woman stood by the sales counter talking together in low tones. It took Liss a moment to recognize the second customer as Felicity Thorne.

"Good afternoon, ladies. How may I help you?"

"Do you have more Tiny Teddies, too?" Thorne's ex wife asked.

"No. Sorry. I—"

They didn't wait to hear her explanation. Both women were out the door and heading for Marcia's place before Liss could finish her sentence.

"Nice chatting with you, too," she called after them.

Paying customers trickled in for the rest of the day. In between, Liss rearranged stock and checked on the kitten. Each time she found it sound asleep on the towel.

The nearer it got to closing time at five, the harder Liss had to fight not to yawn. Her restless night was catching up with her. She handed a Moosetookalook Scottish Emporium bag to a woman in a suede coat, wished her happy holidays, and shifted her attention to the next person in line.

The woman, a small-boned, rather thin creature in a herringbone wool coat, had her head down, digging for something in her purse. All Liss could see at first, beneath a matching herringbone wool hat, was gray-blond hair and a bit of darkly suntanned skin. The latter was an unusual sight, especially in Maine in winter, but in the last few days customers from all over the place had been in town. It didn't surprise Liss that one of the snowbirds—northerners who spent the cold months in southern states—had come to Moosetookalook to shop.

Then the woman looked up and Liss realized she wasn't just any snowbird.

"Hello, Liss. You're looking well."

"Aunt Margaret!" Liss felt her jaw drop. "You're not supposed to be here until Friday!"

That wasn't the only surprise, but it was the only one Liss dared voice. Where was the comfortably plump Margaret MacCrimmon Boyd she'd last seen at her parent's house in Arizona a year ago? Where was the brightly colored hair, a different shade every time, but always red?

"I came early when I heard about the Tiny Teddies." Margaret sounded a trifle defensive. "It was all over the Internet and last night you made the national news on NBC."

"So someone told me." The local report had run the day after the five golden rings ceremony and then been picked up by the network. Liss hadn't seen either clip. For the last few days, with hordes of tourists descending upon Moosetookalook, watching television had been the last thing on her mind.

"I thought the shop would be busier."

"We're out of Tiny Teddies, but we're still attracting some customers."

Now it was Liss's turn to feel defensive. Her aunt was still half owner of the Emporium. What if she didn't approve of what her niece had done with the place? Maybe Aunt Margaret would have raised the price on their supply of Tiny Teddies.

"The profits for the month will be way up," Liss blurted. "Don't worry about that."

"I wasn't." Aunt Margaret had turned her attention to the shop, her gaze taking in the many small changes Liss had made since she'd been in charge. In all the years Aunt Margaret had run the place, she'd kept the arrangement of stock exactly the same—"a place for everything and everything in its place," as she'd been in the habit of saying.

Racks of kilts and tartan skirts had run along one side of the big sales room. Now kilts were on one side, women's wear on the other. The wall display of bagpipes, practice chanters, and pennywhistles hadn't been moved, but there were subtle changes everywhere else. All the cabinets, shelves, and tables gleamed, redolent of lemon-scented furniture polish, just the way they had when Aunt Margaret was in charge. They still held an assortment of Scottish-themed gifts. But they weren't in the same places anymore. Liss had gradually moved every single one of them. She bit back the urge to apologize.

Aunt Margaret wandered over to the display window to peer out into the early evening gloom, no doubt watching customers exit The Toy Box. The streetlights around the town square kept total darkness at bay, but from Liss's perch on the stool behind the sales counter she couldn't see much beyond the pale glowing circles at the top of each pole.

"I do hope all those folks have hotel rooms for the night," Aunt Margaret said in a worried voice. "The roads are terrible. I wasn't sure we'd make it here from the airport, what with the storm and all."

"Storm?" Liss echoed the word, feeling a frown crease her forehead. She scrambled off the stool to join her aunt at the window. Big, wet flakes drifted past the glass at an angle, falling fast.

Aunt Margaret chuckled. "You *have* been out of touch with the rest of the world. It's been snowing for hours."

Liss stared in astonishment at the street and the town square beyond. No longer could a single blade of brown grass be seen. At least two inches of the white stuff had already accumulated on the ground and the storm showed no sign of letting up any time soon.

Standing there, side by side with her aunt, looking out at the snow, Liss felt the tension between them dissolve. Impulsively, she embraced the older woman. "Welcome home, Aunt Margaret."

"It's good to be back. Time to close up?"

"May as well." Liss turned the dead bolt and lowered the shade on the front door. "What did you do with your luggage?"

"It's already in the apartment. I had the shuttle driver help me carry it up the outside stairs. Then I came back down the same way and walked around to the front. I didn't want to scare you to death by popping out of the inside stairwell behind you. Come up with me? You can help me unpack."

"Sure. Why not?"

"The shuttle driver thinks we're in for a good old-fashioned northeaster. He was some tickled by the prospect. According to him, business taking folks from the jetport to ski resorts has been slow all month, even to the places that make their own snow."

"Driving conditions may be poor until the storm winds down and the plows can do their thing, but the skiers will be on the road to the slopes the minute they have a prayer of getting through." She followed her aunt up the stairs and into the apartment.

"Isn't that the truth, and the snowmobilers won't even wait that long. They may not go out *during* a blizzard, but the moment they can see well enough to blaze a trail, they'll be on it. You couldn't pay me enough to ride on one of those things." Aunt Margaret led the way toward the master bedroom.

"They're kind of fun. I had a friend in high school who

had a two-up. You know—a two-person machine. He took me for a couple of rides. It's an expensive hobby, though. Not one I'd ever want to take up."

Liss whistled softly at the size of the stack of luggage piled in the corner and wondered how her aunt had managed to bring so many suitcases with her on the plane. "Did you buy an entirely new wardrobe while you were away?"

"Just about," was the cheery answer. "Oh, I almost forgot. Your folks send their love." She had been staying with Liss's parents in Arizona, on and off, for most of the last year and a half.

"I wish Mom and Dad had been able to come back to Moosetookalook for Christmas, too."

"They've wanted to go on this holiday cruise for years."

"Really?"

"You don't think you know everything about them, do you? Take my word for it—even your next of kin can have a side you just don't see."

Liss hesitated, hearing the bitterness in her aunt's tone. She knew full well how devastated Aunt Margaret had been by what had happened when Liss first came back to Moosetookalook, but the subject had to be broached sometime.

"Aunt Margaret, about—"

The thin, gray-haired woman who had replaced Liss's plump, flamboyant, red-haired aunt turned an icy glare on her niece. "I do not want to talk about those terrible days. Not *ever!*"

Liss gave in without an argument. "Whatever you say, Aunt Margaret."

"Well, then . . . good!" She busied herself transferring clothing from a suitcase to a dresser drawer. "There's another thing I've decided, and this isn't open to discussion, either. We're business partners now. Have been for some time. I want you to drop the 'aunt' and just call me by my first name."

"That will take a little getting used to . . . Margaret."

Liss reached for a small padded bag and started to unload the bottles of perfume she found carefully packed inside, lining up Emeraude, White Shoulders, Wind Song, and My Sin on top of the dressing table.

"You'll manage, I'm sure."

*What next?* Liss wondered. *Shorten Margaret to Maggie? Or Meg? Or Mags?*

"Are you okay, Aunt—I mean, Margaret? I mean . . . well, you've lost some weight—"

"I could stand to, don't you think?" Wry amusement tinged the question.

"And the hair?" Liss tugged on one of her own light brown locks.

"I got tired of fussing with it. Let it grow out. Who was I trying to kid with that all that red, anyway? I'm almost sixty years old and I've earned every one of my gray hairs. People should be proud of their age, not try to hide it."

Finishing the unpacking and putting away Margaret's things took up the best part of the next hour. Liss's aunt chatted nonstop, telling anecdotes about her travels and giving Liss an update on what her parents—Margaret's brother and sister-in-law—had been up to.

"I'm starving, and you must be, too," Margaret said as she folded the last sweater and tucked it away in a drawer.

"I was going to go to the market for you before Friday but I hadn't gotten around to it yet. I doubt there's anything but peanut butter and stale cereal in your cupboards."

"Then I say we go to your house to eat. Besides, I want to see what you've done with the place."

"I updated the kitchen, but everything else is pretty much the same as it always was." Liss had inherited the house under difficult circumstances, but she'd always been comfortable there as a visitor and she liked the way the previous owner had decorated and furnished the rooms, especially the small combination library and office.

"Still got Lumpkin?" her aunt asked as they started back down the inside staircase.

Liss stopped short on the landing, horrified. "Oh, no! I forgot about the kitten. And I've got to check on the birds."

Aunt Margaret looked startled. "Are you keeping a menagerie on the premises?"

"Damned near."

She told her aunt about the kitten first, then launched into an explanation of the Twelve Shopping Days of Christmas. Margaret took the announcement that her stockroom was currently serving as a chicken coop calmly enough, only murmuring, "No one mentioned *poultry* on the evening news."

"I'm sorry, but I'm stuck housing them until the pageant on the last day. That's when we trot out all the gifts mentioned in the song."

"Wasn't it turtle doves and French hens?"

"The closest we could get were carrier pigeons and Rhode Island Reds, and I'm afraid there's a bit of a smell in here." She flung open the door.

Aunt Margaret wrinkled her nose. "I don't expect you'll be able to have your ceremony tonight, not in this storm."

"The swans will be devastated." She indicated that morning's delivery. Swans being in short supply in Maine, especially in winter, she'd turned her problem over to the same high school art teacher who'd offered to make the pear tree. Seven papier mâché swans sat atop the large crate containing the six geese.

With Margaret's help, it didn't take long to see to the needs of her livestock.

"Now for the tough part," Liss said, collecting her coat and the kitten. "Introducing Lumpkin to his new housemate."

Lumpkin, as usual, was waiting for her just inside the

kitchen door. It was time for his supper and he accepted no excuses for tardiness.

He did not notice the kitten at first. He was too busy expressing his disapproval of the snow on Liss's shoes. It rapidly turned into small puddles on the floor and Lumpkin did not like getting his feet wet.

In retaliation, he attempted to bite Margaret's ankle.

She smacked him with her hat. The soft wool didn't hurt the big cat one bit, but it did spook him. He tore out of the room at the speed of light.

Liss set the kitten down on the floor and watched as it began to explore. After a moment, it headed straight for Lumpkin's food dish, which still contained the dried up remains of the last can of cat food.

"This could be an interesting evening," Margaret mused.

# Chapter Six

Following the snowplow wasn't the fastest way to travel in a stormy, predawn hour, but it was the smartest. Dan had spent most of the night at the hotel, even though he had only a few miles to drive to reach home. Once the weather became really bad, white-out conditions and the steep road from The Spruces down to the rest of the village were enough to convince him to stay put. He'd been needed at the hotel until midnight to work in the bar. After that, he'd caught a few hours sleep in one of the unoccupied rooms. Now all he wanted was to get safely home and use the snowblower to clean out his own driveway. He'd shower, change his clothes, and then head for his real job at Ruskin Construction.

Tired as he was, he couldn't help but appreciate how peaceful Moosetookalook appeared with a fresh blanket of white to cover the rough edges. The precipitation falling now was the light, fluffy stuff. Once the roads were cleared and the sun came up, it was guaranteed to be a glorious day. Already the first faint pink and gold hint of sunrise crept above the horizon.

As the plow made the turn by Willett's Store and headed down the twisting road that led to the center of town, Dan caught movement out of the corner of his eye. Squinting, he could just make out the shape of a snowmobile cutting across a field.

Dan shook his head, grateful for the blast of warmth from the heat vents that kept the windshield from fogging and his fingers toasty as they gripped the steering wheel. Give him a nice enclosed truck and a paved road anytime!

A few minutes later the plow driver, one of Dan's lifelong acquaintances, turned down Birch Street. He cleared a short distance up Dan's driveway, making a space to pull in off the street.

Dan hopped out of his truck, waved his thanks, and paused to take in the scene. The snow had all but stopped. The town square was quiet and pretty, all that pristine white reflecting the glow of the streetlamps.

He saw that there were lights on in Margaret Boyd's apartment. She always had been an early riser. She'd called his father the night before to say she was home. The two of them were planning to get together later today. Margaret, after all, had been one of the earliest investors in the hotel project.

There were no lights at Liss's house. She wasn't a morning person. Dan expected she was still asleep. He hoped she wasn't upset about having to cancel last evening's ceremony because of the storm. She could always combine the swans with the maids a-milking. He supposed he should have called her to suggest that, but he'd been right out straight at the hotel.

As he headed into the house to make coffee, he reviewed his plans for the day: make coffee; blow snow; shower; put on clean clothes; get to work. There was no room for Liss MacCrimmon in that schedule.

Better *find* room, he warned himself as he climbed the stairs two at a time. He'd let things drift far too long as it was.

*   *   *

Liss had to drag herself out of bed when her alarm clock went off. She wasn't surprised that she hadn't slept well. First Lumpkin had wanted to keep her company. She'd shoved him off the bed at least a half dozen times before he'd given up. She'd just managed to doze off, or so it seemed to her, when the passing snowplow woke her again. The darn thing was noisy enough to wake the dead! She'd finally resorted to the same desperate measures she'd used the night before, jerking the pillow over her head to drown out the noise. She'd caught another thirty winks that way, but it wasn't enough.

Halfway through the short version of her morning exercises, Liss remembered the kitten. She'd had to leave it in the downstairs bath overnight. Every time Lumpkin had caught sight of the poor little thing, he'd hissed or growled. Liss hadn't trusted him not to hurt the smaller feline.

In the shower, all her other concerns rushed down on her head, pounding at her with greater force than the spray as she soaped up and rinsed off. After they'd eaten supper the previous evening, Aunt Margaret had unearthed one of the yellow-lined pads Liss kept handy for list making. Since Liss had picked up the habit from her aunt, she had not been surprised when Margaret took felt-tip pen in hand and started itemizing. The resulting list had been a simple one with only four items:

bank
lawyer
hotel
Ernie

Reading the last item upside down, Liss had choked on the sip of the white wine she'd just swallowed. "Ernie Willett?"

"You have a problem with that?"

Liss had held up both hands, palms toward her aunt. "Not at all. It just caught me off guard."

Margaret's smile had surprised her even more. It had softened her whole face. "We've been writing to each other since last year."

*Ernie Willett?*

As if she'd sensed Liss's dismay, Aunt Margaret had said nothing more on the subject. She'd gone back to her list and added two more items, but this time she'd covered the writing with her hand so that Liss couldn't see what they were.

Liss turned off the water in the shower and reached for a towel. Ernie Willett, she thought again. Sherri's divorced father. The implications of Ernie Willett being on her widowed aunt's to-do list weren't any easier to accept this morning than they had been the previous evening. True Ernie and Aunt Margaret had dated when they were young, before each of them married someone else, but the Ernie Willett Liss knew was an irritating old curmudgeon. He owned a combination convenience store and service station—the only gas pump in the village—and in her recollection had never numbered courtesy among the services he provided to his customers.

But Ernie Willett was the least of Liss's worries this morning. Just before Aunt Margaret had left Liss to go back to her own place, she'd said she wanted to have a long serious talk with her niece about the future of the Emporium.

If not for the tired look on her aunt's face, Liss would have insisted they hash things out then and there. Instead, she'd resigned herself to spending a restless night before she found out what Margaret really thought of the changes Liss had made since she'd been in charge.

When Liss had dried her hair and dressed for the day, she ventured downstairs to look for Lumpkin. She found him standing in front of the closed door that shielded the kitten, his tail enlarged to twice its normal size. The expression on his furry face was one of affronted dignity.

"Give it a rest," she told him. "You have a visitor. He . . . or she . . . has had a rough time of it. You are to be polite." Mentally crossing her fingers, Liss reached for the knob.

The black kitten bounded out into the hall. Not at all put off by Lumpkin's hiss or his stiff-legged stance, it stopped only long enough to give the larger cat an inquisitive look before gamboling straight toward him. Apparently too astonished to move, Lumpkin just stood there while the kitten stropped itself against his side, then ducked under his belly.

Liss stifled a snicker. It was trying to nurse.

"No joy there, little one," she told it, scooping it up just as Lumpkin recovered enough to growl.

Two mugs of coffee later, Liss entered Moosetookalook Scottish Emporium with the black kitten cradled in her arms. It was only 7:30, but Margaret had already opened for the day. She was standing in the shop doorway, breathing deeply and smiling as she looked out across the snow-covered town square.

"It's good to be home."

"I'm glad you're back." Liss meant it, but she was still uneasy about what Margaret might plan to say to her.

"So, any new gossip I should know about? Did Marcia's husband ever come back?"

"Nope." Liss shared Moosetookalook news as it happened in her regular letters and e-mails to her aunt and to her parents.

"Poor Marcia."

"She seems to be coping. To tell you the truth, she seems happier without Cabot Katz. Did I tell you she took back her maiden name? She's Marcia Milliken again."

"When does The Toy Box usually open?" Margaret had already lost interest in Marcia. "I'm curious to meet this Gavin Thorne and to get a look at a Tiny Teddy. I've never seen one except in pictures."

"He's been opening at eight since the madness started." His usual hours, and hers, had been ten to five, Tuesday through Saturday, until the advent of the Tiny Teddies had changed all that.

"He's got a customer waiting," Margaret observed.

Having put the kitten in the shop's bathroom, already furnished with a litter box and water dish, Liss poured herself yet another mug of coffee from the pot her aunt had brewed. She came out from behind the counter so that she could see past Margaret. It *was* a glorious day. A scene right off a Christmas card. Anyone who came to Moosetookalook to Christmas shop should be delighted with what they found.

Except for the guy pounding furiously on the front door of The Toy Box.

Margaret came inside and moved to the Emporium's display window so she could continue to watch the stranger without getting chilled. Sipping her coffee, Liss ambled over to stand beside her, then took a step back when she got a whiff of her aunt's perfume. It wasn't unpleasant—jasmine, Liss thought, and citrus, and a hint of sandalwood—but it was strong.

The man on Thorne's porch alternated between knocking at the door and banging on the plywood that covered the cracked glass. He tried to peer into the shop, but Thorne had done a thorough job. The panels were flush and contained no convenient knotholes to look through.

"Maybe I should go over there and check on your Mr. Thorne," Margaret murmured. "It's odd he's not opening up when he's obviously got a customer."

"Maybe that guy is a bill collector." The suit and topcoat were very formal attire for rural Maine.

"Don't be facetious." Her eyes twinkled. "Bill collectors are *much* more aggressive."

They watched for a few more minutes, but there was still no sign of life from inside The Toy Box.

"Unless Thorne has changed the locks, I can get inside with Warren's spare key," Aunt Margaret said.

Warren Alden's small appliance repair shop had occupied the building for years, and Alden himself had been a nice old guy who'd have been grateful for Margaret's concern. The current proprietor was something else again.

"He might just be sleeping in," Liss warned.

"Or he might be ill. Good neighbors have an obligation to look out for each other." Margaret rummaged in the junk drawer beneath the sales counter until she produced a key ring. "Warren gave me this four or five years ago, after he accidentally locked himself out."

Margaret grabbed the coat Liss had just hooked over the coatrack, slung it around her own shoulders, and sailed out the door. Moments later, before Liss's aunt had even reached the corner, Sherri Willett appeared on the Emporium's porch, coming from the other direction.

"Was that Margaret?" she asked.

"It was. She got home yesterday afternoon during the storm."

"Where's she headed?"

"Straight for trouble if Gavin Thorne is in a bad mood. Her curiosity seems to have gotten the better of her common sense. She *says* she's worried that Thorne is sick and needs help. He looked perfectly healthy the last time I saw him. He was gloating about all the money he's raking in. He's probably just taking his own good time about opening up this morning. Either that or he's recognized that man pounding on the door and doesn't want to talk to him."

"Maybe that's his wife's lawyer," Sherri speculated.

"The possibilities are endless. Quiet night?"

"Yes, thank goodness. Not even any traffic accidents, in

spite of the storm. There were a few fender benders down Fallstown way, though. I heard Pete a couple of times on the radio." Her voice faded as she ducked behind the counter to help herself to coffee.

"Any reports of a missing black kitten?" Liss continued to watch her aunt through the display window. Margaret trotted up the porch steps to the front door of The Toy Box and said a few words to the stranger. Whatever she told him sent him scurrying back to his car to wait until The Toy Box opened. He started the engine to keep warm but didn't drive away.

"Missing kitten?" Sherri repeated. "No one called the P.D. about one."

"Take a look in the bath."

Behind her she heard the door open and Sherri's delighted chuckle. "Well, aren't you the little sweetie."

Back on Thorne's porch, Margaret fiddled with the lock. After considerable jiggling, her key finally worked and she slipped inside the shop, closing the door behind her. Liss glanced over her shoulder, unsurprised to see that Sherri had a squirming ball of black fur tucked under her arm.

"Where did Sweetie come from?"

"Wandered into the shop yesterday. I put a sign in the window." Liss gestured toward the notice, glanced that way, and froze.

"What on earth . . . ?" Sherri took a step forward, staring through the glass, as Liss was, at The Toy Box.

The door left standing wide open behind her, Margaret stumbled down the porch steps and into the street. Oblivious to the fact that Dan Ruskin, headed for work in his pickup truck, was bearing down on her, she ran right out in front of him. Tires squealed as he stopped inches from a collision.

Margaret kept going. Her face ashen, she burst into the

Emporium. "Call 9-1-1," she gasped, her voice barely audible above the jangle of the sleigh bells attached to the door.

"Sherri's right here." Liss had never seen her aunt so upset. She was literally shaking.

"What's wrong?" Sherri asked.

The sleigh bells over the threshold erupted once more as Dan rushed inside. His face was almost as pale as Margaret's.

"What the hell were you thinking?" he shouted. "I almost hit you!"

Margaret didn't seem to hear him, nor did she respond to Sherri's blue uniform. Her eyes locked with Liss's. "There's a dead man in the toy store!"

"What?" Liss didn't think she could have heard correctly.

"Are you certain?" Sherri was already moving toward the door.

A horrible grimace distorted Margaret's features. "I'm sure. Hearts tend to stop beating when someone fires a bullet through them."

*Ohmigod,* Liss thought. *Just like the Tiny Teddy!*

# Chapter Seven

The words of a lecture on crime scenes came back to Sherri as she stepped cautiously through the open front door of The Toy Box. "Think like a criminal," the instructor had said. "Witnesses are not the most important factor. They're unreliable. The *scene*, however, *does not change*."

It did if it had been messed with.

A strange man knelt next to Gavin Thorne's body.

"You! Stand up and turn around. Slowly." Sherri didn't see a weapon, but she drew her own. Better safe than sorry.

The man blinked at her in confusion. Hands in the air, he tried for an innocuous smile and missed. He wore a dark gray wool coat that shouted expensive but the faint greenish tinge of his complexion was common as dirt. "I'm sorry. I think I'm going to—"

"Outside. Now!" She barely had time to get out of his way before he rushed past her to deposit his breakfast in the bushes beside the porch. She followed him, giving him a moment to recover before she spoke again. "You done?"

He nodded, eyes closed.

"Name?"

"Mark Patton. Innocent bystander. I swear."

"Then why did you go inside?"

"Something upset that woman."

"Try again."

"I was looking for a Tiny Teddy, okay?"

"Okay. Stay put. You'll have to give a statement." She wasn't sure she trusted him to follow orders, but she had his name and made a mental note of the license number on his car before she went back inside. If he took off, she could find him.

The basics of murder investigation had been drilled into Sherri at the police academy. There were only three departments in the entire state that handled them—the cities of Portland and Bangor and the State Police. The local P.D., however, had its role to play. Sherri was the one responsible for making initial observations. She might be asked to assist the state police further, if she had special knowledge of the case to offer. What she did in the next couple of minutes could be crucial, not only to solving Thorne's murder but also to her career in law enforcement.

Secure the scene? No. Not until she'd made sure Thorne was really dead. Although she wasn't in much doubt, she wasn't supposed to take a civilian's word for it. A few steps inside the shop she stopped to brace herself for the sight and smell of violent death.

It wasn't as bad as she'd feared. There was blood, but not buckets of it. Thorne lay sprawled on the floor on his back. His Harry Potter glasses had landed a short distance away. One lens was cracked.

Her gaze shifted back to the body. Gavin Thorne had been shot in the chest. Good aim, Sherri thought. She wasn't a doctor, but it looked to her as if the bullet had struck the heart, just as Margaret had said.

And just like the last victim she'd eyeballed in The Toy Box.

After one long stare to verify that there was nothing anyone could do to revive Thorne, Sherri turned her attention to her surroundings. She wasn't the one who'd examine blood-spatter patterns or ballistic evidence or determine cause of death. The experts in those areas would arrive soon enough.

Quiet engulfed her, the silence of a building empty of life. No one, she was certain, was hiding on the premises. Whoever had killed Thorne was long gone.

It was warm in the shop. No doors left open, then. Not for long, anyway. Thorne might even have been killed the previous evening, since he was fully dressed and did not seem to have turned the thermostat down. It had been considerably chillier in The Toy Box the night she'd come to investigate the broken window and mutilated bear. On the other hand, he might have gotten up early and been preparing for the day when someone shot him.

Surveying the shop from her central vantage point, she tried to determine if anything had been vandalized or stolen. Thorne's arm had struck a small table as he fell, knocking it over and spilling a display of American Girl products onto the floor. Other than that, nothing seemed to be out of place or disturbed.

Giving the dead man a wide berth, she approached the high sales counter and climbed the steps at the back to check if Thorne's computer and cash register were still there. Both looked intact and untouched. Using only her fingertips, she opened the drawer where she'd seen him stash his gun. There was no sign of it now. That wasn't good, but she knew better than to mess with the crime scene by continuing to search for it.

The distant wail of a siren warned Sherri that she didn't have much time left for observation. From her lofty vantage point, she gazed down at the shop. The boarded-up front window cut out most of the natural light, but the overhead fixture showed her much the same arrangement she remembered from her previous visit with Liss and Marcia. If anything had been taken, the thief had been neat about it.

Had the light been on when Thorne was shot? She hadn't

flicked the switch beside the door, but Margaret might have. Or Mark Patton. Sherri frowned, staring at Patton through the still-open door. There was something familiar about him. It came to her a moment later. He was the disappointed customer who'd been swearing so creatively because Thorne's prices were too high. When had that been? Sunday, she thought. The day the news crew came to town. She couldn't help but wonder what would bring Patton back to Moose-tookalook three days later.

She was about to go out and ask him when she realized something *was* different about The Toy Box. She didn't see a Tiny Teddy anywhere. Sherri hadn't expected clowns or ballerinas—they'd sold out—but Thorne had supposedly acquired a new supply. Could they all have been bought up so quickly? More likely, having learned his lesson, Thorne had put them elsewhere for safekeeping overnight. She moved cautiously toward the back of the shop, intending to take a peek into Thorne's storage closet.

"Officer Willett?" Jeff Thibodeau's shout came from just outside the front door.

"In a minute!" she hollered back.

"Get out of there," he ordered. "Now."

Jeff knew the ropes, particularly what *not* to do. He had no intention of entering the crime scene himself.

"I'm just making sure the killer isn't still on the premises," Sherri called, using the first reasonable excuse she could come up with. "I want to check the apartment upstairs."

"You need backup?"

"I'm okay. Just being thorough."

"Don't mess anything up. Go up from the inside of the building but exit by way of the outside stairs."

"I knew that," Sherri muttered, but she didn't sass her boss.

Jeff had been in law enforcement for a long time. He'd

been the policeman who'd visited the local elementary school as Officer Friendly when Sherri was a kid. Even then he'd had a Santa Claus build and a distinct shortage of hair. Granted, his promotion to chief had been more reward for long service than vote of confidence in his ability to run the department—the selectmen had been looking for someone whose salary wouldn't break the budget—but Jeff was no dummy. He'd heard too many cautionary tales of murder scenes contaminated by local cops who didn't know what they were doing to let any of his officers be careless.

Sherri made her way around the perimeter of the shop, careful not to touch anything except the doorknob and the stairwell light switch. Someone else would have to examine the contents of the storage closet.

Like most of the old Victorian houses around the town square, The Toy Box had started life as a private home. Over time, a business had taken over the lower floor and the upstairs had been turned into living quarters.

Thorne's apartment had a Spartan appearance, with few pieces of furniture and no curtains. Only shades covered the windows, pulled down so that the whole place was full of shadows. At a guess, although he'd won the contents of his old toy store in the divorce settlement, his ex wife had kept the household goods.

Sherri didn't take time to inspect the boxes and cartons that filled the spare bedroom and half the space in the living room. Instead, she poked her head into the master bedroom. She couldn't tell how recently the bed had been slept in. A spread had been haphazardly thrown on top of the blankets and pillows. It might have been left that way only hours earlier or be untouched since the morning before.

In the kitchen, the dish drainer next to the sink was full of clean, dry dishes. Did that mean he'd had supper last night and washed up before he was shot? Sherri had no idea. She wasn't familiar with Thorne's habits and didn't know what was normal for him. Maybe he never put dishes away.

She glanced at the coffeepot—a French press. There was no indication he'd made himself a cup that morning. Then again, maybe he didn't bother with breakfast. She couldn't imagine starting a day without coffee herself, but she wasn't Gavin Thorne.

With no excuse to linger—no perpetrator; no conveniently discarded gun with fingerprints; no Tiny Teddies—Sherri unlocked the apartment's back door and made her way carefully down the slick, snow-covered outer stairs. Her boots sank down a good five inches, adequate proof that no one else had come this way since the storm. Relieved that she didn't have to worry about messing up evidence on her descent, she hurried as fast as she could, anxious to report to her boss.

It took some time to circle the house. The wind during the night had swept much of the snow off the stairs only to deposit it in drifts three times as deep elsewhere. Sherri's steps slowed even more when she saw that Jeff Thibodeau had been joined by Pete Campbell, her fiancé.

Pete worked as a patrol deputy for the Carrabassett County Sheriff's Department. He was supposed to be off duty but she wasn't surprised that he'd heard the call on the police-band scanner he left on 24-7. That he'd come running both pleased and annoyed her. She was a big girl now. She didn't need a protector. She had her own gun and everything.

"You okay?" Pete slung one arm around Sherri's shoulders and hauled her up against his side.

He had eight inches of height and a good seventy-five pounds on her, but she managed to squirm out of the embrace by elbowing him in the ribs. At a distance of a few feet, she glared at him. "Why wouldn't I be?"

His dark brows lifted into a hairline of the same deep brown shade. "Defensive much?"

"Sorry. Long night."

Pete let it go, but she knew she'd be hearing about her testiness again later. The engagement ring he'd given her the previous February weighed heavily on her finger. This murder had happened on her watch. She wanted in on solving it. The last thing she needed was her fiancé hovering like a mama bird watching a fledgling take its first flight.

Pete backed off when Gordon Tandy showed up. As the local state police detective, he was in charge of the case. That meant he decided who stayed in the loop and who got booted out. First off, he wanted to talk to the witnesses— Margaret, the "innocent bystander," and Sherri.

While Jeff and Pete secured the scene, making sure no one except the medical examiner and the officers Gordon had called in from the state crime lab entered The Toy Box, Gordon questioned and dismissed Mark Patton. Then he turned to Sherri.

"Officer Willett."

"Detective Tandy." She met his steady stare with one of her own.

He had eyes of such a dark brown, except for a few lighter flecks, that they almost looked black. Now that he was in his early forties, the fact that he looked younger than he was no longer created problems for him. Liss found those "boyish good looks" sexy, but Gordon was a bit intense for Sherri's liking.

"Want to fill me in?" he asked.

Standing a little over six feet tall, Gordon Tandy looked every inch a cop. It didn't matter that his job allowed him to wear a suit instead of a uniform. He had the walk, the attitude—he even kept his thick, reddish brown hair trimmed military short.

"The first thing you should know," Sherri said, "is that this is the second shooting this week at The Toy Box."

"You don't need to stick around, Dan," Liss said when she heard the clock in the cozy corner of the Emporium strike nine. "Gordon said you could go."

He caught her arm as she started for the stairs behind the sales counter. "And he told you to stay put in the shop while he questions your aunt."

"It's pretty horrible to find a body." Liss knew that firsthand. "She's upset. Having me with her might—"

"You can go up after Tandy's done with her. Stay out of it, Liss."

She rounded on him, slapping his hand away. "It isn't as if I *want* to have anything to do with investigating Thorne's murder."

"Good. Let's keep it that way. The less you know, the better."

"I really hate high-handed men," she muttered.

Part of her agreed with him, but another part was afraid she wasn't going to be *able* to stay out of it. It had been her bright idea to force bear collectors to come to Moosetookalook and she had the feeling that, somehow, the shooting was tied to the Tiny Teddies.

"Did you see *anything* on your way home?" she asked him.

He rolled his eyes. "I give up. If I tell you what I told Tandy, will you give it a rest?"

"If I can."

"Come and sit down, then. You're as nervous as that kitten."

"Poor little thing." Liss let Dan lead her to the cozy corner and settle her into one of the comfortable chairs. Sherri had been halfway out the door after Margaret's announcement before she'd remembered she was still holding the black kitten. She'd all but thrown it at Liss, who had promptly passed the cat off to Dan so she could look after her aunt. "Sorry about the scratches."

"At least it doesn't bite ankles."

"Maybe Lumpkin will teach it that trick, if he ever stops hissing long enough." Rather than talk about murder, she found herself filling Dan in on Lumpkin's opinion of his new housemate. "I had to bring the kitten to work with me. I was afraid to leave it at the house."

"Sounds like you plan on keeping it."

"Oh, no. I mean . . . well . . . I don't know what I mean." She ran one hand over her face. "I'm babbling. I hate it when I babble, but I just can't seem to take this in."

"Do you really want to know what I told Tandy?"

Did she? Dan was right. It was none of her business.

He didn't wait for her to answer. "I came home at dawn, following the plow. Margaret's light was on. Your place was dark. The town square looked like a picture postcard. I didn't notice if there were lights on at Thorne's place, or anywhere else for that matter. I didn't see anyone out and about except one stray snowmobiler. End of statement."

"Oh."

"Yeah. I wish I *had* seen something. I didn't care much for Gavin Thorne, but no one deserves to be murdered."

"I doubt his ex would agree with you."

"Well, there you go. She killed him."

"That would be good." Liss gave a nervous little laugh. "Well, not *good*, exactly. Better than the killer being someone, well . . . local." She shook her head. "I'm babbling again, aren't I?"

"You're entitled. Are you going to open the shop today?"

"Not unless Aunt Margaret wants to." She sent a fulminating glare at the ceiling. "I'll ask as soon as I'm allowed in."

"The Emporium is your shop," Dan reminded her.

"Only half of it. The other half belongs to my aunt."

He frowned, hearing more than she'd intended in her tone of voice. "Are you worried about that now that she's back?"

Liss shrugged. "A little. You saw how she's changed, Dan. I don't know what to expect next."

"Change can be good. And if she wants the Emporium back, there are other things you can do." His smile was gentle. "I might have an idea or two to suggest for your future."

Liss scarcely heard him. Her thoughts were still on the shop. She'd poured all her energy into making it a success online. She didn't want to give that up.

"Think positive," Dan said.

"You're right. Maybe I'm making too much of the gray hair and the 'call me Margaret' and it will all work out just fine."

Too restless to sit still any longer, she left the cozy corner and returned to her post by the window. The mobile crime lab van had arrived. So had several other official-looking vehicles. Drawn by the yellow crime-scene tape, a crowd of gawkers had gathered in the town square. Liss recognized Lovey FitzPatrick at once.

"See that woman in the bright blue coat?" she asked Dan, who had joined her at the window. "Is she staying at the hotel?"

"Oh, yeah. Ms. FitzPatrick. Quite a character." Abruptly, his voice hardened. "And here comes the news van. Damn."

"And to think we *wanted* them here for the pageant. . . . Oh, my God! The pageant! What am I going to do about tonight's ceremony? We already had to postpone last night's event and for tonight I've got eight girls set to dress up as milkmaids. If we're going to have to cancel, I need to call them."

"Wait a bit longer. Maybe—"

"No." Liss's heart sank as she considered all the ramifications. "The Toy Box and the town square are just too close together. There's no way we can pretend not to see the crime scene tape, and no way that the news media will let us get away with ignoring it. Besides, what's the point now? The only Tiny Teddies were in Thorne's shop. They're evidence, right? No one will be able to do anything with them until the investigation is finished."

The hard grip of Dan's hands on her shoulders brought her head up with a snap.

"Are you listening to yourself?" he demanded. "You didn't get into this for Gavin Thorne's benefit and there's no reason why his death, tragic as it is, should bring everything to a grinding halt. Move the ceremony to the hotel. Hell, bring stock from the all shops in town and sell it in the lobby. We have *snow*, Liss. It's eight days till Christmas. Do you honestly think Thorne would have closed his place if some other Moosetookalook businessperson had been murdered?"

"Crass commercial—"

"Common sense. It's called making a living. No one expects you or me or anyone else to go out of business just because Thorne got himself killed."

That he was right didn't make Liss feel any better about the situation. She couldn't quite shake the conviction that she'd been responsible for putting the events in motion that had led to Thorne's murder.

# Chapter Eight

The sound of footsteps on the stairs heralded Gordon Tandy's return to the Emporium. He scowled when he saw Dan.

"Thought you'd have been on your way by now, Ruskin. Didn't you say you were headed to work when you almost ran over Mrs. Boyd?"

Ignoring the other man, Dan turned to Liss. "I can stay if you want me to."

"That's okay. Gordon has to interview me, and you do have a job to go to. Will you make the arrangements at the hotel for tonight's ceremony?"

"No problem."

As soon as Dan had left—with flattering reluctance—and driven away, Gordon greeted Liss in a slightly more personal fashion with a peck on the cheek. "What ceremony?"

"Where have you been hiding? Surely you've heard about the Twelve Shopping Days of Christmas?"

"Oh, that. Yes, I did. Thought it was a stroke of genius, if you want to know the truth."

She acknowledged the compliment with a little mock curtsey and a "Thank you kindly, sir."

"Sorry I haven't called lately, Liss, but you know how it is at this time of year. Everybody's supposed to be happy. Hey, it's Christmas! The added pressure is just too much for some people. They get drunk and crash their cars. Domestic violence calls increase. And the really screwed-up cases shoot, stab, poison, or otherwise do harm to their nearest and dearest."

"Lovely job you have. Is that what you think happened here? The ex wife flipped out?"

He shrugged. "It's too early to say and I couldn't share any theories with you even if I had one. I need to examine the crime scene."

"You didn't do that first?"

He shook his head. "I collect what facts there are before I go in." He steered her back to the cozy corner and pulled out his notebook. "Did you hear anything unusual last night?"

"No shots fired, if that's what you mean. The snowplow went by at least once, but I don't know when."

He took her through the morning's events, but since Liss hadn't seen anything out of the ordinary except a man in a gray coat banging on the door to The Toy Box, the interview quickly came to an end.

"I've been wanting to call and ask you out to dinner," Gordon said when he'd closed his notebook and returned it to a pocket. "The job's been in the way. Now this murder is really going to interfere with my personal life."

"Look at the bright side. If you're spending time in Moosetookalook, we'll be able to talk to each other now and again. You can come by for coffee."

"True. Maybe even lunch." He leaned forward, taking her hands in his. "It's damned frustrating, Liss. I spend more time than I should thinking about you, and have less time than ever to spend with you."

"I'd like to see more of you, too, although I'd really prefer it didn't take a crime scene to bring us together."

His grip tightened. "Stay out of this investigation, okay?"

"Trust me, I have no plans to get involved. I've got too

much else on my plate as it is." She tried for a lighter tone. "It would be a really good thing if you could solve this case quickly. Moosetookalook doesn't need the bad publicity."

"My plan exactly, after which I have another plan, a remedy for that other problem . . . the one where I don't see enough of you."

This time the kiss was much more than a peck on the cheek. Liss was still reeling from the impact when the jangle of sleigh bells told her Gordon had left the building. She touched her fingers to her lips. The man did know how to kiss.

Then again, so did Dan.

Just after noon, Sherri knocked on Liss MacCrimmon's kitchen door.

The first words out of Liss's mouth were, "Please tell me there's been an arrest."

"Sorry, but no. I'm just here to bum lunch."

"You'll have to settle for peanut butter and jelly."

"I can live with that. Heck, I can live *on* that. So, did your two gentlemen friends come to blows?"

"Oh, please."

"Hey, I caught sight of Dan's face when he left the Emporium. He was not a happy camper."

They exchanged idle chitchat while Liss made a sandwich for each of them. Sherri bit into hers and chewed thoughtfully, her eyes on Liss's face.

"What? Do I have peanut butter on my nose?"

Sherri chuckled. "I was just wondering what kind of Christmas presents they have in mind for you."

Liss's eyes narrowed. "What are you getting at?"

"Christmas is a very romantic time of year."

"Oh, no. Nobody's getting serious here."

"You sure? I mean, you ought to give it some thought. Could be there's a diamond ring in your future."

"Just because you and Pete are getting hitched, doesn't mean everyone else wants to tie the knot."

They ate in silence for a few minutes.

"Damn!" Liss exploded. "Now I can't get the idea out of my head. Dan did say something this morning about having a few suggestions for my future. And Gordon—Gordon said he thought he might have come up with a way to see more of me. Damn!"

"Hah! Told you so." Sherri polished off the PB&J and reached for the soda beside her plate.

"It seemed like such a good idea at the time. Two attractive, personable men, both interested in being more than friends. I wasn't able to choose between them, so I decided to go out with both of them. It was supposed to be oh-so-civilized and, eventually, I was *sure* I'd be able to pick one over the other." Liss fingered the nubbly pattern on the tablecloth, a grim expression on her face.

"Didn't work, huh?"

Liss shrugged. "I've gotten to know both Dan and Gordon much better over the last nine months, and if I'd been aiming to be lifelong friends with them both, I'd be completely satisfied."

Satisfaction, Sherri thought, in line with the old Rolling Stones song, was probably the one thing Liss was *not* getting.

"After all this time, shouldn't I know it if I'm in love? And if I'm not, doesn't it seem unlikely I ever will be?"

"Can you see yourself having sex with one or the other of them?" Sherri asked.

"Sure. They both get the old juices flowing. But that isn't the same thing, and I'm not about to sleep with two men at the same time."

"You haven't actually seen much of either one of them for the last few weeks," Sherri reminded her.

Liss sighed. "Maybe that says it all. Proposal of marriage

or not, I'm going to have to choose one of them soon . . . or dump them both. A fine heck of a note," she added in a mutter. "Here I am, only a couple of years short of thirty, and I'm still doing a dog paddle in the dating pool!"

Sherri polished off lunch without further comment. She sympathized, but only to a point, and was glad she had only one ornery man to worry about. "How's Margaret doing?"

Liss chuckled. "After Gordon left, I went up to her apartment. I found her lying on the sofa, one arm over her eyes. She moved it just far enough to squint at me and tell me to go away because she was having an attack of the vapors."

Sherri laughed out loud. "Margaret Boyd never had the vapors in her entire life."

"Well, she's decided she wants to have them now. She said she thought those Victorian ladies had a good thing going. Slightest little setback and they'd take to their fainting couches." Liss made a derisive sound. "They had to, I told her. They were stuffed into corsets laced so tightly they couldn't breathe."

"And here I thought you were a fan of Gothic novels."

"Only some of them. If one of them has a TSTL heroine, it makes me want to throw the book across the room."

"TSTL?"

"Too stupid to live. You know the type. They hear a loud noise in the basement—or the attic, or the crypt— and they charge right in, unarmed and without backup, to find out what it is."

"Usually wearing a flowing white nightie, right?"

"Only in the cover art."

Since Liss had finished clearing the table, Sherri stood. "Are you going to open the shop this afternoon?"

"No. Margaret needs time to collect herself and she won't have any peace if she can hear customers coming and going downstairs. It was a shock finding a dead man."

"Of course it was."

"Margaret's also upset because she didn't think she was much help to Gordon. She was up early, you see, but the only sounds she can remember hearing were normal. You know—engines revving, the snowplow doing its thing."

Liss took a bag of kibble out of a cupboard and refilled the cat feeder. As if by magic, Lumpkin appeared, closely followed by the black kitten.

"What about you, sport," Sherri asked the cat. "Did you see or hear anything suspicious?"

"I don't think you want to hear Lumpkin's thoughts today. He's not happy about his little buddy there." The kitten insinuated itself between Lumpkin and the food, but for a miracle Lumpkin allowed the incursion.

"Are you going to keep it?" Sherri asked.

"I don't know yet. The owner may still turn up. Why? Are you looking for a pet for Adam?"

"I wouldn't mind, but my mother would have fits." Ida Willett had moved in with Sherri and her son when she'd divorced Ernie and now cared for Sherri's son while Sherri was at work. Sherri tried not to rile her. Finding a good day care provider wasn't easy and it cost a small fortune.

The kitten stopped eating to strop itself against Lumpkin's front legs. The larger feline bristled and hissed.

"Get over it," Liss told him. To Sherri, she said, "If no one claims it by Christmas I'll probably call the vet and make an appointment for a rabies shot and all the other vaccinations it needs."

Sherri wasn't at all surprised. Liss had a kind heart. "Have you named it yet?"

"It's too soon."

Sherri glanced at her watch. "Nope. It's too late. I've got to get back to work." She couldn't suppress a grin or control the tremor of excitement in her voice.

Liss's eyes narrowed. "Have you been at the crime scene all this time?"

"Yup. And I'm going to stay on the case." She preened just a bit. "You are looking at their local expert."

"Better you than me!"

"I even provided Gordon with a clue." She leaned closer to her friend and lowered her voice. "You can't tell anyone this, Liss, but all the Tiny Teddies, the new ones, are missing."

"Are you sure? Maybe he sold them already."

"How many did he have?"

"I don't know. I don't even know for certain where he got them or what costumes they were wearing. Not kilts. I'm pretty sure of that much."

"And?"

Liss hesitated, but her internal debate didn't last more than thirty seconds. "I don't want to get anyone in trouble, but this *is* a murder investigation. Tell Gordon he should probably have a little talk with Eric Moss."

Liss meant to stay clear of the murder investigation. She had other things to worry about—the change in venue for the ceremony, the presence of frustrated shoppers in town, and the press, not to mention possible proposals of marriage. And yet one question kept nagging at the back of her mind as she spent the afternoon making phone calls and fending off reporters: had the presence of Tiny Teddies in The Toy Box been responsible for Gavin Thorne's murder? Each time the possibility surfaced, she shoved it firmly aside, even when it was asked by the same smiling television newswoman who'd covered the five golden rings ceremony.

On the theory that the best defense is a good offense, Liss left the safety of her own house for the porch of the

Emporium when she saw the news crew head that way. She'd already made a brief statement about how saddened the entire community was by the loss of one of its members. She intended to make an announcement about the evening's entertainment—they'd decided to wait until tomorrow to continue the ceremonies—and then retreat.

The woman with the microphone wasn't interested in Liss's spin. She had her own agenda. "Surely you must have some idea why he was killed? I understand Mr. Thorne had been charging outrageous prices for the remaining Tiny Teddies."

"I really can't speculate." Liss heard the hint of panic in her own voice and wished she'd left well enough alone. She wrapped her arms around herself, feeling a sudden chill that had nothing to do with the freezing temperature.

"Were the Tiny Teddies stolen by the killer?"

"I have no idea."

"Any idea how many are left, then?"

"I have not been inside The Toy Box, and even if I had, I don't think I should be telling you anything. Talk to the police." *Vultures*, she thought, moving closer to the entrance of the shop. Next they'd be asking her what she knew about Thorne's love life.

Instead, the reporter latched onto an even more troubling subject. "Is there any connection between this murder and the last one to take place in Moosetookalook?" The woman's eyes were avid, as if she scented blood in this line of questioning.

"Don't be ridiculous." Liss had one foot on the porch but turned back, eyes flashing with annoyance. "Mr. Thorne didn't even live here back then. I repeat: if you have questions about his death, talk to the police. The only news story I have for you concerns tonight's portion of our Twelve Days of Christmas Pageant."

"A little heartless, isn't it? Going on with the festivities when there's been a death?"

"I am certain that Mr. Thorne would have wanted us to continue as planned."

That was certainly true. As Dan had suggested, had someone else been murdered, Thorne would have been the last one to miss a sale because of it.

"However," she continued, "tonight's portion of the program has been postponed until tomorrow night and the combined seventh, eighth, and ninth days of Christmas will be celebrated at The Spruces, a lovely old hotel that has just been completely renovated. You may recall that it opened to the public last July. The festivities start at six o'clock."

Firing the last part of her announcement over her shoulder, Liss scuttled inside the safe haven of Moosetookalook Scottish Emporium and shut the door in the reporter's face. Instinctively, she engaged the dead bolt and was glad she had when someone turned the knob, then rattled it aggressively. Fists thudded against the wood, louder than ordinary knocking.

Determined to ignore the clamor to be let in, Liss stood with her back pressed against the inside of the door. The second round of pounding was violent enough to reverberate through her entire body. Or maybe that was trembling. She held one hand out in front of her and, sure enough, it was shaking.

"This is a disaster," she muttered.

The creak of the stairwell door opening made her jump.

"It's just me."

Margaret stepped into the shop, casting a nervous gaze toward the display window. One obnoxious reporter had his nose pressed to the outside of the plate glass. Liss hoped it froze to the surface.

"I was thinking about getting a breath of fresh air, but maybe not."

Liss crossed to her aunt, peering anxiously into her face. She had a hollow-eyed look but she'd brushed her hair and put on makeup and doused herself in perfume, a different scent from the last time. This one was muskier, with hints of carnation and maybe heliotrope.

"How are you feeling?" Liss asked. "Should you be out of bed?"

Margaret sniffed. "I'm not some frail old lady who needs cosseting, and don't you dare offer to make me a nice cup of tea."

"What happened to having the vapors?"

"Been there. Done that."

"Bought the T-shirt," they finished in unison and suddenly Liss felt much better.

"Let's slip out the back way and go to your place," Margaret suggested. "If we move fast enough, maybe no one will notice."

A few minutes later they were settled in Liss's living room. Margaret had a rum and cola in hand, in spite of the early hour. Liss had poured herself a glass of white wine. "Good thing there's no pageant tonight," she murmured as she sipped. "I don't think I'm up to making a speech."

"What was scheduled? Milkmaids, right?"

"Yup. Eight maids a-milking."

"So . . . cows?"

Liss managed to keep a straight face. "No space to house them in the stockroom."

"Papier mâché cows?" Margaret suggested with a faint smile.

"Eight girls from the middle school, dressed as milkmaids. They're going to present a program of winter-themed songs. Their music teacher will start off by explaining that they're milking the occasion for all it's worth."

Margaret groaned loudly and had another sip of her drink. "So, tell me, Liss. What have you got planned next for the Emporium?"

Well here it was—show time! "I was thinking about reducing the Emporium's hours and relying more on mail orders and online sales for business. That's where most people go to buy these days. If the shop wasn't part of the house, if you had to rent retail space, it wouldn't be profitable at all."

"What if more folks interested in things Scottish decided to come to Moosetookalook?"

"Like that's going to happen! Besides," Liss waved a hand, almost overturning her glass, "look how badly this Tiny Teddies thing turned out."

"First of all, the Tiny Teddies haven't turned out badly at all."

"You're just saying that to make me feel better."

Aunt Margaret sent her a quelling glance. "I never sugarcoat the truth. You had a brilliant idea and it is not your fault that man got himself killed. But I'm getting off track. What I really wanted to tell you is that I won't be working at the Emporium any longer."

There was a note of defiance in her voice. She flung her announcement at Liss as if she expected to be challenged. Very deliberately, Liss set aside her glass. "What *do* you have planned?"

"I want to sell you my share of the shop."

Stunned, Liss couldn't think of a single thing to say. With a sense of surprise, she realized that her mouth was literally hanging open. She closed it with an audible snap.

"I intend to get out of the retail business," Aunt Margaret continued. "Even before . . . everything that happened . . . I was growing tired of being tied down to a store, and I have no interest in all this online stuff."

"But . . . but . . . I thought you came back to—"

"I returned to Moosetookalook because it's my home. I am moving back into my apartment. But I don't want to do the same old thing for the rest of my life. I was in a rut,

Liss. Now that I've climbed out of it, I don't intend to tumble back in."

"But what will you do? I can come up with the money to buy you out. That's not a problem. But that won't give you much to retire on."

"Who said anything about retiring? I have a new job lined up."

"Please tell me you're not going to be pumping gas for Ernie Willett."

Her aunt burst out laughing. "Ernie is part of the personal side of my life. He's not involved in the business end."

Somehow, Liss did not find that information as comforting as Margaret intended. "What are you planning to do, then?"

"I'll be working at The Spruces as events coordinator. I'll be in charge of bringing in conferences, conventions, and social gatherings like weddings."

"That's . . . great."

"That's good for us both." Margaret's eyes sparkled. Gray hair or not, she suddenly looked years younger. "Do you have any idea how many groups revolve around the Scottish heritage of their members? If even a fraction of them come to The Spruces, you'll have a built-in customer base."

Liss picked up her wineglass. "A toast, then. To our future."

Margaret drank, draining her tumbler. "Now, then, on to another important matter." She ran an assessing gaze over her surroundings before she fixed her niece with a gimlet stare. "Amaryllis Rosalie MacCrimmon, this house of yours is a disgrace!"

"What?" Affronted, Liss surreptitiously searched for dust bunnies, dirty socks, or discarded cutlery. She saw nothing to warrant criticism in her neatly organized and more-or-less recently dusted and vacuumed living room. "What do you mean?"

Margaret laughed at the expression on her niece's face. "I mean, Liss, that here it is almost Christmas and you haven't put up a single holiday decoration!"

# Chapter Nine

"This was a good idea." Dan's approving gaze scanned the revelers in Liss's living room and came back to rest on Liss herself. She was looking especially fine in a bright red sweater and snug jeans. She'd tied back her hair with a length of green and red striped ribbon. A tiny wreath pin decorated the right side.

A helpless shrug accompanied a slightly embarrassed smile. "I have no idea how this turned into a party. It was just going to be Margaret and me, putting up a tree and a few other do-dads. Then Ernie Willett showed up—I think Margaret phoned him and invited him over—and you dropped by, and before I knew it I had a house full of people."

"So you didn't invite Tandy?" Dan hoped that sounded casual.

Liss's speaking glance told him the attempt at subtlety had failed. "I didn't invite *anyone*. They just turned up. Not that I'm complaining, mind you, but this isn't the quiet evening at home I envisioned."

In addition to Ernie Willett, Gordon Tandy, Sherri and Pete, and Dan himself, the entire Hogencamp family had joined the party. Pete had brought pizza and Patsy had sent over a box of cookies in the shape of snowmen from the coffee shop.

"Heard you took the whole day off from work," Dan said. "Hope you weren't bored."

"Hardly. And I actually managed to spend a few quiet hours with a good book."

"Have you read everything in the house yet?"

Liss laughed. In the adjoining room was the sizeable library she'd inherited along with the house and Lumpkin. "Not quite, but that hasn't stopped me from adding to the collection." She took a sip of the eggnog Margaret had made. "I hate to say it, but I may have to weed out some titles. I'm rapidly running out of shelf space."

"Have you got a star for the top of the tree?" Aunt Margaret called from the other side of the room.

"I've no idea." Liss bent to look through the large cardboard box she'd just opened. "I don't have any decorations of my own," she explained to Dan as she burrowed through an odd collection of Christmassy bits and bobs. "I didn't bother to buy any last year because I spent the holidays with Mom and Dad and Aunt Margaret in Arizona."

"A pitiful excuse," Margaret said with a sniff as she joined them in exploring the contents.

"So where did these ornaments and the lights and all come from?" Dan pulled a moth-eaten Christmas stocking out of the mix.

"There were five boxes of them up in the attic, clearly labeled XMAS DECS."

Margaret stood back, hands on hips to survey the room. "There's something missing. Where's the choir?"

Liss gave her aunt a blank look, but Dan knew what she meant. "Those little candles shaped like choirboys and choirgirls, right? I remember them. They go on the mantel. There should be one big one—the choirmaster—in blue." The little ones, representing children, were dressed in choir robes with red skirts and white tops. Last time he'd seen the display, there had been at least a dozen pieces.

"I didn't see any more boxes in the attic," Liss said.

"They wouldn't be stored there. It gets too hot in the summer. How about the root cellar."

"What root cellar?" Liss asked.

He gave her an incredulous look. "How long have you lived here?"

She glared back. "You know exactly when I inherited this house and all its contents. I admit I don't spend a lot of time in the cellar, but I don't remember seeing any separate rooms down there."

"Come with me." Grabbing her hand, he towed her out into the foyer and down the hall to the combination dining room and kitchen. Off the dining area were two doors, one that led to a closet and the other to the stairs to the cellar. Before they started down, he pointed to the window opposite. "What do you see when you look out there?"

"Snow." She made a face at him.

"Under the snow?"

"Grass? Come on, Dan. I'm no good at guessing games."

"Your cellar has an outside entrance through a set of bulkhead doors."

"Oh. That's right. It does."

"I'm betting you've never even had them open."

"No bet." She followed him down the steep steps and across the cement floor of the basement to the door that clearly led to the other way out. "We can't use this exit now. There's too much snow on top of it."

"We're not going out." He opened the door and ushered her through, pulling the cord for the lightbulb hanging in the tiny space at the foot of the stairs. "There." He gestured to the right. "That's the root cellar."

What looked like a solid wooden surface turned out to have a latch. When Dan lifted it, the metal screamed. It had been awhile since anyone had been inside.

Dan ducked and passed through the low door into a

small, chilly room lined with shelves. Liss followed, gaping at the number of homemade preserves stored there. On the top shelf were assorted boxes, all carefully labeled.

"I had no idea this room was here."

He shouldn't be surprised, Dan thought. His house—the one Liss knew best from living there while she was growing up—didn't have one. Some of the other places around the square did, others didn't. "You could use it to store produce like apples and potatoes," he suggested. "Stock up for the entire winter."

"Or, as some of my favorite mystery authors might say, this would make a great place to hide a body!"

Chuckling, Dan rummaged through the boxes until he located the one marked CANDLES. Opening it, he burrowed in the tissue paper packing and pulled out three of the little wax figurines.

"They're adorable!" Liss exclaimed in delight. "And they're in great shape. How old to you think they are?"

"Older than either of us, that's for sure."

"Probably collectible," Liss murmured, turning one of the small figures over in her hand to look at the manufacturer's name. Carefully, she placed all three back in their tissue paper nest.

"Could be," Dan agreed. If they were, he hoped they weren't one of the more popular items with collectors. One Christmas craze per year was more than enough for him.

Carrying the box, he headed back across the cellar. He stepped aside to let Liss go up the stairs first, then almost ran into her when she stopped abruptly on the landing. The low murmur of voices reached him from the other side of the door. Recognizing Gordon Tandy's voice, he kept silent.

"Give her my apologies," Tandy said, "but no details. I'm counting on your discretion, Sherri."

Dan stood too close to Liss to miss her reaction. At

Tandy's words she went rigid. Her hands clenched into fists at her sides.

"No problem, boss." Sherri said.

Dan pictured her wearing a cheeky grin. He heard the back door open and close as the state police detective left. A light patter of footsteps marked Sherri's return to the living room.

When Liss remained frozen in place, Dan wondered if she was counting to ten. Was she upset that Tandy had taken off? Or was it the fact that the state trooper had warned Sherri not to confide in her that ticked her off? By the time Liss cautiously opened the cellar door, Tandy was long gone. The kitchen's only occupants were feline. Lumpkin perched on top of the refrigerator while the kitten was crouched below, trying to figure out how to climb up there with him.

"Something's going on," Liss muttered.

"Police business," he reminded her.

"Maybe I can worm it out of Sherri." But she made no move toward the living room. "No, maybe not."

Dan set the box on the kitchen counter. Taking Liss by the shoulders, he gently turned her toward him until he could see her troubled expression.

"What we just overheard . . . I hadn't realized till then how much Sherri risks every time she confides in me. I don't want to put her on the spot."

"So you won't ask her any questions about the case. Why is that a problem? You were going to stay out of the investigation anyway, remember?"

"How could I forget with you and Gordon reminding me every five minutes!"

"Whoa! Don't bite my head off." He dropped his arms and stepped back.

"Sorry." One hand went to her forehead, rubbing it as if

to ward off a headache. "I just . . . I like tossing ideas around with Sherri. That's all. I'm not getting involved!"

Dan thought the lady protested a bit too much, but there was no point in saying so. Let her be mad at Gordon Tandy, not him. Retrieving the carton, he carried the candles into the living room, entering just in time to hear Pete suggest that everyone sing Christmas carols while they finished decorating.

Liss waved her hand in the air in the manner of a pupil trying to get a teacher's attention. "No musical talent whatsoever, remember?"

"I thought you learned to play the bagpipes when you were a kid," Dan teased her.

"I *tried* to learn. It was not a success. My best effort sounded like cats strangling. And I'm definitely no singer."

Dan tried to think if he'd ever heard her vocalize. Nothing came to mind. He found himself intrigued. Something Liss couldn't do well? This he had to hear.

She remained stubbornly silent while the others belted out "Good King Wenceslas."

Dan poked her in the ribs. "Come on," he whispered. "You can't be *that* bad."

"I can't carry a tune."

"No one cares."

"So you say *now*."

"I may not have much tolerance for bagpipes, but I can put up with a little off-key singing." He winked. "Besides, if it's really awful, I'll just stick my fingers in my ears."

In a cheerful mood and well rested, Liss stepped out onto her front porch to check on progress at the crime scene before going to work the next morning. The yellow tape was still up, flapping in the breeze, but there didn't seem to be anyone inside The Toy Box. There were, how-

ever, a great many cars parked along Liss's end of Pine
Street and onto Ash, where Thorne's shop stood. Puzzled,
she turned the other way, toward the Emporium . . . and
froze.

More vehicles of every shape and size, including a Win-
nebago, lined all four sides of the town square. At the corner where Pine met Birch Street, they were double parked
and creating a traffic jam in front of Second Time Around,
Marcia's consignment shop. Liss narrowed her eyes against
the glare of the winter sun on snow. A half dozen people
were crowded onto Marcia's front porch and two of them
looked as if they were about to pummel each other. Wondering if someone was going to have to call in the riot squad,
Liss hastily did up the buttons on her coat and headed that
way. Opening the Emporium could wait a few more minutes.

All the "regulars" were there. Lovey Fitzpatrick—wearing
bright crimson this time—and the man in the gray coat, and
two or three others Liss recognized as people who had bought
one of her kilted bears and gone on to shop at The Toy Box.
Just as Liss started up the porch steps, Marcia unlocked the
door and the crowd surged inside.

Liss followed more slowly, taking time to read the sign
Marcia had posted. Second Time Around did not have a
display window, or even a bow or bay window in the front
room. Two normal-sized windows flanked the door. A notice
had been taped to the inside of one of them: NEW SUPPLY
OF TINY TEDDIES AVAILABLE NOW. FIRST COME, FIRST SERVED.

Lovey Fitzpatrick's shrill voice rose above the hubbub
inside the shop. "What do you mean you're holding some
back?"

"Just what I said." Marcia glanced Liss's way and grinned
at her. "I intend to auction off the last of the lot to the high-
est bidder on the final afternoon of the pageant."

"How many?" the gray man demanded.

"Which design?" someone else wanted to know.

Marcia whipped out a stack of fliers, complete with pictures. Hands grabbed them away from her. She laughed and reached under the sales counter for more. Eventually, one made its way to Liss.

She waged a brief battle with herself over whether or not to stay and find out where the bears had come from, but Marcia's plan to auction off some of them at the pageant made that information Liss's concern. She waited for a break in the buying frenzy—a near riot by Moosetookalook standards—and slipped close enough to speak privately with a flushed and excited Marcia.

"Where did you get the bears?" she asked in a low voice.

"They're not counterfeit, if that's what you're thinking," Marcia whispered back.

"I wasn't." Liss hastily made the "cross my heart" gesture. She truly didn't suspect Marcia of anything underhanded.

Marcia took money from a customer and rang up the sale. She was charging $150 a bear. Reasonable, Liss supposed, at least compared to Thorne's prices.

Things got busy again after that, but Liss stubbornly stuck around.

"You still here?" Marcia asked a half hour later. The rush had subsided to a trickle.

"I'm still here."

Marcia sighed. "Okay. Okay." She peered around the store, as if to make sure no one was eavesdropping on their conversation. "I suppose you've got a right to know, since you're the one in charge of the pageant and the auction."

"Yes. The auction I didn't know we were holding."

Marcia just grinned at her. "But it's a brilliant idea, isn't it? It will keep people here through the weekend."

"The bears, Marcia—where did they come from?"

"Spoilsport. Well, I kept a couple of the elves back. I said I was sold out but I really wasn't." She shrugged. "I saw what Thorne was doing to the prices, so I thought, why not? See how high they go, then reveal my own 'last bear in New England' to the world."

"You've got more than a couple of elf bears now," Liss persisted. "Did you buy them from Eric Moss?"

"Second thoughts? Too late, Liss. He may have offered them to you first, but you turned him down. Your loss. My gain."

"No problem. I thought his price was too steep. You know that. I left you a phone message to tell you so." Marcia looked smug. "So you bought them? The entire batch?"

"Yup."

"I thought you only took things on consignment." And she'd *thought* Moss had sold his bears to Gavin Thorne.

"That's the way it usually works, but this deal was too good to pass up." She chuckled. "You know what they say about something that sounds too good to be true, but as far as I could see there wasn't any downside to this deal."

"But what took so long? Moss had the bears days ago." And why, come to think of it, had *Moss* been ready to let them go for only fifty bucks a bear?

Marcia shrugged. "We've been negotiating. He finally agreed to my counteroffer and delivered them this morning."

A rosy-cheeked woman with a child in tow approached the counter with two Tiny Teddies and a credit card in hand. Marcia lit up like a Christmas tree.

"Do you know where Moss got them?" Liss asked.

"Don't know. Don't care. I own them now and they're selling like hotcakes." Ignoring Liss, she waited on her customer.

In a thoughtful frame of mind, Liss left Marcia's shop and belatedly opened Moosetookalook Scottish Emporium. It was a slow morning, and would no doubt get even slower once Marcia ran out of the Tiny Teddies she was prepared to sell that day. She had a different selection of bears set aside for Friday and yet another batch selected for Saturday. Any left over on Sunday—and Liss expected there would be only those Marcia had already decided to hold back for the auction—would be sold at the end of the pageant.

Marcia Milliken was either a very clever businesswoman or an extremely shady character. Liss tried to imagine the other woman shooting Thorne in order to steal his bears but the picture refused to come into focus. For one thing, it was a pretty stupid reason to kill someone. For another, Liss had begun to suspect that Marcia's business plan for the little bears had been devised only in part to maximize her profit. Making just a few available for sale at a time meant she could take the rest of each day off. Liss was sure she was right when Marcia drove by an hour later . . . towing her snowmobile trailer.

It continued to be quiet into the afternoon. Margaret had gone to the hotel, leaving Liss with no one to talk to. Before long she found herself doodling on a notepad. Eventually, the doodles turned into a list of names.

Eric Moss was number one. He'd supplied Marcia with Tiny Teddies. Had he also supplied Gavin Thorne? Then, had he turned around and taken them after killing the man? She'd always thought Moss was honest. Then again, he *had* met Jason Graye in suspicious circumstances at the town office the night of the selectmen's meeting. What had that been about?

Graye styled himself an entrepreneur and it was an open secret that he'd run for town selectman only to give himself an "in" to decide zoning questions. That went along with his main occupation—shady real-estate broker. He'd walked a thin legal line in the past, and Liss had no doubt he'd do it again. The question was whether Eric Moss was cut from the same cloth. Maybe, she thought, she should ask Moss that question . . . and a few others.

No. Maybe *Gordon* should question him. She was supposed to stay out of it. Funny how hard that was to remember.

Telling herself she was engaging in harmless speculation, nothing more, Liss continued to the second name on her list: Felicity Thorne.

Thorne's ex wife was the most obvious suspect, she supposed. There had been no love lost between them. They'd quarreled shortly before his death. And Felicity had been in town at least once after that. She'd been in the Emporium with Lovey FitzPatrick. Had it only been yesterday afternoon?

Liss wondered how well the two women knew each other. She could ask, she supposed. She had a feeling Lovey would be sticking around until after Sunday's auction. She might complain about the prices, but she was an avid collector. Such people were addicted to the hunt. Maybe tonight at the hotel, in between the milkmaids and the leaping lords—actually the high school's men's gymnastics team— she could find a moment to chat with Ms. FitzPatrick.

The next name on her list wasn't exactly a name. She'd written "man in gray coat" as number three.

Stu Burroughs was number four on her list. Stu hadn't liked Gavin Thorne, but Liss had a hard time believing he'd murder the other man. She started to cross out his name, then stopped. Everyone was a suspect at this point.

The sleigh bells over the door jangled loudly and Sherri breezed in. From her happy-as-a-clam expression, Liss concluded that Gordon must still be keeping her in the loop. She felt a small stab of envy.

Sherri zeroed in on Liss's list. "Your man in the gray coat is named Mark Patton. He's in the clear as far as we can tell."

"He's still in town."

"There are still bears." That seemed to say it all.

"Collector?"

"Worse. Dealer. He's got customers waiting back in Connecticut."

"You sure he's off the hook? That's *two* counts against him."

"Funny, Liss. There's a third strike, too. He was in town last Sunday and pretty steamed over Thorne's prices. He didn't buy any Tiny Teddies that day."

"So maybe he helped himself to some later?"

"Then why stick around? Why call attention to himself by pounding on Thorne's door after the murder?"

"Good point, but I'm not crossing him out." She gave Sherri a sharp look. "Are you supposed to be sharing information like this?"

"Some things are general knowledge, or soon will be. For example, Felicity Thorne was looking good. Seems her ex never changed his will. She gets The Toy Box and anything else he owned. But she's got an alibi."

Sherri skimmed Liss's list again, then tapped Moss's name with one short, unpolished fingernail. "Why did you put him at the number one spot?"

Liss gave her a quick recap of Moss's whispered conversation with Jason Graye at the town office and Marcia's confidences about her source for the Tiny Teddies. "Has anyone talked to Moss yet?"

"I passed on your suggestion to Gordon, but no one's been able to track Moss down. He may be off on a buying trip."

"Marcia saw him just this morning," Liss said. "Talk to her."

# Chapter Ten

The eight little milkmaids, including ten-year-old Beth Hogencamp, were charming to look at and sang on key. Liss envied them. Her own performance the other night, when Dan finally coaxed it out of her, had left him with a strained expression on his face and a sudden desire, she suspected, to purchase earplugs.

As Liss and Margaret and about two hundred others watched, the nine lords a-leaping launched into a gymnastics routine in the ballroom at The Spruces. They showed enthusiasm and considerable skill, but Liss couldn't help but be a trifle disappointed.

"They don't quite match my image of the stanza from the song," she whispered to her aunt.

"Beggars can't be choosers," Margaret reminded her. "At least they're crowd pleasers."

And they *had* given in on the costumes. It couldn't be easy for teenage boys to appear in public in green tights and tunics. Liss joined in the appreciative applause at the end of their act.

The hotel's largest function room had been decorated in grand style for the holidays. The scent of evergreen boughs drifted into every corner. Festooned with garlands and twinkling lights, the room was dominated by a twelve-foot Christmas tree placed midway along the window wall.

After the evening's ceremony closed with another appearance by Jeff Thibodeau as Santa Claus, spectators and performers alike milled about. Hotel employees threaded their way through the crowd with free eggnog, punch, and sugar cookies. An array of other nibblies had been set out on a buffet table and a cash bar at the far end of the room provided stronger libations to those who desired them.

Liss abandoned her aunt to sidle up to Lovey FitzPatrick as the bear collector loaded a plate with fancy crackers, assorted cheese cubes, and carrot sticks. "Good evening, Ms. FitzPatrick. I didn't think you'd still be in Moosetookalook."

"I came for the Tiny Teddies. There are still Tiny Teddies to be had."

"Yes, indeed. You'll stay for the auction on Sunday, then?"

"That's the plan." She moved steadily along the length of the buffet, adding tidbits to the collection on her plate.

"I wonder . . . do you happen to know how I might contact the former Mrs. Thorne?"

Ms. FitzPatrick's hand jerked in the act of spearing a thin slice of raw zucchini. "Who?"

"Felicity Thorne. I'm sorry. I assumed you knew her. Her hair is very black but just starting to go gray and I'd say she's about the same age as her ex husband. She was in the Emporium at the same time you were the other day."

"Oh. Yes, yes I do vaguely remember someone like that. Didn't get her name." Moving more quickly now, Lovey FitzPatrick left the buffet table and sped toward a single empty chair at one of the small tables arranged around the room. To judge by the startled expressions on the faces of those already seated, she was a total stranger to them. That didn't stop her from plunking herself down and starting to eat.

**Interesting, Liss thought.** Lovey didn't want to talk

about Felicity Thorne. She wondered why not. She was still pondering that question, considering whether to mention Lovey FitzPatrick's odd behavior to Gordon, who had just entered the ballroom, when Dan Ruskin materialized behind her. A faint stirring of the air and a whiff of familiar aftershave identified him a moment before he spoke.

"How's it going?"

"Not too bad." She glanced over her shoulder to smile at him, but quickly returned her attention to Gordon. She frowned as she watched him make his way toward Stu and Marcia. He had that "official" air about him, which meant he was on duty.

"People seemed to like having the ceremony here," Dan remarked.

Still keeping her eyes on Gordon, Liss murmured something affirmative.

"You might want to consider continuing to use this venue."

"What?" That remark captured her full attention.

"I've heard several people say how nice it is to be inside and warm. There's really no reason you have to go back to the town square for the remaining—"

"No reason? There's every reason! The whole idea was to get customers into our shops and they, in case you've forgotten, are located downtown."

"But by the time you hold the ceremonies in the evening, stores have closed for the night anyway. Why not move all that here, where it's more comfortable?"

"And the final pageant? What about that? It's scheduled for Sunday afternoon."

"Hey, don't bite my head off. I'm just trying to help. Do you really want people to see the boarded-up window and the crime scene tape when they're supposed to be thinking happy thoughts about the holidays?"

He was right, drat him!

"You could start off in the town square and march everyone—well everyone who *can* march—up here for the final performances. A parade."

"In winter?"

"Why not? Farmington just held their annual Chester Greenwood Day parade a week or two ago." Chester Greenwood, Liss recalled, was the native Mainer famous for inventing earmuffs.

The change in venue wasn't a bad suggestion, but she hated to have to alter her original plan. Again. "I'll think about it."

Pointedly ignoring Dan, she once more looked around for Gordon, but he'd done a disappearing act. So had Marcia and Stu.

Marcia? Should she have put the other woman on her list of suspects, after all? Could the consignment shop owner have lied about how she'd acquired her current batch of Tiny Teddies? If she'd stolen them from Thorne's inventory instead of buying them from Eric Moss . . . wait a minute!

Inventory!

Liss gave herself a mental slap upside the head. Why hadn't she thought of that before? Thorne must have made a list of the Tiny Teddies he had in stock. Maybe he'd even indicated where they'd come from—Eric Moss or some other source. If Sherri could get a look at it. . . .

"I don't like that look in your eye," Dan muttered.

"I was *thinking*, that's all."

"Thinking about Gordon Tandy?"

"I want to tell him to talk to her." Liss gestured toward the table where Lovey had taken refuge, but Lovey FitzPatrick was no longer sitting there. Only her plate remained, still overflowing with food from the buffet. "Well, pooh!"

"You were going to stay out of this investigation," Dan reminded her.

Liss sighed. "I don't want to be involved. Really. But if I have an idea that I think might help, then there's nothing wrong with sharing it with the authorities." It *was* frustrating not knowing what was going on, but she didn't confide that feeling to Dan. He was overprotective enough as it was.

"I'd think you'd have too much on your plate to have time to worry about solving Tandy's case for him, what with the two remaining ceremonies and the pageant and all. And I still think—" He broke off when Liss slanted him a quelling look. He sent her a sheepish grin. "Can't blame me for trying. I'm *supposed* to look out for the hotel. Bring in new business and all that."

Liss considered for a moment longer and felt a slow smile creep over her face. She stuck out a hand to grasp his and shake it. "Congratulations. You talked me into it. We'll move everything here for tomorrow evening and Saturday evening and Sunday afternoon."

Because he knew her so well, suspicion tinged Dan's response. "Great, but . . . ?"

"Oh, didn't you realize? You'll have to take charge of the . . . participants. I'll see to it that the crates of poultry are delivered to The Spruces first thing in the morning."

"So I was thinking," Sherri said, "that if you boot up the computer you took from The Toy Box and take a gander at Gavin Thorne's inventory, you might find a description of the Tiny Teddies Thorne acquired to replace the first lot."

"And this would help how?" Gordon Tandy wore his skeptical face.

"Well, then you'd know for sure if any were taken from the crime scene."

God! This had sounded so simple when Liss suggested it. Take a peek at the inventory. Discover if the bears that were missing had been wearing the same outfits as those now in Marcia's consignment shop. Liss had even given her a flyer with some of Marcia's bears pictured.

Gordon, however, wasn't making things easy. He'd been working at his laptop when she rapped on the door of the P.D. Her own office had been commandeered for temporary use by the state police. Gordon hadn't stopped tapping on keys once since she started her spiel.

At last he looked up at her. His expression was not encouraging, so his words surprised her. "It's not a bad idea."

Silence.

Sherri rolled her eyes. "But?"

"We've been working on the theory that Thorne surprised a thief who was after the money in his cash register. Why do you think the bears were the target?"

"Because they're *missing*." She restrained the impulse to add a "duh!" to the end of that sentence. It would be a really bad idea to tick off the man in charge.

"Or they were sold."

"Or they were sold," she conceded.

Gordon drummed his fingertips on the desktop. "The cash register was empty. The gun Thorne usually kept nearby was gone. Those facts we know. Anything concerning stolen Tiny Teddies is pure speculation."

"That doesn't make theft any less possible," Sherri argued.

His lips twitched. "And I assume you're about to suggest that I assign you to take a look at the records, right?"

"Why not? I used to work at the Emporium. I know how inventories are set up." At his skeptical expression, her back stiffened and her chin came up defiantly. "Look, Gordon, you're the one who wanted me for local intel. This is part of the package. Furthermore, I could be a lot more effective if you'd share *all* the information you have.

Right now, half the time, I feel like I'm playing blindman's buff!"

"This isn't a game, Sherri."

"I know that. And I'm not an amateur. I've had police training. Okay, I don't have as much experience as you do, but I know I can help find Thorne's killer."

Oh, Lord! She was *whining*. That wasn't going to help her case.

She had the uneasy suspicion that Gordon Tandy was laughing at her, but at least he *tried* to hide it. Her knees went weak with relief when he turned the screen of his laptop toward her. She sank into the visitor's chair she'd been too agitated to take before and scanned the file in front of her.

It didn't show an inventory page, but rather a ledger sheet on which Thorne had recorded the purchase of the new batch of bears. Under Tuesday's date he had entered an expenditure of "two thousand dollars (cash)" for "forty Tiny Teddies (assorted)."

"That's it? No descriptions? No source?"

"Dead end," Gordon affirmed, leaning back in Jeff Thibodeau's rump-sprung chair.

"How many sold? Could he have run out?"

"There Thorne's bookkeeping stops being helpful. He didn't enter the bears into his inventory program. They don't show up all nicely itemized on his cash register receipts. In fact, my guess is that he sold them off the record, hoping to avoid the hassle of income and sales tax. It's possible he unloaded all forty, but there's no way to tell."

Sherri bounced to her feet again and began to pace the confines of the small room. "No. No, he'd want to keep a few back, just the way Marcia has. He'd know he could get even higher prices for them. There must have been at least one or two in the shop, or in his apartment, when he died."

Gordon's intense dark eyes bored into her. "You really think the killer was after the bears?"

"I know it sounds absurd, but yes. And suddenly, after Thorne's death, Marcia Milliken has more bears."

"That's Marcia Katz, right? From the consignment shop?" Gordon scribbled a note to himself but Sherri could not decipher his handwriting.

"Did you know Marcia and her husband when they lived in Waycross Springs?" Sherri was aware that Gordon had been born and bred and still lived there. Waycross Springs and Moosetookalook weren't far apart as the crow flew but it took almost an hour to drive between them along the winding, roller-coaster roads of rural Carrabassett County.

"Slightly." He shrugged. Residents of small towns tended to know all their neighbors, at least to nod to.

"Anyway," Sherri continued, "I know Marcia bought her Tiny Teddies from Eric Moss, but—"

Gordon's chair hit the floor with a resounding thump. "Back up. What's this about Marcia and Moss?"

Genuinely surprised, Sherri blurted out the first thing that came to mind: "But I thought you questioned Marcia last night. Liss saw—"

"Liss MacCrimmon! I should have known. I thought I warned you about talking to her."

"She just mentioned that she saw you—"

"She didn't see me talking to Marcia because I didn't talk to Marcia." Gordon glared at Sherri, which put her back up.

"Small town, remember? Liss saw you. She saw Marcia. She jumped to a conclusion."

Gordon rubbed his temples, as if the entire subject of Liss MacCrimmon gave him a headache. "Sorry. Overreacted. I don't want her involved."

"I know."

He was worried Liss would get herself into trouble . . . again.

Wearily, Gordon waved Sherri back into the visitor's chair. "You are not to repeat one word of anything you hear in this office to Liss MacCrimmon, is that clear? She almost got herself killed the last time she meddled in a murder investigation. I'm not taking any risks with her safety this time around."

"No problem." Sherri perched on the front edge of the seat. "But you should know that it was Liss who made me think that what the bears were wearing might help. It was a good thought. They're limited editions. If Marcia's bears are wearing the same outfits as some of the ones Thorne had . . . well, that would make her supplier—Eric Moss— a suspect, right?"

"My officers interviewed every Toy Box customer they could locate. Some of them gave descriptions of the Tiny Teddies they saw. Others showed off the bears they bought on Tuesday. None of the descriptions matched those we identified as being in the consignment shop. Someone *did* check, even on the Tiny Teddies Marcia is keeping back for the auction on Sunday."

"Thorne didn't have a new supply of bears until Tuesday afternoon," Sherri mused aloud. "The storm was already pretty bad by five and he closed up around six. It seems to me that he must have had a few bears left."

"Did you see the size of the mob that descended on The Toy Box?"

Remembering, Sherri had to admit that Thorne *could* have sold them all. "Dead end?"

"Dead end."

Sherri hesitated, then blurted out a question. "Why *were* you at the hotel?"

"I went to The Spruces last night to track down Eddie Bruce, the snowplow driver."

"Did he see anything the night of the murder?"

"Nothing out of the ordinary. Lots of snow. A few cars and trucks, including Ruskin's. One idiot was out on a snowmobile before the sun even came up."

"A snowmobile? Maybe that's how the killer fled the scene of the crime."

Gordon cracked a smile. "Don't think so. It was Doug Preston's boy, Frank. He snuck out of the house and took off on one of the family machines to go see his girlfriend. He's fourteen."

"I don't suppose *he* saw anything suspicious?"

"A lot of snow, especially after he got hung up in a thicket. Had to use his cell phone to call his father for a rescue. He's been grounded till after Christmas."

Sherri heaved a resigned sigh. "Dead end?"

"Dead end."

Liss first noticed unusual activity at The Toy Box when the crime scene tape came down. Surprised, since it had been only a bit more than forty-eight hours since the discovery of the body, she cast an occasional glance that way as the afternoon wore on.

A truck from a local glass replacement company pulled up in front of the shop at two and in short order the delivery men had installed a new display window. Next to arrive was the crew from a cleaning company that specialized in putting things to rights after blood or other bodily fluids had been spilled. Sherri had mentioned them to Liss once. They did regular cleaning, too, but the police often recommended their services to victims of violent crimes.

By the time Margaret returned from The Spruces at four o'clock, smelling strongly of gardenias, Liss could no longer contain her curiosity. She left her aunt in charge of the Emporium and headed for the scene of the crime.

Inside The Toy Box, Liss found Felicity Thorne supervising the cleaning and repair efforts. Well turned out in a dark green pantsuit, her hair coiled into an elaborate twist at her nape, Felicity looked every inch the business owner. Her temperament, however, showed no improvement over their previous encounter. She scowled at Liss and sounded as irritated at the interruption as she looked. "What do you want?"

"I'm just being neighborly." Liss surveyed the shop, noting that the cleanup was nearly complete. "Is there anything you need? Anything I can do to help?"

"Try minding your own business."

"Your late husband—"

"Ex husband."

"Your late ex husband was a member of the Moose-tookalook Small Business Association. He was a big part of our Twelve Days of Christmas promotion. I don't think it's out of line for me to ask if you plan to reopen the toy store. This is a small, friendly community, Ms. Thorne. We've found that pulling together makes the sleigh go faster."

Felicity's gimlet-eyed stare lasted a moment longer. Then she blinked twice. When she had Liss in focus again she sent a hard, assessing look her way before a slow smile curved her lips. For just a moment, Liss thought she seemed approachable, but the impression was only an illusion.

"Sleigh, huh? What century do you live in?"

"There's nothing wrong with being a little old-fashioned." Liss's muscles had tensed to the point where it was physically painful to hold her ground, but she hadn't finished with Felicity Thorne. "Is there to be any sort of funeral or memorial service? I assume you're in charge of that, as well."

"He didn't like funerals," Felicity snapped. "Neither do I."

Liss couldn't say she cared much for displays of public

mourning either, but she found the other woman's attitude offensive. Without another word, she turned on her heel and headed back toward the door.

"Wait. There's something you can do for me, after all."

One hand on the doorknob, Liss glanced warily over her shoulder. "Yes?"

"Spread the word that I'll be having a going-out-of-business sale. Then I'm putting this building on the market and getting the hell out of Dodge. If I never set foot in this one-horse town again, it will be too soon."

"And you have a good day, too," Liss muttered as made her escape. It took considerable will power not to slam the door behind her.

Late Friday evening, after the ceremony at The Spruces—the ten ladies dancing—Liss and Sherri found a quiet spot in the lobby, shielded by a large pillar, and settled into two deep plush chairs angled toward each other to make private conversation easier.

"What's happening with the investigation?" Liss asked.

"I'm not supposed to talk to you about the case." In contrast to the prim-sounding words, Sherri dug into a pocket and handed over several pieces of yellow-lined paper, folded in eighths.

Liss hesitated. "I don't want you to get into any trouble."

"A good detective, according to the textbooks, uses any and all resources to help solve a crime. The state police have made me their local expert. I'm soliciting your input for the same reason."

"Thanks." Liss glanced around to make certain they weren't being observed, then quickly read through Sherri's notes. "Not Marcia or Stu," she murmured, coming to the part about Gordon's reason for being at the hotel the night before. "The plow driver." Sherri's summary of what the driver had told him was a succinct "nothing relevant" with no details.

Most disappointing to Liss was the lack of detailed inventory records for Thorne's stock. "Maybe he didn't have time to list the new acquisitions properly."

"Gordon thinks he didn't intend to record them, that he was trying to save paying sales tax. You know—cheat the government while turning a profit."

"No indication of who supplied the bears?"

"Nope. Just the price. He paid fifty bucks apiece for forty bears."

"Then I expect he got them from Eric Moss, just as Marcia did. That's the price Moss quoted to me."

"No sign of Eric Moss yet," Sherri volunteered, "but Gordon seems to regard his absence as a minor and unimportant mystery." She grimaced, apparently remembering she wasn't supposed to "talk" to Liss about the case. "I can't tell you where his focus is, but it's not on Moss and that's *all* I'm saying." She mimed zipping her lips.

"There isn't much mystery in where this new supply of Tiny Teddies came from. The only logical source is the other side of the border. They entered this country illegally from Canada."

Sherri's nod encouraged her to go on.

"Moss, or one of his contacts, must be smuggling them in."

"Let's say you're right. Your hypothetical smuggler has no reason to kill Thorne. As long as Thorne was profiting from the arrangement, which he must have been, he wasn't likely to go to the cops."

"A falling out among crooks? Whatever happened, there has to be a connection between Thorne's murder and the Tiny Teddies."

"Why?"

Liss just looked at her.

"Think about it. Really, the idea is pretty far-fetched, especially when—" She broke off, waving away any questions about what she'd almost said.

Liss didn't push. Sherri was conflicted enough as it was, forced to choose between her friendship with Liss and her career prospects. But whatever lead Gordon Tandy was pursuing, Liss was convinced it was the wrong one.

"It's the timing," she murmured, thinking aloud. "And the fact that the Tiny Teddy, the one in the chef's outfit, was also shot through the heart."

"A warning?"

"Maybe."

Sherri sighed. "I wish we knew for certain if there were Tiny Teddies in The Toy Box when Thorne was killed."

"I wonder if The Toy Box's going-out-of-business sale will include any little bears? I spoke with the not-so-grieving widow this afternoon. She's out for a quick buck."

Sherri's sudden stillness and the avid gleam in her eyes caught Liss's attention as she was about to launch into a recap of her encounter with Felicity Thorne. So that was the way the wind blew, she thought. Gordon was trying to break the former Mrs. Thorne's alibi. He thought she'd murdered her ex.

"Say Felicity doesn't pan out," Liss said carefully. "Will Gordon look for Eric Moss then?"

Sherri shook her head, but was careful not to answer aloud.

"There's nothing to tie him to the murder, I suppose," Liss mused. "No known quarrel with Thorne. Drat!"

What other suspects were there? Liss wondered if Stu Burroughs had been checked out. He and Thorne had certainly been at odds, but would Stu kill just because the other man refused to sell him a few bears for resale in the ski shop? And what about Mark Patton, the gray man?

And Lovey FitzPatrick, the woman in the blue coat? They'd both exhibited suspicious behavior.

Liss glanced again at Sherri. Her friend's lips were set in a thin, grim line. She'd said all she was going to. Probably more than she should have. The guilty look on her face and the anxious glance she directed at someone coming up behind Liss were ample proof of that. Liss hastily stuffed the yellow pages Sherri had given her into a pocket. Their tête-à-tête was over.

Expecting to see Gordon Tandy appear in her peripheral vision, Liss was relieved when Pete Campbell came around the side of the chair and bent down to give his fiancée a quick kiss on the forehead.

"Hey, gorgeous. Ready to head out?"

"What are you doing here? I don't need a ride." Sherri's attitude was anything but loverlike.

Pete ignored the rudeness. "No, but I do."

"You expect me to drive you to your place? It's a good fifteen miles out of my way."

Beginning to get the message, Pete shuffled his feet and shot Liss an apologetic glance. "I thought you might enjoy a sleepover. It's been awhile."

"I have a kid, remember?" Sherri's voice grew increasingly testy with every word she spoke. "I can't just run off any time I feel like it."

What was wrong with the two of them? Liss wondered. They were getting married next year. They shouldn't be sniping at each other like this.

"You *can* take a little time for yourself once in a while," Pete said. "I've already talked to your mother. She thinks it's a great idea. She's not expecting you home tonight."

Sherri exploded out of the chair. "*I'm* expecting me home. I've got things to do. And I've got to go to work at midnight."

"I thought you might like to spend the time between now and then with me."

"I've got things to do!" From the stiff set of her shoulders and the stubborn tilt to her chin, Liss could tell Sherri had no intention of relenting.

"Fine!" The backs of Pete's ears had gone red and he could no longer keep the frustration from creeping into his voice. "Can you at least give me a lift home?"

Unspoken was the plea that they finish this discussion in private. They were drawing unwanted attention from patrons in the lobby of the hotel.

It was touch and go for a minute, but Sherri finally managed to unclench her teeth long enough to spit out an answer. "Fine. Let's go. See you later, Liss."

She stomped away, leaving Pete to follow. He had to sprint to catch up.

Shaking her head, Liss watched them exit the hotel together. Dan had been right. There was trouble in paradise.

# Chapter Eleven

The next day there was trouble at the Emporium, too.

Liss slammed the phone receiver into the cradle, wishing she knew more creative swear words. It landed off center, bounced, and slid off the sales counter to dangle over the side by the cord, revolving slowly. She ignored it until it started to beep at her. Then, very carefully, she hung up.

One of the eleven bagpipe players she'd so laboriously rounded up for the Saturday evening ceremony at The Spruces had just canceled on her. She had less than twelve hours to find a replacement.

One man was the obvious person to ask, but Liss needed a few minutes to convince herself that she had the right to put him on the spot. The only other alternative she could think of was to fill in for the missing piper herself. The world wasn't ready for that! Bad enough some of her closest friends had listened to her attempt to sing. First taking a few deep, calming breaths, she punched in Gordon Tandy's cell phone number.

An hour later he showed up in person.

"I got your message, Liss. What's so urgent?"

Belatedly, Liss realized he must think her request to see him had something to do with the murder case. Hastily she explained. His expression grew more thunderous with every word.

"Gordon, please. I wouldn't ask if I wasn't desperate."
She put one hand on his arm and sent him her most be-
seeching look.

His features softened but he still hesitated. "Liss, I
haven't had time for hobbies since I joined the state police.
First, I gave up skiing. Then, I sold my snowmobile. Finally, I stopped entering piping competitions. Do you have
any idea how long it's been since I played?"

"It doesn't matter."

He gave a snort of laughter. "Oh, yeah, it does. And you
know it."

She did. To perform well, a piper had to practice. "How
about this—you stand there with the other ten pipers and
*pretend* to play. The important thing is that there be eleven
of you."

That she could have done that same thing herself belatedly occurred to Liss, but she knew in her heart that she
wanted Gordon to agree. If she meant anything at all to
him, he'd *want* to help out.

"It's only for one evening. The piper I originally had
lined up can be here for the pageant on Sunday. Please?"
She stopped short of adding "pretty please with sugar on
top." That sounded too much like begging.

"I don't have time to go home for my pipes."

"You can use those." She gestured toward the wall.

If he wasn't really going to play, it didn't matter that
"those" had been hanging in the Emporium for as long as
Liss could remember. They were decoration, not inventory. Once upon a time they might have been for sale, but
that had been way back when her father, the only serious
piper in the family, had still lived in Moosetookalook. For
years, that set of pipes had been kept on display solely to
enhance the Scottish decor. People who expressed an interest in learning to play the bagpipes had been referred to

Gordon's brother, Russ, who owned a music store in Waycross Springs.

Gordon inspected the instrument, looking doubtful.

Liss slanted him a sunny smile. "Really, it will be enough if you just show up and pretend to play. You don't need to drive all the way back to Waycross Springs." She caught his hand and dragged him toward the rack that held the kilts. "You can borrow piping regalia from the Emporium, too."

"I've got my own kilt."

She took that as a "yes," but didn't dare breathe a sigh of relief quiet yet. The kilt, presumably, was in Waycross Springs with the pipes.

"My brother is one of the eleven, right?"

Liss nodded, barely able to contain her elation.

"He's been after me to start playing again. I'm sure he'd be glad to pick up my pipes and regalia on his way here. If he can come over a little early, I might even be able to work in a short practice session."

"Thank you!" Liss went up on her toes to give him a quick kiss on the lips. "I really appreciate this."

"Yeah, yeah." But he was smiling as he headed out the door.

Shortly after noon, Marcia closed Second Time Around for the day. She stopped in at Moosetookalook Scottish Emporium soon after. For once she did not look particularly thin. Her beanpole figure was covered head-to-toe in a one-piece snowmobile suit. The material, the same as that used in ski parkas, bulked up her entire body, but the dark green color made her milk-white complexion look even paler than it really was.

"Have you seen Sherri?" she asked.

"Not recently. What's up?"

"I wanted to ask her to keep a close eye on my place. When I stepped out for a minute earlier, I returned to find Lovey FitzPatrick creeping around my back door, trying to see in through the windows. I'm afraid she, or one of the other nutcases, may try to break in and steal the bears I set aside for the auction tomorrow."

Liss couldn't quite imagine Lovey as a sneak thief, but she understood Marcia's concern. "If you're that worried, maybe you should stick around and guard your stock."

"Are you kidding? The day's too perfect to be cooped up inside."

Looking where Marcia pointed, at the bright blue sky and pristine snow visible through the display window, Liss experienced a sudden longing of her own to breathe fresh air. She understood the frustration of being stuck at work. That was one reason she wanted to convert the store into an online business. It would be heaven to pick and choose her own hours.

"Going out on the snowmobile?" she asked.

"Every chance I get."

"Then wouldn't it be easier just to put the Tiny Teddies in a safe place when you're not open?"

The other woman smirked. "I've got that covered."

"Bank vault?"

"As good as." She leaned closer, her snowmobile suit making swishing sounds as the fabric brushed the counter. "You've got a root cellar in your house, right?"

Had everyone known but her? Liss nodded.

"Well, so do I, but Cabot did some work on ours during his survivalist phase. Made it into a panic room."

"You're kidding!" Liss had heard of such things, even seen one in that Jodie Foster movie, but she had never imagined someone installing something like that in a house in Moosetookalook, Maine.

"Climate controlled," Marcia boasted. "The perfect hiding place for all sorts of things."

"Well, then, if the bears are secure, why do you need to have Sherri keep an eye on the place?"

"I don't want to come home to a jimmied lock or broken glass. I don't need the hassle."

Remembering the bullet that had gone through The Toy Box's display window, Liss saw Marcia's point. "How about I get hold of Sherri for you? She can't have gone far."

Most likely she'd simply walked into one of the many "dead zones" where her cell phone wouldn't work. There were several in the low spots on Moosetookalook's hilly streets.

"That'll work." With a cheery wave, Marcia headed for the door. "I'll be back in a few hours."

"It'll be dark by then," Liss protested.

"That's okay. My machine has lights."

"Marcia! Wait a minute." Liss crossed the sales floor toward her.

The other woman paused with one hand on the doorknob, clearly impatient to be gone.

"Just one quick question," Liss promised. "You know Eric Moss better than I do."

"Not all *that* well."

"Do you know if he still lives in that ramshackle old farmhouse out on the Ridge Road?"

"Last I heard, he did. Why?"

"Because I think he smuggled those Tiny Teddies in from Canada. Have you read the newspapers lately? Customs keeps catching people crossing the border with hundreds of them in the trunks of their cars like miniature illegal aliens."

A pained expression flickered across Marcia's face as

she let go of the knob and turned toward Liss. Her voice changed, too, sounding reproachful. "Don't be flip, Liss. You don't know what you're talking about."

"I beg your pardon?"

"Illegal aliens are not something to joke about."

"Well, no. I get that." Liss hadn't meant to offend. "Terrorists—"

"No." Marcia stood with her back propped against the door, as if to prevent anyone from entering. The shop was presently empty of customers, but she lowered her voice all the same. "I have a good friend, a Canadian married to an American. She lived in this country for years but she kept her Canadian citizenship because she wanted her kids to have a choice when they grew up. Then along came all the new antiterrorism rules and one fine day, after my friend visited Canada to spend some time with her elderly parents, she was stopped at the border and told she couldn't return to the U.S. and her husband and kids. Stupid government red tape kept them separated for months."

"That's appalling, but they finally let her go home, right?" Liss tried to imagine what being forcibly separated from loved ones would be like and found herself sympathizing with Marcia's obvious disgust with a system that allowed such things to happen.

"Not exactly. She got fed up with waiting and slipped back into the U.S. at a spot well away from any official border crossing. Now she really is an illegal alien."

"I'm very sorry about your friend's troubles," Liss said, "and I didn't mean to make light of folks in her situation, but my point was that Eric Moss may be smuggling in Tiny Teddies and—"

"I bought those bears in good faith and no one can prove otherwise!" Sudden temper flashed in Marcia's narrowed eyes.

Liss had to fight an urge to back up a step or two. "I'm

not trying to interfere with your business, Marcia. I just want to talk to Eric Moss."

"I have no idea where he is!" Marcia gave Liss one last fulminating glare and then stormed out of the Emporium. A few minutes later, Liss saw her drive by with her snowmobile on its trailer.

After Marcia's abrupt departure, Liss tried to keep busy making lists—items she wanted to order for her spring catalog; names for the kitten—but her thoughts kept drifting back to Eric Moss and his bears. Marcia's bears.

"Stay out of it," she muttered to herself. "Smuggling is police business, just like murder."

But the police were not pursuing this angle.

What had Sherri said? That she, Liss MacCrimmon, had special knowledge that might be useful?

Not at the moment, she didn't, but she would if she could just find a connection between Moss and Thorne. She had only to match the description of a single Tiny Teddy in Thorne's shop with one Marcia now had. Then she'd pass the information on to Gordon. Let him track down the elusive Mr. Moss.

Liss doodled on a blank sheet of paper as she contemplated what she did know. At least two people—individuals who were still in town—had probably seen all of Thorne's bears and most of Marcia's too. One of them might even have gotten a glimpse of the ones Marcia was keeping back.

Without allowing herself time to think better of the idea, Liss called the hotel switchboard. Within fifteen minutes she had talked both Lovey FitzPatrick and Mark Patton into stopping by at Moosetookalook Scottish Emporium to talk with her.

Just under an hour later, as it was starting to get dark on this day before the shortest day of the year, Ms. FitzPatrick sailed into the shop. Liss invited her to make herself comfortable in the cozy corner. She had coffee and a plate of sticky buns from Patsy's ready and waiting.

"Thank you so much for coming in, Ms. FitzPatrick."

"You made it sound urgent." Lovey removed her coat, sat, and placed her heavy shoulder bag on the floor beside her.

"It is. You see, the reason I want to talk to you, and the reason I was asking questions at the hotel the other night, is that I am afraid whoever killed Gavin Thorne may still be right here in Moosetookalook."

"Felicity Thorne isn't," Lovey said. "She's in Fallstown."

Liss blinked at her, startled. "You think Mrs. Thorne murdered her ex?"

"Stands to reason, doesn't it? She hated the bastard."

"I'm surprised to hear you sound so certain. I was under the impression that you barely knew the woman."

Lovey FitzPatrick grimaced. "You'll find out anyway, I guess. The police certainly did. I met both Gavin and Felicity Thorne years ago. I'm a collector. They were dealers. She still is, but that doesn't make me a *friend* of hers."

"I see."

Liss took a sip of coffee to keep herself from making a rude remark. If they'd had no more than a long-term business relationship, why had Lovey ducked out on Liss at The Spruces rather than just say so? There had been no reason for her to panic.

"Well, then, I'm sure you'll be delighted to hear that Mrs. Thorne is here in Moosetookalook supervising repairs on The Toy Box. She plans to reopen before Christmas for a close-out sale."

"How interesting." The cup rattled slightly as Lovey returned it to the saucer.

"Have you seen her since Mr. Thorne's unfortunate death?"

Lovey glanced around, as if she expected someone to pop out from behind the nearest display of Scottish imports. Like Marcia earlier in the day, she lowered her voice to a whisper. "This is just between you and me, right?"

"Of course," Liss lied.

The proverbial lightbulb had come on. Liss remembered Gordon Tandy walking into the hotel ballroom just after she'd tried to question Lovey. The woman's vanishing act hadn't been about avoiding Liss's questions. She'd been trying to stay out of the sights of the state police detective in charge of the murder investigation.

"That woman is a real piece of work," Lovey said. "A troublemaker from the get-go. When I ran into her the other day, *before* the murder, she yammered on and on about what a raw deal she got in the divorce and how she had nothing but their old store—empty—in Fallstown and no money to buy new stock. It was ages before she shut up long enough to listen to *my* complaints."

"I wonder if she knew she stood to inherit her ex husband's estate?" Liss murmured.

"I doubt it."

Liss gave Lovey a sharp look. She sounded very sure. "Does Ms. Thorne live above the store in Fallstown?"

Lovey sampled a sticky bun. "Oh, this is good! I, uh, believe the Thornes had a house on the outskirts of town."

Liss said nothing, practicing a technique she'd learned from reading mystery novels. As she'd hoped, Lovey felt compelled to fill the silence.

"Felicity got the house in the divorce settlement. And all the furniture. And the dog. I don't see that she had anything to complain about myself."

Lovey FitzPatrick knew a great deal about a woman she claimed was only a business acquaintance, Liss thought. And she was nervous, fidgeting with her cup, her pastry, and the strap of her purse. Although Liss could neither guess why nor pinpoint what made her so certain of that fact, she was sure Lovey was lying to her about something.

"I find it a trifle odd that Felicity Thorne confided in you at all," Liss said carefully. "Was that on the day you were both in here? Tuesday?"

"No. Earlier in the week. I met her over at the coffee shop. Is that where these buns came from? They're wonderful." Lovey's face was set in a rather desperate-looking smile.

Liss refused to be distracted. "So, you're saying Felicity Thorne was in Patsy's Coffee Shop *before* Tuesday? Do you remember which day?"

Lovey FitzPatrick shook her head. "I've been here since Saturday afternoon. I've stopped in at that coffee shop every single day. How could I resist such wonderful pastries? It could have been Sunday. Or maybe Monday."

Making a mental note to ask Patsy if she remembered seeing Mrs. Thorne, Liss shifted her line of questioning. "What I really need to know, Ms. FitzPatrick, is what bears were included in Mr. Thorne's second lot of Tiny Teddies. You see, he didn't enter any description in his inventory, and there may be some missing."

Lovey's eyes lit up at the possibility. "More bears?"

"Could be. The descriptions? Were they all the same?" She already knew the answer to that question, but she asked it anyway.

"Only in being overpriced! The nerve of that man, increasing the prices every time you turned around!"

"How many different costumes were there?"

"I'm not sure. You see, I suspect he was holding some back, just as he did the first time around. I saw a bride and a nurse and one in a cap and gown and another in a big Mexican hat and a serape."

"Did you buy any of them?"

"One, because it was the only one in a bridal gown. He said there weren't any more like it, not that I believed him."

With a sinking sensation in her stomach, Liss remembered seeing a Tiny Teddy dressed as a bride in Marcia's shop. It had been one of those offered for sale the first day, the day Marcia said Eric Moss had delivered the bears. "You've been in the consignment shop. Did you—?"

"Different bride," Lovey declared. "I bought one of those, too. Here. I'll show you."

She hauled the huge purse into her lap and began to burrow through the contents. Bemused, Liss watched item after item pile up on her coffee table. Lovey had everything in her shoulder bag but the kitchen sink.

"Here you go!" Victorious, she produced two small bags, one with The Toy Box logo and one with no logo at all—the kind Marcia used at Second Time Around.

She pulled out the two bears, but by then Liss had lost interest. From where she was sitting, she had a clear view of the interior of Lovey FitzPatrick's purse. It was almost empty . . . except for what looked suspiciously like the barrel of a gun.

Struggling to concentrate on what Lovey was saying, at least to the point of giving coherent responses, Liss angled for a better look.

Lovey shoved her purse aside, cutting off Liss's view but leaving the bag balanced on the very edge of the coffee table. With a minimum of encouragement, Liss thought, it would tumble to the floor and the remaining contents would spill out.

"This little darling is my favorite." Oblivious to Liss's growing consternation, Lovey held up one of Thorne's ballerina bears. "Isn't the construction on the skirt adorable?"

Liss stared blankly at the Tiny Teddy and nodded, giving Lovey sufficient encouragement to launch into a detailed description of her entire collection. She segued from bears into talking about other passions she'd indulged over the years. They all involved toys of one sort or another.

Liss bumped the table with her knee but the shoulder bag didn't budge. She reached forward, as if to pick up one of the Tiny Teddies. Deliberately, she jabbed an elbow into the bulky purse. It landed on the area rug with a dull thunk . . . right side up.

"Oh, sorry! I'll get that." Subtlety, she decided, was highly overrated.

"Thank you, dear." Preoccupied with admiring the Tiny Teddy in the bridal gown that she'd purchased from Marcia, Lovey paid no attention at all to what her hostess was doing.

Liss reached into the purse and seized the weapon by the barrel. Pulling it out, she turned it around and pointed it away from both herself and Lovey. She was careful to keep her finger well away from the trigger. She knew almost nothing about firearms, except that they were damned dangerous to play around with.

On the other side of the coffee table, Lovey froze. Her voice was as icy as the expression on her face. "Replace that in my purse, if you please. It is not a toy."

Liss kept hold of the gun as her gaze darted to the other woman's face. A worried frown added wrinkles to Lovey's forehead, but otherwise she seemed no more threatening than before.

"Why do you have a gun?"

"For protection, of course."

"Generally speaking, small towns in Maine are pretty safe places."

"A lot you know. There are criminals everywhere. Home invasions are up. Wackos are always breaking into houses, looking for money to buy drugs." Pushing herself out of the comfortable chair, Lovey held out her right hand, palm up. "Give that back, if you please."

"I'm sorry. I don't think I can do that."

"It's mine. You have no right to keep it." Her nostrils flared slightly, instantly putting Liss in mind of a bull about to charge.

She wished she knew how to tell if a gun was loaded. She wished she were wearing gloves, because she was undoubtedly messing up fingerprints. And she wished she weren't so far from the phone, which was on the sales counter on the opposite side of the shop. Not that she could use it even if the telephone sat on the coffee table in front of her. She needed both hands to hold the gun steady. They were trembling already. If she let go with one, she'd be sure to lose her grip on the gun. Or accidentally fire a shot.

Liss swallowed hard, then very carefully lifted the weapon until it was pointed at Lovey. "I think, Ms. FitzPatrick, that we need to have a little talk."

# Chapter Twelve

"**I**s this the weapon you used to kill Gavin Thorne?"

"Oh, for heaven's sake!" Annoyed, Lovey flopped back down, landing so hard that she made her chair bounce.

"Is it?"

"No!"

"Then why are you so upset about my finding it?"

"Because you're aiming it at me!"

That probably meant it *was* loaded. Liss felt sweat bead up on her forehead.

"Answer my questions honestly and you'll be fine. Do you have a permit to carry a concealed weapon?" Liss had no idea if such a thing was required in Maine or not, but the question sounded good.

"Well, no, but—"

"Then I believe I'm obliged to turn this over to the police." A thought occurred to her. "You're from Massachusetts, right? Aren't all handguns illegal there?"

"I have a summer place in Kennebunkport. I keep my weapon there. Not that the fact that I own a gun is any of your business."

That resort community was on the coast. It would take almost three hours to reach from Moosetookalook by car. No wonder Lovey was staying at The Spruces rather than make that round-trip every day. What still did not make sense, however, was the idea that she thought she needed a gun for protection. She must have another reason for carrying it.

"This gun has been fired." Liss had no way of knowing if that was true, but she figured that if she was going to bluff, she should go all out.

Lovey's face, which had been edging toward purple, abruptly lost all its color.

"Spill it," Liss ordered.

Heaving a deep sigh, Lovey FitzPatrick folded her hands over her midsection and glared across the coffee table at her interrogator. Sounding more grumpy and put upon than either remorseful or scared, she once more denied killing Gavin Thorne.

"I shot the bear," she confessed. "Just the Tiny Teddy in the window. I did not shoot Gavin."

"You shot . . . the bear?" Liss repeated. That was *not* what she'd expected to hear. "Why?"

"Did you see how much he wanted for it?"

"Too steep for you?"

"That's not the point. I can afford any amount, but the way he kept raising his prices infuriated me on principle. They went up fifty dollars between the time I left his shop last Saturday to come here and when I returned to his store to demand that he show me the bears he'd held back on my first visit."

"Why did he do that?" Liss had lowered the gun, although she kept hold of it. Lovey's motivation for shooting out Thorne's window and destroying one of the Tiny Teddies made no sense to her. Still, Liss was inclined to believe the other woman when she said she hadn't killed anyone.

Lovey hesitated.

"Ms. FitzPatrick, you lied to me earlier."

Silence.

"You've been calling both Mr. and Mrs. Thorne by their first names. Was Gavin Thorne more than a business acquaintance?"

Lovey's face twisted into a grimace. "Are you suggesting I was *intimate* with Gavin Thorne? Bite your tongue! It's Felicity I'm friendly with. *That's* why Gavin was being so beastly to me. He thought he'd take a stab at her by giving someone she likes a hard time."

"So you shot his bear."

"It seemed like a good idea at the time." Suddenly Lovey grinned. "I waltzed right up to the window and popped it one!" She pantomimed firing a gun. "It *was* a good idea. Best way to hurt him—hit him in the pocketbook."

"Pretty good shot."

The grin widened. "I took lessons."

"In Massachusetts?"

"On visits to Maine, not that it's any of your business."

Liss leaned forward, her gaze intent on Lovey's face. The gun dangled, forgotten, from her fingers. "So, the decision to shoot the bear—did you act on impulse or was it premeditated?"

Lovey hid her reaction an instant too late.

"Was it even your own idea?"

"Well, I did think of it because of something Felicity said when we were talking in the coffee shop."

"Didn't it occur to you that you were committing a crime?"

"It's only a crime if you get caught or if someone rats you out." Lovey sulked for a moment. Then a sly look came into her eyes. "*Are* you going to turn me in?"

"I don't see that I have any choice. The police need to

know that the vandalism and the murder were two separate crimes." Liss frowned, wondering if they *were* unrelated. Had Lovey's action given the killer the idea?

"I'll pay you to keep quiet about this. How much do you want? A thousand dollars? Two thousand?"

"I don't want your money, Ms. FitzPatrick. I just want to make sure no one gets away with murder."

Sleigh bells jangled. Distracted, Liss turned toward the door. Her hand lifted. Aunt Margaret, home from her new job at The Spruces, stopped in her tracks and gaped at the tableau in the cozy corner.

"Amaryllis Rosalie MacCrimmon, what are you doing with a gun?"

Liss glanced down at the weapon in surprise. Hastily, she lowered it.

At the same moment, Lovey threw herself across the coffee table, ramming Liss's shoulder. The gun flew out of Liss's hand. She hit the floor with bruising force, catching one last glimpse of the weapon as it landed several feet away and skittered beneath a display of kilts.

Lovey landed on top of her, driving the air from Liss's lungs. At once, the older woman began to squirm, trying to right herself while at the same time patting the floor around them, searching for the gun.

Liss shoved her away, scrambling to her feet just as Aunt Margaret scooped up the weapon and carried it back with her to the sales counter. She'd punched the speed dial for 9-1-1 before either Lovey or Liss could reach her.

"Give me that!" Lovey screeched.

Liss seized Lovey's arm as she reached for the gun, twisting it behind her back. Margaret whisked the gun away, hiding it beneath the counter. She plucked a tartan scarf from a display as Liss caught hold of Lovey's free hand. The scarf made an excellent restraint.

Within an hour, the state police had come and gone, taking Lovey FitzPatrick and her gun away with them.

"Well," Aunt Margaret said when she and Liss were alone again. "That certainly broke up the monotony."

Liss's laugh was a trifle shaky. "I think I could stand a bit of boredom right now."

"Did she kill Gavin Thorne?"

"She says not."

Under Gordon's expert questioning, Liss had gone over everything Lovey had told her. She'd come away from the interview convinced that Felicity Thorne had somehow planted the idea of shooting the Tiny Teddy in Lovey's head. A petty desire for revenge might explain away Felicity's manipulation of her friend, but had there also been a darker motivation behind it? She'd certainly been angry enough at her ex to kill him that day Liss had witnessed them quarreling.

Gordon intended to question Felicity. He'd told Liss that much, but he'd refused to say more. Once again, he'd warned her to stay out of police business.

"I'm glad you weren't hurt." Aunt Margaret accompanied her words with a hug so fierce it left Liss nearly breathless.

"I'm fine." Liss eased out of the embrace, but not before she'd identified the day's perfume as Wind Song. "No more than a couple of bruises from when Lovey tackled me." Ruefully, she rubbed her elbow. It embarrassed her to have been taken down by a woman more than twice her age.

"What on earth were you thinking? That woman said you *invited* her here."

Gordon hadn't looked happy about that part, either.

"I did. I wanted to ask her what bears Thorne had in his shop right before he was killed. I'd intended to compare them with the Tiny Teddies Marcia has."

"You can't think Marcia killed Thorne! I know she's always had a short fuse, but—"

Aunt Margaret looked so upset that Liss hastened to reassure her. "Of course not! But Marcia didn't just pull her Tiny Teddies out of thin air. She bought them from Eric Moss, who may have sold bears to Gavin Thorne. The thing is, *he's* nowhere to be found, so—"

"So you think Moss killed Thorne?" Aunt Margaret shook her head in disbelief. "I find that hard to accept. I've known Eric for years."

Liss gave her aunt a hard look. "You didn't ever *date* him, did you?"'

Margaret's bark of laughter reassured her. "Nothing like that, but I've always found him to be pleasant to deal with."

Liss started to remind Margaret that, given the right circumstances, *anyone* could kill. Just in time, she realized what a bad idea that would be. Instead, she made a production of looking at the clock in the corner. "Well, will you look at that! It's past closing time. What do you say we lock up and call it a day?"

"What did you say?"

The desk clerk looked startled by Dan's vehemence. "That Ms. MacCrimmon said she'd be in Mr. Patton's room if anyone was asking for her."

Dan ignored the elevator and took the stairs, arriving outside Mark Patton's door out of breath and short of temper. He pounded on the wood with both fists. "Open up, Patton!"

From the other side of the door, Liss's voice responded to his shout. "Dan?"

"Liss? Are you okay? Did—?"

The glower on her face when she opened the door froze the question before it passed his lips but did nothing to blunt the fierce anger he felt. With a curt nod at Mark Patton, he grabbed Liss's wrist and hauled her out into the corridor.

"Hey!"

"Shut up. Just shut up." He dragged her down the hall and into the elevator, punching the button for the lobby.

"You're hurting me."

He released her at once but did not apologize. "I don't suppose it occurred to you that if Mark Patton killed Gavin Thorne you could be hurting a lot worse right now?"

"He didn't kill anyone."

"You don't know that."

"I . . . Gordon just arrested Lovey FitzPatrick."

The elevator doors opened on the lobby. For a moment they stayed put, glaring at each other. Then he seized her arm—more gently this time—and escorted her through the public areas and into the less grand environs where Joe Ruskin had created office space.

"Dad, I need the conference room," Dan hollered as he steered Liss past the medium-sized office where his father sat hunched in his chair in front of a computer. Joe gave him a wave in response but he didn't take his eyes off the spreadsheet on the screen.

The conference room contained a long table surrounded by chairs and a side table with a coffeepot and accessories. Dan closed and locked the door and gestured Liss toward a chair. "Now, what's all this about Lovey FitzPatrick?"

Liss did not sit. She paced the room like a caged lioness as she recounted that afternoon's altercation with Lovey. He read the subtext all too easily.

"You're not satisfied that Lovey's arrest solves the murder, are you?"

"I believed her when she said she only shot the bear."

"Felicity Thorne, then?"

"Seems logical."

Dan studied her face. "I know that look. You have someone else in mind. And you decided, all on your own, to meet in private with Mark Patton."

"He's a witness, not a suspect. I wanted Patton's description of the bears he saw in The Toy Box, as well as the ones he bought."

"Why?"

"To see if they match any of Marcia's stock."

"Do they?"

"Not so far as I can tell."

He thought about that for a moment. "If you seriously believe that someone killed Thorne in order to steal the bears, then I'd think Mark Patton would be a prime suspect. He is buying for resale, after all."

"But he wouldn't still be here if he had the Tiny Teddies. Besides, I really hadn't considered the possibility that someone stealing bears might have been surprised by Thorne and shot him. Maybe I should have, but I've been focused on the smuggling angle."

And he had to go and give her ideas! Dan wanted to kick himself.

"*Maybe*," he said, "you should be more wary of talking to strangers all by yourself."

"He was coming to the Emporium to talk to me. Patton. I saw him through the display window just before Gordon arrived. He must have caught a glimpse of all the uniforms. He drove off without stopping."

"And you decided this made him safe to talk to alone in his hotel room?"

Abruptly, Liss sat down in one of the conference room chairs.

"You okay?"

"Fine," she muttered.

Dan took the chair opposite and reached across the

table to slide his knuckles under her chin and lift. Reluctantly, she met his eyes.

"I only get pissed at you because I care, Liss."

"I know that."

"You're impulsive."

A faint smile answered that observation. "No. Lovey FitzPatrick is impulsive. I suffer from a lack of patience."

"Whatever. The point is that I don't want you to get hurt."

"I've been careful. I told the desk clerk I was going to Patton's room. Didn't take her long to pass the word along, did it?"

He released her. "No, it didn't."

Her impatience, combined with curiosity, was a more potent force than she realized. Looking for answers on her own had put Liss in harm's way in the past. Dan didn't want her to wind up there again.

"How about you tell me who you're going to talk to next," he suggested, "and I go with you?"

A shrug said it all. "I don't have anyone else on my list except Eric Moss."

"Why Moss?"

"I'm pretty sure he supplied both Thorne and Marcia with Tiny Teddies."

"Let me get this straight. You suspect Moss of killing Thorne just because he found some mysterious source for more Tiny Teddies?"

"That and the fact that he seems to have vanished off the face of the earth. Oh, I know he goes off on buying trips, but I don't ever recall hearing that he stayed away this long."

She was right about that. Moss wasn't a close friend, but Dan had known him for years and Moosetookalook was a small town. Moss had been heard to say, more than once, that he liked sleeping in his own bed. He rarely spent more than a night or two on the road. Now that Dan thought about it, he realized that Moss ordinarily went off picking only in good weather. He mostly stayed home during the cold months.

Dan checked his watch. He could get someone to cover for him here at the hotel for an hour or two.

"What do you say we take a run out to his place? See if he's home?"

Liss caught his hand and turned his wrist so she could see the time. A horrified expression on her face, she leapt up. "I can't! I've got to get ready for this evening's ceremony!"

Rising more slowly, Dan grimaced. "Eleven pipers, right?"

But she was already out the door.

"And I'm betting they're playing *bag*pipes," he muttered. He wondered if the ear protectors he wore when he used his noisiest saw would be able to drown out the sound.

He did not take the time to go home and get them, but that evening, when he heard the first blat of a bagpipe from the ballroom, he wished he had. The performers were tuning their instruments but it sounded more like they were torturing cats.

Several of the musicians—Dan used the term loosely— were people he knew. He was only slightly surprised that Gordon Tandy was one of them. Dan had known for some time that an interest in all things Scottish was one of the things Liss and Tandy had in common.

Over the course of the next few minutes, every adoring sigh and approving comment Dan heard from women in the audience sent his mood spiraling downward. What was it about females and men in kilts? He just didn't get it.

Rather than be forced to endure the sight of Liss fawning over Gordon Tandy, Dan headed for his father's office. There was always paperwork to catch up on and maybe, just maybe, he'd be out of range of the bagpipe serenade.

Annoyed at himself, Dan sat and stared at the screen saver. He made no move to bring up data files. That old devil, jealousy, had raised its ugly head again. He'd really thought he had it under control. He certainly knew by now that it did no good to glower at Gordon Tandy. Diss him and he'd just drive Liss further away . . . straight into the other man's arms.

She *liked* the guy.

*Even if Liss married me,* Dan thought, *she'd probably still want to be Tandy's friend.*

Whoa! Where had that come from? He and Liss had agreed months ago that they weren't going to rush things. She wasn't interested in getting hitched and settling down.

Neither was he. Was he?

Maybe he was. Every time he watched her talk and laugh with Gordon Tandy his chest got tight and his hands automatically curled into fists. He was tired of sharing, but he had no idea how to remedy the situation.

Beating up on Gordon Tandy wasn't an option, even supposing he'd come out the winner. Too bad duels were out of fashion. As Dan attempted to settle down and work on the hotel accounts, a curiously appealing fantasy played out in his head, a particularly bloody scenario in which he was the swashbuckling hero who rescued Liss from a dastardly villain who just happened to look a lot like Gordon Tandy.

Dan always had liked old Errol Flynn movies.

The ceremony would start a little late.

Liss had been about to introduce her eleven pipers when one of them announced that he needed to change a reed. Left to twiddle her thumbs while he did so, Liss sidled up to Gordon.

"Still mad at me?"

"I should be."

She smiled at him. "You look wonderful in that kilt."

"I smell like moth balls. Stop trying to butter me up."

"Pipes sound a little rough."

"You know what they say: old pipers never die; their bags just dry up."

Liss obligingly groaned at the corny T-shirt slogan. "You should give some thought to playing regularly again," she said as she watched him adjust the drones. "All work and no play and all that."

"I guess it's more likely than going back to either of my other old hobbies, though I have to admit I sometimes miss owning a snowmobile."

Suddenly he stiffened and looked down at his sporran. The leather pouch, suspended around his hips on a chain so that it hung at the front of his kilt, was vibrating.

Liss bit her lip to hold back a laugh.

"If you say one word about me being happy to see you. . . ." Gordon opened the flap and extracted his cell phone. Turning away, he answered the call, listened for a few moments, then said "okay" and broke the connection. "Ms. FitzPatrick has been released on her own recognizance."

"So that means you believed her when she said she didn't kill Gavin Thorne."

"Different guns were used for each crime."

"Nice of you to share that tidbit."

He didn't reply.

"Was Thorne shot with his own gun?"

That got Gordon's attention. "How did you know he had one?"

"Sherri told me. And you needn't look so grim. She passed along that information before the murder. She saw the gun after Lovey shot the Tiny Teddy. She was worried about Thorne having it in the store. A loaded gun in a toy store didn't strike her as a real good idea. What if a child had gotten hold of it?"

Grudgingly, Gordon agreed that Sherri had been right to be concerned.

"So, do you *have* a suspect?"

No answer.

"Will you at least consider Eric Moss? If you asked for a search warrant for his house—"

"I am not interested in searching Moss's house at this time. I'm only going to say this once more, Liss: stay out of police business." The brusque command put an end to the discussion. With one parting glare, Gordon stalked off toward the stage.

"He looks good in a kilt," Marcia observed, coming up to stand beside Liss and admire Gordon's backside.

"Yes, he does." Liss sighed.

"What's the delay?"

"I'm still waiting for the signal that everyone's ready."

"I heard you had some excitement at your place this afternoon," Marcia said.

"It was a tempest in a teapot as they say. Lovey Fitz-Patrick was the one who shot the bear through the window of the Toy Box but she didn't kill Gavin Thorne. In fact, she's already out of jail. I wouldn't be surprised to see her show up at the ceremony this evening."

"Lovey FitzPatrick," Marcia marveled. "Who'd have thought?"

"No one, apparently."

"So who do the police think the killer is?"

"Beats me. I suggested—again—that they look more carefully at Eric Moss. The fact that he hasn't been seen for days should be enough to get a warrant to search his house."

Marcia looked thoughtful. "I suppose so."

"Have you ever been inside his place?"

Marcia shook her head. "He's not the type to entertain." Her gaze shifted to the stage at the other side of the ballroom. "Looks like the pipers are ready to begin."

Excusing herself, Liss mounted the steps to the low platform. Once she'd introduced each of the eleven men and women who were to be the evening's entertainment, they launched into "Scotland the Brave."

Liss looked around for Dan, but he was nowhere in sight. She was pleased to see that they had a good crowd, however, and most of them looked as if they were enjoying the bagpipe music.

The sound reverberated through the large room, echoing off the ceiling and penetrating every corner. Conversation was impossible but no one seemed to mind.

The second tune was a strathspey. Liss's feet itched to dance. That was only to be expected, since she'd spent so many years of her life performing to just such pieces. The wave of regret caught her by surprise.

Turning away from the stage, she made her way toward the exit. A reel was scheduled next. Suddenly she didn't think she could bear to listen to it.

Liss left word at the front desk for Dan and for Gordon, saying she'd gone home early with a headache. What was really sending her off into the night alone was an overwhelming need to escape the flood of memories. She'd loved being onstage, loved performing.

In the privacy of her car, she rested her head against the steering wheel. She'd thought she was done with these sudden bouts of intense longing for the career she'd once had as a dancer. Apparently not. At least they came less frequently now. Shaking off depressing thoughts, determined not to wallow in self-pity, she started the engine.

It had been a long and eventful day. Curling up with a good book for the rest of the evening sounded like a fine plan. Liss had a towering TBR pile—books she had yet to read—stacked by the chair in her little library. Her biggest problem would be making a choice between mystery, romance, paranormal, and nonfiction.

She slowed down at the fork in the road at the foot of the hill below the hotel. A left turn would take her to the town square and home. As she looked both ways for traffic, Liss remembered what lay in the other direction.

Driven by an irresistible impulse, she turned right.

# Chapter Thirteen

Sherri Willett sat tailor-fashion in the middle of her bed with the notes she'd made spread out around her. Her son was asleep. Her mother was fully occupied with one of the dumber reality shows. Sherri figured she should be safe from interruptions until it was time to go in to work at midnight.

She picked up the first page. Something here had to be significant. She was certain of it.

Thorne's glasses had been broken. Had there been a fight before he was shot? She shook her head. There had been no indication of that in the autopsy report. The glasses had probably been damaged when he fell, *after* the bullet struck him.

Time of death was difficult to pinpoint, but it had probably occurred sometime between eight and midnight. That was really no help at all.

Methodically, and for at least the tenth time, Sherri went over every detail she could remember from the crime scene, adding in the information gathered by other officers. The absence of Tiny Teddies was undoubtedly significant, no matter what Gordon Tandy thought. Sherri had her doubts about Liss's theory, but she had to admit she didn't have a better one. She was no closer to finding out who killed

Thorne or what had happened to his little bears than she had been on the day the murder was discovered.

The last thing Sherri had written down in her report was that there were no tracks in the snow on the outside steps. The killer probably hadn't entered Thorne's apartment. He, or she, had most likely come in the front door and gone out the same way. Well after dark, no one would have noticed either the arrival or the departure.

On a fresh sheet of paper, Sherri sketched a rough floor plan of The Toy Box. She knew there was a rear exit because she'd checked it when she'd been called in to the bear shooting. She had not gotten near that door after Thorne's murder. When Jeff had hollered at her to come out, she'd opted to check the upstairs before leaving the scene. She'd relinquished the task of searching the rest of the shop to someone else.

Had that someone thought to check for footprints on the other side of the back door? She'd seen no report of it if they had. Then again, she didn't suppose she'd seen every bit of paperwork connected to the case. She'd have to ask Gordon about it the next time she saw him.

"Damn," she muttered. If the case files didn't include that information from another officer's report, then she was out of luck.

Or was she? It hadn't snowed again since the storm. The days had been clear and cold with little melting. Might there still be something left to find? First thing in the morning, she promised herself, she'd take a look.

Two miles west of Moosetookalook village, Liss slowed down as she came to Eric Moss's house, a cape with dormers. There was no car in the dooryard, not his beat-up old pickup or any other vehicle. No lights showed inside the building. Unless he was one of those people who went to bed with the chickens, he was not at home.

Liss turned her car around in Moss's driveway and headed back toward town but temptation got the better of her before she'd gone a hundred yards. Pulling off onto the dirt side road that was one of Moss's property lines, she drove a short distance over the rutted surface and stopped on the shoulder. She cut the engine and killed her headlights.

It was a clear night and the moon was almost full. From across a field she could easily make out the south side of Moss's house. From this vantage point, it appeared deserted, just as it had from the road in front.

If Gordon Tandy didn't consider Eric Moss a suspect, Liss told herself, then he could scarcely object if she checked out the house for herself. Besides, Gordon would be busy at the hotel for at least another hour. He'd never know she'd been here.

Before she could change her mind, Liss grabbed the big flashlight she kept in the car for emergencies, opened the car door, and got out. She didn't turn the flashlight on. The moon was bright enough to guide her, at least on the first part of the journey.

Glad she was wearing knee-high boots, Liss clambered over a low stone wall and crunched her way across the field to the back of the house. Her mid–calf-length tartan skirt wasn't the most practical garb for walking in deep snow. Jeans would have been much better, but Liss wasn't about to go home and change her clothes. She'd just take a quick look around, she promised herself, then scram.

The driveway had been plowed—Moss probably bartered with someone to do that for him—but the front sidewalk had not been shoveled and the area around the small back stoop looked equally untouched. That it wasn't a foot deep in snow was due solely to the way the wind had sculpted the landscape during the storm.

Liss hesitated, her hand on the knob. It looked as if no

one had been here since the night before Thorne's murder was discovered. Had Moss killed him and taken off without even bothering to come home first?

No—that didn't make sense. Marcia had seen him after that. She'd bought her Tiny Teddies from him the morning *after* Margaret found Thorne's body.

A semi rumbled past on the two-lane road out front, rattling the glass in the windows. Since the shades had been left up at the back and sides of the house, the truck's headlights sent eerie shadows bouncing into the interior of Moss's house.

*Stop procrastinating,* Liss told herself. *Either try the door or go back to your car.*

She turned the knob and wasn't surprised when nothing happened. No one was very trusting anymore, not even the old-timers. More out of habit than in expectation of finding anything, she ran her gloved fingers over the top of the lintel. The key she dislodged landed at her feet with an audible smack.

A sign? Maybe even an invitation?'

Liss fished it out of the cold snow and let herself into the house.

The back door led directly into Moss's kitchen. An ancient refrigerator hummed, but there was no other sound. She sniffed cautiously and was relieved to smell nothing worse than a faint mustiness. She'd harbored a secret fear of discovering another dead body.

Liss risked using her flashlight. There were no neighbors close enough to be alarmed by its bobbing light. On closer examination, the room proved to be filled with old-fashioned appliances. Other than a light layer of dust, it was scrupulously clean.

Passing through a small dining room. Liss entered the adjoining living room. All was quiet there, too. Magazines lay scattered on a table beside a worn recliner, next to the remote for the television. That appliance was probably the newest thing in the house and still needed the digital converter box that sat on the shelf beneath it.

Since the drapes had been drawn across the front windows, Liss continued to use the flashlight freely. Another semi passed while she was checking the magazines. Liss had met two others during the short drive from the village. She had no idea what they were hauling, but obviously this was a regular route for truck traffic.

Liss replaced the periodicals. She hadn't really been expecting to find *Guns and Ammo* or *Soldier of Fortune.* Old copies of *Down East, Yankee,* and *Newsweek* seemed innocuous enough, even if they did have someone else's address label on them. At a guess, one of Moss's neighbors passed them along once he was done reading them.

In the basement, the furnace kicked in with a low rumble. Liss glanced at the thermostat. Moss had it set at fifty-five degrees. Did he always leave it that low when he was out, or had he planned to be away and left the heat on only so that the pipes wouldn't freeze?

She contemplated the ceiling. If she was going to search the place, she should be thorough. Invading Moss's privacy this way troubled her conscience and left her feeling a little queasy, as well, but she'd come this far. If he'd killed Gavin Thorne, or even if he was only a smuggler, Eric Moss had forfeited his right to fair treatment.

Liss went up the stairs.

The second floor consisted of two small bedrooms and a bath. In common with the downstairs, everything was clean but a trifle shabby, as if money had been tight for some time.

It didn't take Liss long to search Moss's bureau and closet. He was almost painfully neat and didn't seem to have many clothes. It occurred to Liss that he could have packed some and taken them with him but a check of the bathroom revealed a toothbrush and other personal items still in place, including several tubes of Ben Gay. She found a battered suitcase and a duffel bag stored in the hall closet, further indications that he probably hadn't left for good.

Liss moved on to the back bedroom, which contained a desk and a file cabinet but no computer. Moss's office. She felt a little surge of anticipation. She supposed it would be too much to hope for that she'd locate a ledger itemizing sales to Thorne and Marcia, but there might be something useful.

Her search of his desk drawers yielded nothing of interest. She was about to open the file cabinet when she noticed the Maine atlas sitting on top of it. It was one that contained detailed road maps of the entire state. A bright yellow sticky note protruded from one side.

Curious, Liss opened the oversize volume and studied the two-page spread Moss had bookmarked. It encompassed the northern half of Carrabassett County along with a bit of Franklin and Oxford Counties on either side. It also showed part of Canada, Maine's neighbor on the north.

Someone had circled one small section of the border in red with a felt-tip pen.

Liss carried the atlas back to Moss's desk and spread it out on the flat surface. She wasn't familiar with the area he'd circled, but she could see that it wasn't all that far from Moosetookalook. She reached for the desk lamp, needing more light. Her hand froze in midair at the sound of a door creaking open.

Heart pounding, Liss switched off her flashlight with fingers that were none too steady. There was someone downstairs.

An eerie silence lengthened as Liss sat in the darkness of a room lit only by the moon, waiting for her eyes to ad-

just, ears stretched for any further indication that she was
no longer alone in the house.

She tried to tell herself that it was possible she hadn't
completely closed the door she'd unlocked earlier, but
there had been no wind blowing when she entered the
house. And then, in the stillness, she heard a distinctive
click—the sound of a latch catching as someone carefully
closed the door.

Liss swallowed hard. She was close to panic, her heart
racing, her breath hitching, her palms sweating. Every instinct she possessed screamed at her to get out of there, but
she had nowhere to run without being seen.

Hide, then. She was tempted to slide out of the chair
and squeeze herself into the kneehole of the desk, curling
into a ball to avoid discovery.

*TSTL!*

Maybe that would work for some idiot heroine of a
gothic novel, but this was real life. She had to think. There
had to be a way out of this.

Who was downstairs?

No lights came on. Not Eric Moss, then. And not the
police, either. An intruder. Like herself.

Listening intently, Liss heard footsteps cross the hardwood floor below. Whoever it was would be coming upstairs soon. She had to find a place to hide.

Ducking into a closet was out. So was crawling under
the bed.

In desperation, as the footfalls came closer and the person who had entered Eric Moss's house approached the
foot of the stairs, Liss scrambled out of the desk chair and
high-tailed it into the tiny upstairs bathroom. Hopping
into the tub, she pulled the thick shower curtain closed behind her. The back scrubber she almost stepped on made a
poor defensive weapon, but she grabbed it anyway. Clutching it tightly in one hand and holding her flashlight ready

in the other, she waited in an agony of suspense to see if she would be discovered.

The bath was not the first place that the intruder searched on the second floor. Liss heard movement in the other rooms. The screech of a metal drawer opening fixed his location at the old file cabinet. Was that the rustle of papers? If he found what he was looking for, would he leave without ever coming near her hiding place?

He?

Not necessarily, Liss realized. She had no particular reason to think the searcher was a man. Would she stand a better chance if she came face to face with another woman? Maybe not. Weren't females supposed to be deadlier than males?

Footsteps left the spare room and came closer to Liss's hiding place. The bathroom door opened and someone stepped inside. Liss didn't dare breathe.

A flashlight beam played over the opaque shower curtain and a sudden image of Janet Leigh's death scene in *Psycho* flashed into Liss's mind. That was all she needed! She hastily replaced it with the Mel Brooks send-up in *High Anxiety*. That helped calm her, but only a little.

The movement on the other side of the shower curtain abruptly stopped. Had she been spotted? Liss tightened her grip on her pitiful arsenal. She held the flashlight backwards so that the handle could be used as a club, but what use would that be against a knife or a gun? She fully expected the next sound she heard to be the rattle of rings along the rod overhead as the intruder jerked the curtain aside and revealed her hiding place.

Instead a scraping sound reached her ears—the lid on the toilet tank. A lightbulb went on in Liss's head. She'd seen that trick in old movies: hide something inside, protected by a watertight pouch. Had Eric Moss resorted to such tactics? If he had, she'd never know. The lid settled back into place with a dull clunk. The footsteps moved rapidly away.

Liss stayed where she was for what seemed like an eternity but in fact was less than ten minutes. When she could stand the waiting no longer, she gathered her courage and stepped out of the tub. She peered cautiously into the hall. It was empty, and silent until another truck passed by outside.

Moving rapidly but with as much stealth as she could manage, Liss darted into Moss's bedroom and looked out the window. No car was parked in the driveway or on the road in front of the house. She ducked into the other upstairs room and peered through the curtains at the backyard. Nothing. The field she'd crossed was empty, too, although from this height she could make out the tracks she'd left earlier.

Liss listened hard. The only sound she heard was the distant hum of an engine. It grew even fainter as she stood there and finally faded away altogether.

Satisfied that the danger had passed, Liss risked turning on her flashlight—she'd left the back scrubber behind in the tub. A quick survey of the room showed her that the top drawer of the file cabinet was not quite closed.

She opened it, confirming the sound of the screech she'd heard while in hiding. A pity she hadn't gotten around to checking the contents before she was interrupted. There was no way to tell now if anything had been taken.

Swinging the flashlight toward the desk, Liss caught her breath. She'd left the atlas there, open to the page Moss had marked. Now it was gone.

She shone her light on the floor, into the kneehole, even onto the single bookcase in the room. There was no sign of the oversize map book. The only possible explanation for its disappearance, illogical as it seemed, was that the intruder had taken it.

\* \* \*

Sherri looked up in surprise when Liss burst into the police station. A glance at her watch confirmed the early hour. At this time of morning, her friend was usually still in bed. The sun hadn't even come up yet.

Waving Liss into a chair, Sherri headed for the coffeepot. Liss looked as if she needed a shot of caffeine and Sherri was ready for a refill herself.

By the time she brought the two mugs back to the desk, Liss had covered Sherri's papers with a two-page spread of DeLorme's *Maine Atlas and Gazetteer*. All the cops Sherri knew, and most of the civilians, kept a copy of that same map book in every vehicle they drove. It was too easy to get lost on winding back roads without one.

"What's up?" she asked, handing over the coffee.

The story that spilled out left Sherri alternately shaking her head in disbelief and gaping at her friend in astonishment. "Are you out of your tiny little mind?" she exclaimed when Liss finally wound down.

"I didn't think there would be any danger. Moss wasn't home." Clutching the mug in both hands, she took a long swallow of Sherri's coffee. She grimaced at the bitter taste and reached for another packet of sweetener.

"You didn't think. Period. What happened to your common sense?"

"Hey! I was just trying to help!" After another tentative sip, she added still more sugar.

"You broke the law. I ought to arrest you for burglary!"

"I didn't take anything!"

"You'd have walked off with the map book if someone hadn't beaten you to it."

"Maybe. Are you going to lock me up?" Liss gave the door to the cell a wary look.

"Of course not!"

"Then stop looking so . . . so . . . *official!*"

Sherri felt like tearing at her hair. "I give up. You're impossible!" No wonder both Gordon and Dan worried about her.

"I might have discovered something useful." Liss spoke in a calm, matter-of-fact voice.

When she was right, she was right. "Tell me again about Moss's atlas."

"Look here."

On her feet, bending over the desk, Liss indicated a section of the border with Canada in what was labeled "unorganized territory." That meant it wasn't part of any municipality. It was definitely out of Sherri's jurisdiction . . . but not Gordon's. Or Pete's, for that matter.

"That's the area that was circled?" Sherri asked "Pretty remote," she remarked when Liss confirmed it. "There aren't even any roads going into it."

"That's the point. I've been thinking. Dan told me that he saw a snowmobile out before dawn on the morning Aunt Margaret found Gavin Thorne's body."

Sherri could guess where Liss was going with this. "Don't tell me. You think some smuggler came down from Canada on a snowmobile and killed Thorne, then escaped the same way?"

"No. Yes. Well . . . maybe. The thing is, I think it was a snowmobile engine I heard at Moss's house last night."

"Some people do ride at night. That's why the snowmobiles come equipped with headlights."

"Yes, but—"

Sherri held up a hand to stop her. "We know who it was that Dan saw. The snowplow driver saw him, too." She filled Liss in on young Frank Preston's thwarted love life.

Liss plopped back down into the visitor's chair, discouragement plain in her slumped posture. "Damn. I really thought I was on to something."

"Moss had this area marked for some reason," Sherri

said slowly, running one finger along the line that divided Maine from Quebec. There were hundreds of miles of open border with Canada, at least thirty miles of them in Carrabassett County alone. The spot marked on the map would make an ideal crossing.

"We know he had a source for Tiny Teddies," Liss said. "Someone *could* have brought them into this country by snowmobile."

Sherri tried to visualize what Liss was suggesting. The bears were small. A lot of them would fit into a pack, even more onto the size sled a snowmobile could pull. There was only one thing wrong with her friend's reasoning.

"Until the night of the murder, there was no snow. No snow means no snowmobiles."

Liss leaned forward, eyes glittering with triumph as she came up with an answer to Sherri's objection. "Maybe the smugglers used an ATV. An all-terrain vehicle can go any-where a snowmobile can, *without* the need for a foot of ground cover."

Abruptly, Sherri stood. The sun had risen while they'd been talking. "It's light enough now for me to check some-thing out. You coming?"

Liss was right behind her as Sherri left the municipal building, crossed the town square, and circled The Toy Box to reach the back door.

"What are we looking for?"

"Tracks. Watch where you step." Sherri kept her eyes glued to the ground.

She didn't really expect to find anything. The idea that someone might have parked a snowmobile behind Thorne's shop and gotten away on it after the murder was pretty far-fetched. There were no snowmobile trails going through downtown Moosetookalook. Then again, some-one who'd commit murder would hardly worry about sticking to marked trails or following proper snowmobiling etiquette.

She kept an eye peeled for tread marks as well as for footprints.

"Would there be anything left after so many days?" Liss asked. "And don't forget that Felicity Thorne and her workers have been in and out this way dozens of times since the murder."

"I had to see for myself." Lack of sleep, Sherri decided, was catching up to her. Of course there was nothing left to find. There hadn't been even a few hours after the murder. It had been snowing hard all that night and into the morning. Blowing, too. Any tracks would have been filled in well before the state police arrived on the scene.

"Can we go look at Eric Moss's place?" Liss asked. "There hasn't been any new snow since last night. If there are tracks, they should still be visible."

Sherri considered the idea. What would it prove even if Liss were right? On the other hand, there *was* something peculiar going on with Eric Moss. Sherri wasn't convinced that it was tied to Thorne's murder, but it wasn't as if she had a lot of other leads to pursue.

"I guess we could take a little ride."

Ten minutes later, they arrived at Moss's place. It looked as deserted as Liss had described it, but when Sherri circled the building she could clearly make out Liss's footprints coming in from the dirt road. On the opposite side of the house, approaching from the tree line, she spotted a second set.

"Did you walk over this way?"

"No." Liss's eyes gleamed with excitement as Sherri stepped onto the front porch and found another key hidden above that door.

"Looks like your intruder got in the same way you did,

only using the other entrance. He or she never knew you were here." Lucky for Liss!

Sherri backtracked, following the footprints from the front door through a stand of trees and into a clearing. There the signs were unmistakable. Liss had been right—the getaway vehicle had been a snowmobile.

"Now we're making progress," Liss all but danced with glee.

"Only a little," Sherri warned. "Don't get cocky."

"Why would an innocent snowmobiler search Moss's house?"

"Why would a smuggler, let alone a killer?" Back in the car with the heat going full blast, Sherri turned on the seat to face her friend. "You shouldn't read too much into this, Liss. You're jumping to conclusions based on very little evidence."

"So we'll get evidence. Look, let's say I'm right. Thorne was killed because he had smuggled Tiny Teddies in his shop. He got them from someone, probably Eric Moss. Can you find out if Moss owns a snowmobile or an ATV?"

"Liss—"

"What? How hard could it be? Both types of vehicle have to be registered, right?"

"Yes, but I can't just go searching willy-nilly through state databases, not without being called to task for it." Sherri drove toward town as they debated the issue.

"Can Gordon?"

"It would be easier for him to get access to that kind of information than for me to do it, yes."

"So tell Gordon."

"Tell him *what*? That you broke into Moss's house?"

"You could show him the map. Tell him you have a snitch."

"You've been watching too many crime dramas on television."

"Then tell him you're following a hunch. Just get him to check on Moss."

Sherri spent the rest of the trip back to Moosetookalook in thoughtful silence. Liss was so certain she was right. Sherri supposed it couldn't hurt to check the records.

"Let me see what I can find out," she said when she pulled up in front of the Emporium. "I may be able to locate snowmobile and ATV registrations online. As for finding out who owns that parcel of land, this is Sunday. There won't be anyone around to answer my questions until tomorrow."

"What can I do to help?" Liss asked.

"That's easy," Sherri told her with a grin. "Stay out of trouble."

# Chapter Fourteen

Patience had never been Liss MacCrimmon's strong suit. She dealt with a handful of customers during what was left of Sunday morning and made final preparations for the pageant that afternoon, but she was itching to pursue the lead she'd uncovered. When Aunt Margaret volunteered to spell her at noontime, she leapt at the opportunity.

Instead of going home for lunch, Liss crossed Ash Street and continued on down Pine until she came to the corner of Lowe—Jason Graye's house.

Official channels for finding out who owned the land Moss had marked might not be available until Monday, but Jason Graye was a real estate agent. Even though Liss hated to ask him for a favor, she felt a sense of urgency about the matter. If Eric Moss wasn't the villain after all, then the same person who'd killed Gavin Thorne might be trying to find Moss. That could explain the search of his house. In any case, Liss saw no reason to wait another day when she could get an answer now.

"What do you want?" Graye demanded when he opened his door. He had a brusque manner in the best of times and his opinion of Liss was on a par with hers of him.

"Gracious, as always." Liss's lips twisted into a wry smile. "Believe me, I wouldn't bother you if I could think of any other way to get the information I need."

"You intrigue me, Ms. MacCrimmon." Graye waved her inside, chuckling when she hesitated. "I don't bite."

"My aunt knows I'm here."

Both his eyebrows shot up at that, but he did not respond in any other way to her comment.

Curious, Liss took a look around her. Graye's living room was stylishly, even luxuriously, furnished but everything had a sterile quality to it. The place lacked that comfortable, lived-in look that made a house or apartment into a home.

Shoving aside an instant of pity for the man, Liss reminded herself that although he probably wasn't dangerous, she shouldn't let down her guard around him. He had been up to *something* with Eric Moss.

Her reluctant host was a man in his late thirties or early forties with a hawklike nose, a slightly jutting chin, and thin lips. He stood an inch or two taller than she and did not appear to be in very good shape, although he was by no means overweight. Liss was not afraid of him physically, and she had grown accustomed to his rudeness and his tendency to push into everyone else's personal space.

Graye was first and foremost a self-styled entrepreneur. He made his money handling real estate and he was good at turning a profit. His dealings might not always be completely ethical, but he was savvy enough to stay on the right side of the law. Most important to Liss's mind was that he was familiar with properties all over the county. It was her hope that his knowledge extended right up to the Canadian border.

"I'm here about a parcel of land," she announced.

Graye's face brightened and his manner lost some of its aloofness. His voice was only mildly condescending when he asked if she was buying or selling.

"Neither."

His lips pursed into a straight, tight line. "Then I don't see why I should do anything to help you."

Without an invitation, Liss selected a chair and sat. The cushion was rock hard beneath her and tilted back at an awkward angle. In the days right after her knee surgery, she'd have had to be hoisted upright again.

Muttering under his breath, Graye took the sofa. He did not offer coffee or tea. Just as well, Liss decided. She'd be leery of accepting. He'd probably spit in the cup.

Liss folded her hands in her lap and fixed her steady gaze on Graye. She had come prepared to use coercion. "Remember the night of the selectmen's meeting? You had a conversation with Eric Moss out in the hall. You weren't as private as you thought. Would you like to know what I overheard?"

"You expect me to believe you were eavesdropping and I didn't see you?" He scoffed at the notion, but his eyes were wary.

"I admit I didn't listen in intentionally, but I was sitting on the stairs that night after getting a drink of water from the fountain. I heard everything, and I saw you pass an envelope to Moss. A payoff, I assume."

Graye's laugh sounded forced and he looked uneasy. Liss cudgeled her brain. She needed to take advantage, now that she'd shaken Graye's composure. He thought she knew more than she did. Guess right and he'd cooperate. Guess wrong and she'd be out on her ear.

She didn't believe Graye was involved in the smuggling. He'd never have let Moss offer the Tiny Teddies so cheap. Besides, their whispered conversation had taken place only hours after she'd seen that newspaper item.

So, Graye had been paying Moss off for something else, but what? There was probably a connection to real estate. A tip of some sort? Moss did get around in his search for bargains.

Liss considered what she'd heard about Graye's business practices. He'd been known to claim houses had seri-

ous defects—carpenter ants, dry rot, and the like—in order
to get the owners to sell property to him for less than they
might have gotten through an honest broker. He also kept
an ear to the ground for building projects. He'd tried to
outbid Dan's father for the hotel, thinking to tear it down
and erect vacation condos on the site. Once he'd even tried
to buy all the buildings on one side of the town square.
Some scheme involving senior housing, if she remembered
right.

"You're up to your old tricks," she said aloud, hoping
he'd fall for her bluff. "However, I see no reason to mention what I overheard to anyone, as long as you're willing
to share a little information with me."

"You want in on my deal?" He couldn't quite keep the
astonishment out of his voice.

"No! I want to know who owns a certain parcel of land."

"That's all?" From his incredulous look, Liss wondered
if she'd underestimated the scope of his scheme with Eric
Moss.

"That and the answer to one other question."

"Where is this parcel?"

Graye produced detailed topographical maps of Carrabassett County. Liss had no difficulty finding the area Moss
had circled. "Here." She tapped the spot on the map. "Do
you know who owns this property?"

Graye's beak of a nose twitched once as he stared at the
map, making Liss wonder if she'd just put her foot in it.
Was this the very property that had prompted Graye to
give Moss that payoff?

"As far as I know," Graye said carefully, "this land currently belongs to an out-of-stater. It contains a rustic cabin
but has no running water or electricity."

"Currently?" Liss repeated. "Who did it belong to before that?"

Graye allowed himself a small, self-satisfied smile. "I

owned it, briefly, before I sold it for a tidy profit. You see, I purchased that parcel for a song from a couple obliged to unload it as part of their divorce settlement."

"What couple?" Liss asked, although she thought she already knew.

"Gavin and Felicity Thorne."

Participants in the Twelve Days of Christmas Pageant crowded into Moosetookalook's town square. The gala parade to The Spruces was about to begin.

It had taken some doing to find enough volunteers to carry trees, golden rings, and assorted birds, but Liss had managed it. Even Jason Graye pitched in, gingerly pushing the partridge in the pear tree on a dolly. The fact that this meant he led the procession undoubtedly had something to do with his compliance. So long as he helped, Liss didn't care what motivated him.

The weather cooperated. It was another sunny day, warm enough that the snow had begun to melt rather rapidly. Too much of that would not be good for skiers and snowmobilers, but at the moment Liss was more concerned with the comfort of the spectators. Temperatures above freezing suited them very well.

A good-sized crowd also waited at the hotel. Gratified, Liss shooed her charges into the ballroom and a short time later took the stage to start the pageant. She'd assigned herself the job of master of ceremonies. For the next hour and a half she introduced participants and watched their performances.

The pipers, strengthened by the addition of the man Gordon had replaced the previous night, played with tremendous enthusiasm. A few in the audience clapped hands over their ears, but they were smiling as they did so. All except Stu Burroughs, who stood next to Liss wearing a pained expression on his face.

"You have no appreciation of the finer things in life," Liss teased him.

"What?"

She shook her head. There was no sense trying to be heard until the music stopped. She studied the crowd instead, picking out familiar faces.

Liss's neighbor, bookstore owner Angie Hogencamp and her daughter Beth stood off to one side. Beth had already performed and Angie had warned Liss that they weren't going to stick around for the auction. She claimed she couldn't face the constant inaccurate references to "teddy bears."

Sherri, in civvies, had brought her mother and son. With them was Pete Campbell, wearing his dark brown deputy sheriff's uniform. Liss wondered if Jeff Thibodeau had asked for help from the county, or if Pete was just taking a break from his regular patrol. Moosetookalook chief of police or no, Jeff was committed to spending the rest of the afternoon dressed as Santa.

As Liss watched, Sherri scowled at her fiancé. Pete's expression became equally thunderous. Obviously they were still at odds about something.

Nearby, Marcia waited, looking anxious. The auction was scheduled to take place between the performance of the eleven pipers and the concert by the twelve drummers—members of a local drum and bugle corps. Marcia had a lot riding on this, Liss supposed, but there was no way she would lose money. She hadn't paid all that much for her bears in the first place.

It dawned on Liss that she recognized almost everyone in the ballroom, even the ones she didn't know by name. Those who were not residents of Moosetookalook had been among the customers who'd visited the Emporium in the course of the last few days. Mark Patton was present.

So was Lovey FitzPatrick. She looked none the worse for her brief incarceration in the county jail.

On the far side of the room, Liss caught a glimpse of Aunt Margaret. She was working for the hotel this afternoon, still getting the hang of her new job as events coordinator. She'd been a huge help to Liss in making sure everything about the pageant ran smoothly.

Neither Dan nor Gordon were anywhere to be seen. Liss was pretty sure Dan was elsewhere in the hotel, just avoiding the bagpipe concert. She had no idea where Gordon was, or even if he intended to show up today.

Inevitably, thoughts of Gordon led back to Gavin Thorne's murder. Liss hoped she and Sherri could get together soon and compare notes.

What did it mean that the area circled on Eric Moss's map had once belonged to the Thornes? What did it mean that the intruder had taken that map? The location had to have some significance. An illegal border crossing suggested smuggling, but there Liss's logical thought progression ground to a halt. She couldn't connect the dots to produce a clear picture.

Her second question to Jason Graye hadn't clarified matters in the least. Graye claimed he had no idea where Moss was now, or what he was up to. Liss didn't trust Graye as far as she could throw him, but on this matter she believed him.

She glanced again at Sherri. Her friend had given her a bad moment after Liss confessed to sneaking into Eric Moss's house. Until then, she hadn't been too troubled by what she'd done. In fact, she'd been planning to tell Gordon the whole story. Sherri's reaction had made her change her mind. Admitting to her local state police detective that she'd committed a crime would not be a good idea.

A burst of applause signaled the end of the first part of the afternoon's entertainment. Clapping enthusiastically, Liss returned to center stage. She made a point of thanking each of the performers by name. That done, she turned the microphone over to Stu, who had volunteered to be auctioneer.

He wore a bright red sweater with STU'S SKI SHOP emblazoned across the front in big white letters. "Thank you, Liss," Stu said. "Liss MacCrimmon, everyone!"

She acknowledged the round of applause but quickly left the stage.

"Our Santa, Jeff Thibodeau, will bring out each bear in turn and he'll be passing the ones that sell down to our volunteer bookkeeper. That's Patsy of Patsy's Coffee Shop, folks. Don't forget to stop in for her home-baked pastries and a cup of Joe."

Patsy waved to the crowd. She sat at a small table next to the stage to record the prices and collect the money from the high bidders. Those who wanted to participate had already registered and collected numbered paddles to hold up when they bid. They surged forward as Liss pushed through them heading in the opposite direction.

Escaping the crush of potential bidders and enthusiastic gawkers, Liss reached an open space near the door. Sherri's party was just ahead of her. Angie and Beth were already through the door and Jason Graye was right on Liss's heels.

From behind her, she heard Stu start the bidding at fifty dollars. By the time she stepped out into the hallway, it had reached three hundred.

"Why are you being so stubborn about this?" Sherri hissed at Pete.

"Me? You're the one—" He broke off when he spotted Liss. "Here she is now. Talk to her and then you can go home."

"Be with you in a second, Liss," Sherri snapped, and

stalked away from her, chasing after Pete. He'd already corralled young Adam and taken Ida Willett's arm. They were halfway to the elevator when Sherri yelled, "Hold on just a minute, buster!"

"We'll be in the lobby," Pete shot back, hustling his charges into the cage and jabbing the button. The door closed in Sherri's face.

"Stupid . . . bossy . . . pigheaded!" Every epithet was underscored by the stomp of Sherri's feet as she returned to the spot where Liss waited.

"You okay?"

"Sure. Why wouldn't I be?"

Both hands up, palms out, Liss backed off. "Hey. Don't bite *my* head off." She hid a smile as she experienced a flash of déjà vu. Not very long ago, Dan had said almost the exact same thing to her.

"Sorry. Pete has just gotten so pushy lately. I don't know what to do about him."

"Push back?"

"That only makes things worse." Sherri heaved a deep sigh and waved Liss toward a bow window furnished with a window seat. "I've got some information for you, but I'm not sure it's worth much."

"I found out something, too." She told Sherri what Jason Graye had revealed about the land along the border.

Sherri gave a low whistle. "So it belonged to the Thornes. Interesting."

Puzzled, Liss forgot what else she'd been about to say. "Why interesting?"

Sherri drew her deeper into an alcove. "I couldn't tell you this before because I knew about it from the official investigation, but since the checking I did on my own after you left the office this morning led to the same information, I figure that means Gordon can't object if I tell you what I found."

Liss wasn't certain she followed Sherri's logic, but she nodded anyway.

"I was able to get a look at the state's online records for both snowmobiles and ATVs. I checked on everyone I could think of. Felicity, Marcia, Marcia's ex husband, and Stu all registered snowmobiles this year. Stu also has an ATV."

"What about Moss?"

"Nothing. Forget Moss. *Here's* the interesting bit—Felicity Thorne and Cabot Katz listed the same home address on the forms they filled out."

For a moment, Liss didn't see the connection. Then her eyes widened. "Thorne's ex wife and Marcia's ex husband are a couple? They're living together?"

Sherri made a "keep going" gesture, urging Liss to continue that line of thought to its logical conclusion.

"He's her alibi for the time of Thorne's murder."

"Bingo!"

A round of applause reached them from the ballroom. Liss wondered briefly how much the latest Tiny Teddy had sold for. Then she focused her attention on what Sherri was saying.

"I think you may be on to something with the smuggling idea, only it makes more sense if Thorne himself was running the show." Sherri's brow furrowed in concentration as she supplied the details she'd worked out. "Since he once owned that land, the whole scheme could easily have been his idea from the beginning. Then his ex found out what he was doing, they had words, and boom! No more Thorne."

Liss picked up the thread, unraveling it further. "Thorne probably tried to toss her out. He pulled out his gun to convince her to go, but somehow she got it away from him."

Inside the ballroom, someone let out a whoop of triumph.

"Is she strong enough to have wrestled it out of his grip? I've never met her."

"Oh, yeah." Liss tried to visualize the scene. "Or the gun could have gone off during the struggle. Or maybe *she* went for the gun and he was the one trying to disarm her." She could picture it going down any of those three ways.

"Doesn't matter." Sherri's face glowed with excitement. "She's the prime suspect, just as Gordon seems to have thought all along. Cabot Katz lied to protect her."

"I hate to be a wet blanket, but there are a few problems with that theory. Where does Eric Moss fit into it? Where *is* Moss? And why would Thorne have gotten involved in smuggling in the first place? I'd think it would be pretty hard to start bringing in Tiny Teddies unless he already had contacts on the other side of the border."

Sherri's face fell. "Drat! And there's an even bigger problem than any of those. There's not a shred of proof. Unfortunately, the law requires evidence."

"There's the atlas I found at Moss's house."

"What would that prove, assuming we had it, which we don't?"

Liss tried to think logically, but she had the feeling she was still missing too many pieces of the puzzle. "Moss is the one who sold the Tiny Teddies to Marcia, so maybe Katz *isn't* lying. Maybe Moss and Thorne were in it together and *they* were the ones who quarreled and fought over the gun. Maybe *Moss* shot Thorne."

*Someone* had killed him. It made sense that the fatal shooting had occurred during a quarrel over smuggling Tiny Teddies into the U.S. from Canada. But beyond those two assumptions lay a morass of contradictions and unanswered questions. Liss felt as if she were on a merry-go-round, spinning faster and faster and in imminent danger of being flung off.

"The bears Moss sold Marcia are not the same as the ones Thorne had." Sherri sighed. "In fact, there is no concrete proof that there have ever been *any* smuggled bears in Moosetookalook."

"*You* believe it."

"But Gordon doesn't. I've got nothing to use to persuade him, either. Worse, it occurred to me while I was looking up names online that someone using a snowmobile or an ATV to commit an illegal act probably wouldn't bother to register it in the first place."

Back to Eric Moss, Liss thought. "We'll figure it out. We *have* to."

"Why?"

There were more shouts from the ballroom, but Liss ignored them. "What do you mean?"

"I know why I want to solve this crime. I have a career to advance. But why are you so . . . obsessed with finding answers?"

"Because this is all my fault."

Sherri shook her head in disbelief. "Get over yourself, Liss. It's not that I don't appreciate your help brainstorming or the clues you've come up with, but you have no stake in this. Not really. You aren't a suspect. No close friends of yours are suspects. You didn't know the victim all that well. Heck, you didn't even like him. So why are you pursuing this and, more to the point, taking unnecessary risks?"

Liss opened her mouth and shut it again, unable to come up with a good answer. She supposed she should have asked herself the same question long before this, but it simply hadn't occurred to her to do so, not even when she stood trembling with fear behind the shower curtain in Eric Moss's upstairs bath.

She didn't like the first answer that came to mind. Was she really just TSTL?

The second explanation was no better, involving snoopiness, nosiness, and just plain blatant curiosity about things that were police business and none of hers. She certainly had no desire to become a cop, or a private detective, either.

"Liss? Hey, I didn't mean to send you into a fugue state." Sherri looked relieved when Liss blinked at her. "It wasn't my intention to insult you, either. I just . . ." Sherri groped for the right words. "I just worry about you, okay?"

"I worry about me, too. I don't know *why* I feel compelled to find all the answers, Sherri. I just know that I need to do it. I don't think I can stop myself."

"Then swear to me that you'll be careful? No more sneaking into empty houses. No more questioning of suspects on your own."

Liss made the cross-my-heart sign, but Sherri wasn't looking. Head cocked, she was intent on listening to the hubbub on the other side of the double doors.

Belatedly noticing that the clamor from inside the ballroom was steadily increasing in volume, Liss frowned. "What on earth . . . ?"

She and Sherri exchanged a look of alarm and were on their feet an instant later. For a short person, Sherri had a ground-eating stride when she ran full tilt. Liss was halfway across the mezzanine, following in her wake, when she heard a horrendous crash.

A woman screamed.

Pandemonium broke loose.

# Chapter Fifteen

The ballroom was engulfed in chaos. Stu, hopping up and down on the stage, shouted into the microphone but someone had disconnected it. Liss could not make out a word of what he was saying.

Santa Claus jumped into the crowd, shouting for order. No one paid any attention to him. Most people knew he was their chief of police, but that didn't seem to matter. Mark Patton, the dealer who'd been desperate to get into The Toy Box, shoved past Jeff so roughly that he was bowled right over. He fell behind the stage and did not reappear.

Some of the pipers, all of whom had congregated after their performance in the corner where the cash bar was located, advanced toward the center of the disruption, moving like the military unit pipers so often were. Once at the foot of the stage, however, they didn't seem to know what to do next. Gordon's brother Russ attempted to take command, but he was only marginally more successful than Jeff Thibodeau had been. At least no one knocked him down.

Marcia, her face livid, shoved her way through a clump of milling spectators, including several of the elaborately dressed dancing ladies. She caught up with a rapidly retreating man in jeans and a hooded sweatshirt. Leaping onto his back, she began beating him about the neck and shoulders with her fists while she showered him with epithets.

A few feet away, Lovey Fitzpatrick fended off a wild-eyed attacker by swinging her oversized purse at the other woman's head. Liss sincerely hoped the police had confiscated Lovey's gun.

Mark Patton caught Liss's attention again as he reached the far side of the room. He broke free of the crowd and headed for a service door at a dead run. He clutched something—or rather several small somethings—close to his chest. A yard short of his goal, Liss's Aunt Margaret stepped in front of him, blocking his escape.

At that, Liss waded into the fray, shoving people out of her path with every bit as much ruthless abandon as Patton had displayed. Lacking his brute strength, she only made it halfway to her aunt before a deafening whistle stopped every man, woman, and child in their tracks.

Liss spun around, seeking the source of the loud, totally unexpected sound. Sherri stood on the stage, a police whistle held ready to produce another blast if it became necessary.

Taking advantage of the momentary silence, Sherri bellowed, "I'm Officer Willett. I'm ordering all of you to cease and desist!"

The burgeoning riot abruptly dissolved, leaving behind small clusters of people in varying stages of embarrassment. Most of them had the look of schoolchildren caught misbehaving on the playground. Only Marcia refused to release her hold on the young man she'd captured.

Liss looked again at the service exit, prepared to rush to her aunt's rescue, but Margaret appeared to have Mark Patton under control. They stood talking quietly together. Changing direction, Liss headed for Marcia and the man in the hoodie.

From behind the low stage, a large, rumpled figure in red and white rose like Marley's ghost, one hand holding the side of his head and the other trying in vain to shove his fake beard back into place. Jeff Thibodeau took in the scene with an all-encompassing glance and drew the correct conclusions.

"Carry on," he barked at Sherri, and went in search of first aid.

Liss reached Marcia's side just as Dan and his father came into the ballroom. The other woman was breathing heavily but had a triumphant gleam in her eyes. She'd twisted the man's arm behind his back and showed no inclination to let go.

"I was ripped off," her captive whined.

"That's no excuse!" Marcia tightened her hold, making him wince.

"What did he do?" Dan came straight to them while Joe veered off to consult with Margaret.

"He jumped onto the stage, grabbed the Tiny Teddy he'd been bidding on—he was *not* the winning bidder!—and tried to take off with it." If the look on Marcia's face was any indication of her boiling point, steam should already be coming out of her ears.

"Give the bear back," Liss instructed.

With ill grace, the captive reached beneath his hoodie, fished it out, and handed it over.

"Now you let him go," Dan ordered.

Grudgingly, Marcia relaxed her pincer grip and the freed man slunk away, rubbing his sore arm.

"I'm surprised you managed to catch him in this crush," Liss remarked. "Didn't he have a head start?"

"Dumb ass tripped over the microphone cord. That slowed him down some. Besides, I'm stronger and faster than I look." Marcia inhaled deeply. "Sorry. Nasty display of collecting fever. It was building up all through the auction. You could almost smell it in the air. I'd think it was just testosterone, except that some of the women were as het up as the men. That nutcase wasn't the only hothead in the crowd."

Liss and Dan watched Marcia stalk back toward the stage. For a moment, neither spoke.

"She seems . . . rejuvenated by the skirmish," Dan observed.

"I need volunteers to right fallen chairs," Sherri said into the microphone. Her first order of business had been getting it reconnected.

She'd settled everyone down and convinced most of them to take a seat by the time Pete turned up looking for her. The auction was about to resume.

Dan rejoined Liss, having spent the interim helping Sherri, and the two of them, together with Pete, moved off to one side of the room. In a whisper, Liss provided an abridged summary of events.

"Fisticuffs had broken out in pockets all over the ballroom," she said at the end of her account, "but Sherri put a stop to that nonsense. You'd have been proud of her, Pete."

"She should have been at home," Pete grumbled. "She's supposed to be off duty."

Liss eyed his uniform. "And you aren't. Are you jealous of Sherri?"

Her thoughtless question went over like a lead balloon. Pete mumbled a denial and plunged into a brooding silence.

*In for a penny*, Liss thought: "Sherri's good at her job. Give her a break."

Pete continued to stand there like a stone statue while Stu took the podium to sell more Tiny Teddies. Across the room, Moosetookalook's chief of police, minus long white beard and Santa hat, returned from having the cut on his head patched up. He still wore the rest of the jolly fat man's costume.

Dan drew Liss a little apart from Pete. "You did a good job defusing Marcia. Thanks."

"Nice to be able to accomplish something."

"Do I want to know what that means?"

"Sorry. Frustration talking. Don't mind me."

Dan started to say something, but at that moment his father caught his eye and beckoned to him. "Catch you later, Liss?"

"Sure," Liss agreed, but her attention was already focused on the bidding.

The crowd applauded as Lovey FitzPatrick paid a truly outrageous price for one of the bears. Abruptly Pete came out of his brown study to give the toy collector a hard look. "Isn't that the woman Tandy arrested?"

"Sure is. Lovey FitzPatrick. She shot out the window at The Toy Box. Killed her a b'ar."

Pete ignored her poor attempt at humor. Or maybe he'd just never heard the *Davy Crockett* theme song. "If I was running that murder investigation, I'd be taking a real close look at Ms. FitzPatrick right now."

"It wasn't her gun that killed Gavin Thorne," Liss reminded him. "It was his." Neither Sherri nor Gordon had come right out and said that, but it seemed pretty obvious.

"A whacko like her would use whatever weapon came to hand."

"She is hell on wheels with a shoulder bag," Liss admitted, but she wasn't about to put Lovey FitzPatrick on her list of suspects. There were too many others who seemed far more likely to have killed Gavin Thorne.

Dan caught up with Liss just as she was leaving the hotel. She was nearly the last one out, having stayed till the very end of the auction. "My truck's out back if you need a lift."

"Thanks. I walked up with the parade. I figured I could cage a ride home with Aunt Margaret."

"She left an hour ago."

"Then I'll definitely accept your offer."

He drove to his house, then walked her around the corner to hers, all the while keeping conversation light. He talked about the rocking chair he was attempting to build. She mentioned, again, that she'd run out of space for books but added that, somehow, she couldn't seem to stop herself from buying more.

"Come in for a minute?" she asked.

He hesitated. He could see how tired she was and suspected she'd only asked from force of habit. He didn't care. He accepted, plopped himself down on her sofa with the casualness of an old friend, and turned on the late night news while she plugged in the Christmas tree lights.

She sank down beside him. "I'm too pooped to fix anything. Help yourself if you're hungry or thirsty."

"I'm good."

"I hope there were no cameras at the hotel tonight. Entirely too many people make a habit of sending video clips to the local television stations."

"You want me to turn it off?" He reached for the clicker he'd tossed onto the end table. It had landed on top of one of Liss's lined notepads. Curious, he grabbed that, too.

It contained several lists, all of which baffled him. "Ouist? Muck? Orkney?"

"Islands in Scotland."

"Okay." The next one made even less sense: Sookie, Susanna, Watson, Frevisse, Wimsey, Arly, and Dash.

"Characters in various mystery series." She took the clicker from him as the weather report concluded and shut off the news anchor in midsentence. "That's where the name Lumpkin came from, you know. The Lumpkins are a family in Charlotte MacLeod's Peter Shandy series."

The light dawned. "You're trying to find a name for the kitten. Where is the little guy, anyway?"

"Last I knew, *she'd* discovered Lumpkin sleeping on the bed upstairs and curled up next to him. I wouldn't be surprised if they're still there."

"They getting along better?"

"Only when he's asleep." Liss shifted so she was facing him, her legs curled under her.

"What name did you decide on?"

"I haven't yet. Any suggestions? Sherri voted for Sweetie."

The way the tree lights were blinking, sending flashes of red and green across Liss's face, gave him a few ideas. "Yuletide? Jingle Bell? Noel?"

"Oh, please!"

"No! No, wait, I think I'm onto something here. What was that Scottish name for New Year's Eve?"

"I am *not* calling her Hogmanay." But his teasing had the desired effect. Liss relaxed and started to giggle. "That's even worse than naming her Claus!"

The following afternoon, refreshed by a good night's sleep and a leisurely morning at home—Margaret had offered to work at the Emporium and give her a day off—Liss's thoughts inevitably returned to Gavin Thorne's murder.

It bothered her that she remained fixated on the case. There was probably some deep, psychological explanation . . . one she didn't want to hear. Or else she'd been possessed by the ghost of Miss Marple. Whatever, she craved answers. Well, why not? She hated loose ends in mystery novels. They were even more aggravating in real life.

She knew there weren't always satisfying endings to real cases. Some mysteries were never solved. But surely whoever had killed Gavin Thorne would be caught eventually.

Liss considered her suspect list: Eric Moss, Felicity Thorne, Stu Burroughs.

Stu Burroughs . . . who had registered both a snowmobile and an ATV.

He had quarreled with Gavin Thorne right before Thorne was murdered, but Liss hadn't seriously suspected him. She still didn't, but it occurred to her that a few judicious questions might just rule him out. Once she was certain Stu hadn't murdered anyone, he could be an excellent source of information about *other* people who owned snowmobiles.

Liss had promised Sherri she'd stay out of potentially dangerous situations, but she decided there was no real risk in a visit to Stu's Ski Shop during business hours. "Too bad you aren't a dog," she told Lumpkin. "I'd take you along for protection."

The big cat looked offended. Then the kitten, trailing after him, swatted his tail and they were off, chasing through the house with the abandon of a pair of three-year-old children. Hearing no howls, snarls, or hisses, Liss left them to it.

Stu's Ski Shop, after a brief burst of business immediately following the storm, had returned to its usual gloomy emptiness. Eye-catching displays might have helped, Liss thought, taking a look around, and the place looked as if it hadn't seen a dust rag in years. No wonder business was off!

"Oh, it's you," Stu greeted her. "I don't suppose you're here to buy something."

"I might be."

"You don't ski."

"I'm thinking I should get out more." Spotting a rack labeled SNOWMOBILE SUITS, she headed that way. A row of helmets with full face shields sat on a shelf above it.

"Motorized division, eh? You know you'll have to wait for good snow."

"What's wrong with what's out there?"

"The weather warmed up. This is our second day of snow melt. Another day or two and we'll be back to bare ground."

"It's still deep enough to ride on now, isn't it?"

He shrugged. "Snow melts, you get slush. The temperature drops again at night and the slush turns to ice. Let's just say you wouldn't want to drive very fast on that kind of surface."

"I wouldn't want to go very fast anyway." Sliding one hanger after another along the bar, she gave a small portion of her attention to the gear, noting that most of the suits Stu stocked came in two pieces with a high bib in the front.

"Are you serious about this?" An avaricious gleam came into Stu's eyes when she nodded. "Have you ridden a snowmobile before?"

"I rode on the back of one a few times when I was in high school."

"Not the same thing as being the driver. Come on." Grabbing his coat off the back of a chair, Stu led her out through the back door of the store and along a covered walkway toward his garage. Entering though the side entrance, he clicked on the light and pointed at two large lumps covered with bright blue tarps. When he whipped off the nearest covering, clouds of dust billowed up.

Coughing, waving the swirl of mote-filled air away, Liss realized she had just gotten the proof she'd been looking for that Stu Burroughs wasn't the person who'd broken into Moss's house. Neither his snowmobile nor his ATV had been used in a very long time. Since she was convinced that the intruder and Thorne's killer were one and the same—unless Moss was the murderer—she mentally crossed Stu off her suspect list.

"I've been thinking of selling this machine and getting a newer one," Stu said. "I could give you a real good deal."

"What's wrong with it?"

"Not a thing. It's just an older model, that's all."

"It's what they call a two-up, right? Can one person ride it alone?"

"Of course they can. Marcia still uses the one she and Cabot used to ride together."

"Is it difficult to drive? Do I need a license? A safety course?"

He gave her a look that said she obviously knew nothing about snowmobiles. She could hardly take offense. He was right.

"No to the last two questions," Stu said. "As to how hard it is, hop on."

Game, Liss complied, sliding up to the front of the seat. The last time she'd been on one of these, she'd been perched behind a boyfriend, hanging on to his waist for dear life. She hadn't been able to see much and hadn't really enjoyed the experience. Come to think of it, she hadn't found the boy all that appealing, either. The relationship hadn't lasted long.

"See that red button on top of the handlebars? That's called the 'kill switch.'"

"Nice name."

"When you pull it up, the engine can run. When you push it down, the engine shuts off. Pull it up."

Liss did, but nothing happened. She sent Stu a quizzical look.

"Step by step, Liss. Step by step. Next make sure the cord on the key is attached to the steering column. That's a back up to the kill switch. The engine will only run if it's secured."

"Check."

"Okay. Turn the key."

Again, nothing happened. She craned her neck to glare at him. "This is beginning to get old."

Stu grinned. "One more step, sunshine. On the right side of the sled there's a start cord. It looks like a lawn mower pull cord, only bigger."

Grasping it, she sent him an arch look. "And this time the engine's actually going to start?"

"It should."

It didn't. All Liss got for her effort was a loud pop.

Stu chuckled. At his insistence, she pulled the start cord a few more times, but the engine still refused to turn over.

"She hasn't been used in a while, that's all. Look under the right side of the handlebars. That tab pull is the choke. Turn it on."

To Liss's relief, this finally persuaded the engine to fire. Or rather it coughed a couple of times.

"Good!" Stu looked relieved as he flapped around the snowmobile like a nervous rooster. "Now turn the choke back off. If you leave it on too long you'll flood the engine."

"God forbid!" The snowmobile continued to sputter. Liss expected the engine to die at any second. She'd never been mechanically inclined and could only hope she hadn't inadvertently damaged Stu's machine.

"See that lever on the right side of the handlebar?"

Since he was pointing right at it, she could hardly miss it.

"That's the throttle. Work it with your thumb. Push it in a few times but don't hold it down. That can flood the engine, too. When you're riding, you use the throttle to speed up or slow down."

At last, the sputter settled into a steady purr. Liss felt absurdly pleased with herself as she listened to the rhythmic hum.

"Now shut it down," Stu ordered.

"What? I was just getting started."

Stu gave a snort and stood with his hands fisted on his

hips, one foot tapping the cement, impatient for her to follow his orders. "You can't run it on the garage floor. You have to tow a snowmobile to snow and that snow should be at least four inches deep. Then you ride."

"I knew that." As heat crept into her face, she turned off the sled and started to dismount.

"Stay put. I'll run you through the rest of what you need to know. Okay. We're going to pretend you're properly dressed. That includes a helmet, which you fasten securely under your chin."

"Aye, aye, sir." Given the way he was barking out orders, she couldn't resist saluting.

"None of your sass, young lady. I remember you when you were in pigtails."

"I never," she assured him haughtily, "wore my hair in pigtails."

"Tuck your feet under those metal pockets on the lower front section of the sled. Unless you want to fall off on your first turn."

She followed instructions and then listened attentively as he explained how to use the throttle, the brakes, and the handlebars while riding.

"It's easier to turn if you're going faster than fifteen miles an hour. Lean to the inside of a turn to keep the sled on both skis. Lean far left for a left turn. What usually works best is to slide your backside all the way off the seat, with your shoulders out to the side of the handlebars."

She felt clumsy attempting the maneuver, especially on a sled that wasn't moving, but he beamed at her when she managed it.

"It's just a matter of coordination. You should go out in a field and practice. So, you want to buy her?"

"I want that practice session first." She was half serious. She hadn't come to Stu to buy a snowmobile, but she'd gotten a kick out of the lesson.

She asked him about local snowmobile clubs on the walk back to the ski shop and from that topic segued into gossiping about neighbors with snowmobiles.

"There's Marcia, of course."

"Yes." Liss frowned. "I get why she owns a two-up. Why do you?"

He gave a rueful chuckle "Have you noticed the size of my butt? I like the extra room on the seat."

Liss hid a smile as she returned to the rack of snowmobile suits. She rather liked the hot pink number.

Stu rattled off the names of several Moosetookalook snowmobilers as he rummaged through a file cabinet, but he claimed he'd never had much to do with the Fallstown crowd, the Thornes included. With a satisfied grunt, he produced a dog-eared owner's manual.

"You read through this tonight." Stu slapped it into her hand. "Then you take her out for a trial run tomorrow and see if she isn't worth every penny of her price."

Tuesday dawned clear, cold, and bright. Sherri watched the sun come up from the town square. She'd decided to go on "foot patrol" when she caught herself falling asleep in the office chair. Now wide awake and thoroughly chilled, she was about to go back inside when Liss hailed her.

"Time for a cup of coffee?" she called from the front porch of her house.

"Always." Sherri hurried across to her.

She had done some hard thinking during the wee hours, working her way through a boatload of guilt and doing a lot of soul-searching. She'd made a few decisions. One of them was that she no longer had any qualms about sharing what she knew with Liss MacCrimmon.

Ever since the state police had moved their base of operations back to the state capitol in Augusta they'd been slowly but steadily cutting her out of the loop. They didn't really want her input, not even Gordon Tandy. Maybe especially Gordon Tandy.

The upshot was that Sherri realized she was not going to be the one to solve Gavin Thorne's murder. Not unless pure dumb luck came into play. She'd literally have to stumble over the killer in order to be the one making the arrest . . . or she'd have to take advantage of Liss's talent for doing so.

In the warmth of the kitchen, redolent with the smell of freshly perked coffee and newly warmed cinnamon buns, Liss bustled about with an air of barely suppressed excitement. Something was up.

"Win the lottery?" Sherri asked.

Liss chuckled. "Better. I've had a bright idea."

Sherri repressed a groan but at the same time she felt a glimmer of hope. Whatever Liss was up to, it was better than sitting and twiddling her thumbs. "Hit me with it."

"This afternoon I'm going to go look at that property Moss circled on the map."

"Wait a minute. There are no roads. How are you going to get there?"

"Snowmobile, of course. Stu is letting me borrow his. It seats two. Want to come along?"

Sherri couldn't repress a shudder. "On a *snowmobile?*" The sport had never appealed to her. Nor had skiing or ice skating. Sherri couldn't see the sense in any activity that required being out in freezing weather, exposed to the elements for an extended period of time.

"Why not?"

"Well, for one thing, neither one of us knows how to drive one."

"Stu gave me a crash course."

"Oh, that gives me confidence."

"Don't be negative." Lumpkin appeared at Liss's elbow, eyeing the tasty treat on her plate. The black kitten was right behind him. Apparently they'd negotiated a truce. "Do you want to come with me or not?"

"Not."

Liss's face fell. "Oh, I thought . . ."

Sherri kept her eyes on the last inch of coffee in her mug. "I did some serious thinking during the boring section of my shift. I realized a few things about this case and about myself. I . . . well, I need to talk to Pete this afternoon. A long, serious talk."

"You're not going to break up with him, are you?"

To Sherri's horror, she felt herself tearing up. What was going on here? She wasn't usually a crybaby!

"Sherri?"

"I don't know!" The words burst from her in an anguished cry and she stood, heading for the coffeepot and a refill. Her back to Liss, she got control of her seesawing emotions. "Let's change the subject, okay?"

"Sure. Whatever you want." Concern underscored the words.

"I did come up with one more bit of information for you. It's probably nothing important, but Felicity Thorne got a second snowmobile in the divorce settlement, one she didn't register."

"Thorne must have ridden one at some time, then."

"That's my guess." She returned to the table, coffee in hand, and helped herself to a second pastry. The kitten leapt into her lap and nuzzled her hand. "Did you name this little sweetie yet?"

"No. Stick to the subject. Do you think Felicity might still be using the land along the border, even though it was sold to someone else?"

"Who'd know?"

"Someone who went there and took a look."

"Liss, please promise me you won't go alone. If that's your plan, I'll put Pete off."

"No! Don't do that. You two do need to talk."

"But it's dangerous to ride solo, even more so when you're a novice. And that's without the fact that there's a killer running around loose. Be sensible." Absently she broke off a piece of the cinnamon bun and fed it to the kitten.

"I will. I'll . . . I'll ask Gordon to go with me." She gave Lumpkin a chunk of pastry. He carried it off into a corner, growling when the kitten trailed after him.

"Not Dan?"

"Gordon is the cop. Besides, he used to own a snowmobile. And I think I can persuade him to take a few hours of personal time."

"You're not going to tell him—?"

"No. I'll let him think it's a date. After all, the odds of finding something there are pretty slim. I just can't shake the idea that I should go look."

Sherri told herself that Liss was right. It was unlikely she would find any evidence of smuggling at the cabin that had once belonged to the Thornes. Felicity Thorne wasn't that stupid. As for tracks crossing the border, with all the warm temperatures they'd had the last couple of days, it was doubtful that there would be anything left to see.

Tossing the last bit of her cinnamon bun to the kitten, Sherri headed back to the office with a clear conscience.

# Chapter Sixteen

Liss opened Moosetookalook Scottish Emporium a little later than usual and for once hoped no customers would bother her. She'd been trying for an hour to get hold of Gordon and so far had only connected with his voice mail.

Through the window she could see a bright blue sky punctuated by puffy clouds—perfect for the outing she had in mind. Sherri was right, though. It would be stupid to go out into the wilderness alone. She glared at the phone. "Ring, damn you!"

"Doesn't work that way," Aunt Margaret entered from the stairwell that led to her apartment. Liss sniffed, but for once didn't notice any new scent. Her aunt smelled the way she always had in the past—of Dove soap and Prell shampoo.

"No perfume today? What was with that, anyway?"

"Just an experiment."

Liss waited. Margaret's cheeks took on a decidedly pinker tinge.

"If you must know, I was on a nostalgia trip. I found a shop in Phoenix that sells classic perfumes, some of which aren't even manufactured anymore. I bought all my old favorites—Emeraude, My Sin, White Shoulders, Wind Song, White Diamonds." She ticked them off on her fingers. "I used to wear My Sin when I was your age. I'm told it had a pronounced effect on the male of the species."

She preened just a bit and Liss had to hide a smile. "All that trouble and expense for a man?"

"All that trouble for that dolt, Ernie Willett, who never notices how I smell!"

Liss was still trying to think of an adequate response when the phone finally rang. "Moosetookalook Scottish Emporium. Good morning."

Gordon's familiar voice greeted her from the other end of the line.

"I've been thinking," she said when he asked why she wanted to talk to him, "that you've been working straight out and could use a break. Is there any chance you could help me out for a few hours this afternoon? I've been look-ing at a snowmobile Stu Burroughs wants to sell and he's willing to let me take it for a test drive. You said you missed the one you used to own, so I thought maybe. . . ."

She twirled the cord around her fingers as she waited for his response.

"I'm not sure I can get away." His voice sounded muf-fled, as if he had the phone tucked in against his shoulder to free up both hands. Checking his schedule?

"Not even for an hour or two?" She wasn't above wheedling. "Couldn't you say you were following up a lead? Surely there are things here in Moosetookalook that you need to check on."

Too tense to stand still as she waited for his answer, Liss shifted her position behind the sales counter. Her eyes locked with Margaret's and widened in surprise. Her aunt's censorious look did not bode well, but Liss couldn't begin to guess what was bothering her.

"How's one o'clock?" Gordon asked. "I'll have to go home for my snowmobile suit and helmet before I meet you."

"Great." She beamed at the phone, suddenly lighthearted. "See you then."

She disconnected before he could change his mind and shifted her focus to Margaret. Her high spirits plummeted.

"What?"

"You have a business to run. How can you even consider going off gallivanting on a weekday afternoon?"

"Well, you could spell me again." Liss kept her tone light, hoping to tease Margaret out of her obvious ill temper. "Yesterday you thought I needed a break."

"Yesterday I had free time. Today I have a job to go to at the hotel."

Margaret's fulminating gaze meant trouble. Liss suddenly felt twelve years old again.

"In case it has escaped your notice, Amaryllis Rosalie MacCrimmon, that is a real job, not just auntie's little hobby. I don't mind giving you a break when I'm home anyway, but I told Joe Ruskin I'd put in a full eight-hour day today and so I shall."

Wow! Where had that come from? Liss had a feeling it wasn't anything she'd said. Someone else—Ernie Willett, maybe? Or one of Margaret's old friends?—was apparently not taking her new career seriously.

"No problem," she said aloud, forcing a smile. "I'll just close the shop."

But that answer brought a horrified look to her aunt's face. Liss had the feeling she was in a no-win situation, but she made one more game attempt to soothe ruffled feelings.

"You don't want the shop anymore, remember? You've decided to sell out to me."

Margaret still looked unhappy. "You're right. I'm sorry. I'm overreacting. It's just that, well, you seem to have other things on your mind these days. I have no idea what you're thinking half the time. That worries me, Liss. Do you really want to stay here in Moosetookalook at all?"

"Of course I do!" Only then did Liss realize that she hadn't told her aunt very much of what she'd been up to, or why. She supposed she'd been trying to protect the older woman, to avoid upsetting her. Fat lot of good that had done. She was upset anyway.

She crossed the shop to give Margaret a hug. "You'll have to forgive me. I've gotten out of the habit of accounting for myself to anyone."

"You're entitled to a private life, just as I am."

"True, but I didn't mean to keep secrets from you. The truth is, I've been looking into certain aspects of Gavin Thorne's murder."

"Oh, Liss, is that wise?"

"Probably not, but the thing is, Aunt Margaret, I think I've got a lead."

"Then you should tell the police and stay out of it."

"In fact, that's exactly what I intend to do."

When they were ensconced in the cozy corner, Liss filled her aunt in on what she knew about the Tiny Teddies available on the other side of the border. She told Margaret about the land the Thornes had owned until recently, and even related the story of Eric Moss and his map.

"Oh, and apparently Marcia's ex and Felicity Thorne are an item now," she added as an afterthought. "At least they seem to be living at the same address."

"Well for goodness sake! I knew the two couples were acquainted but I had no idea they were *that* close!"

"You've met Felicity Thorne?"

"No, but Marcia used to talk about how she and her husband were friends with people named Thorne. That would have been about three years ago, before you came back home. The four of them would go on snowmobile trips together."

Liss wondered why Marcia hadn't mentioned knowing Thorne before he moved to Moosetookalook and opened The Toy Box. She'd acted as if they'd just met. Brow furrowing, Liss thought back to that conversation. Marcia hadn't lied. She'd just not added any extra information. What she'd actually said was that she'd gone over to The Toy Box to welcome Thorne to town and that he was so rude to her that she didn't go back. Liss supposed that made sense, especially if Thorne knew his wife was carrying on with Marcia's husband. That was probably why they'd gotten divorced.

"Do you think Marcia knows about Cabot and Felicity?" Margaret asked.

"I've no idea, and I'm not about to tell her if she doesn't. Poor Marcia."

"Well, you can certainly cross her off your list of suspects. She'd have no reason to harm Thorne. If she'd been inclined to kill anyone, it would have been her ex."

"Or Felicity," Liss agreed. "Don't worry. She wasn't on my list in the first place."

A little silence fell. "You're determined to take a look at that piece of land?" Margaret asked hesitantly.

Liss sighed. "It's probably a waste of time, but it's a loose end." She shrugged. How could she expect Aunt Margaret to understand the compulsion she felt. She didn't understand it herself.

"And the only way to get there is by snowmobile?"

Liss nodded. "That's why I made arrangements to borrow Stu's machine. Gordon and I will drive up there this afternoon."

"Gordon Tandy," Margaret mused. "Isn't he more than ten years older than you are?"

"We have a lot in common," Liss protested. She wasn't certain if she meant their interest in crime or their interest in things Scottish but she didn't suppose it mattered.

The sound of sleigh bells jangling as the door opened brought both Liss and Margaret to their feet. Liss automatically put on her professional shopkeeper smile for the first customer of the day. It faded when she recognized Ernie Willett.

He went straight to Margaret and gave her a peck on the cheek. They made an incongruous couple. At her new weight, Margaret wore business casual with a professional woman's flair. Ernie sported a quilted, blaze-orange vest all year round. With his deeply lined face, gnarled fingers, and perpetual slouch, he'd always reminded Liss of a particularly sour-tempered gnome.

"Hello, Missy," he greeted her. He rarely used her name.

"Mr. Willett. What brings you to Moosetookalook Scottish Emporium?"

"I came by to talk to Margaret about our plans for Christmas Day." He sidled closer to Liss's aunt and an expression of delight came over his grizzled features. "Hey, you smell good today. Keep this one. Those other perfumes were too danged strong for a delicate flower like you."

Liss smothered a laugh.

Her aunt fixed her with a stern look as she gathered up her coat and the briefcase she'd brought downstairs with her. "Good timing," she said to Ernie. "You can drive me to work and we can talk on the way. I do have one suggestion for you, Liss," she threw over her shoulder when Ernie had opened the door for her and set the bells ringing again.

"What's that?" Liss hoped she wasn't about to receive auntly advice on juggling men friends, especially not while Sherri's father could overhear.

Apparently unaware of her niece's train of thought, Margaret rolled her eyes upward toward the top of the door frame. "Replace those annoying sleigh bells with something that sounds a little more pleasant."

Gordon pulled off the two-lane country road when Liss told him to, but he looked at her askance. "Are you sure this is where you want to start? We could have picked up the same trail five miles back, near an actual parking lot."

He didn't bother to point out that they could also have found a similar trail much closer to Moosetookalook. To reach this point they'd had to drive nearly an hour along the road that ran north through Carrabassett County and into Quebec.

"I just want to take a little test run and I came across a site online that showed all the trails and where they cross streets and highways." That was true enough. The maps she'd found there had told her where to turn off the trail groomed by a local snowmobile club to get to the site marked in Eric Moss's Maine atlas.

"You're the boss."

Gordon had Stu's machine off its trailer in short order. Liss got aboard and started the engine, on the first try, while he locked his truck and made a final check of their gear. Although Liss had seen his wistful glance at the controls, he climbed on behind her without a word of protest, content to let her drive.

Liss passed back the map she'd printed out and marked. "We're looking for the spot with the big red X," she said over her shoulder. "Don't let me drive past it."

His visor was open, giving her a clear view of his skeptical expression. Before it could turn into suspicion, she flipped her own face mask into place and put the snowmobile in motion.

She started off slowly. Stu had been right about the condition of the snow. Even on a well-maintained trail it was rough going. They bumped along, the noise of the engine discouraging conversation. She felt as if every inch of her body had gone numb from the cold and the constant vibration of the snowmobile by the time Gordon shouted into her ear.

"There! That's the place you marked."

Glad she'd read the owner's manual and knew how to stop, Liss brought the snowmobile to a satisfactory if jerky halt and let it idle as she scanned the frozen landscape. It was also a good thing she'd brought Gordon along, she decided. She wouldn't have recognized any landmarks in this sea of white.

"You're sure?"

"The area you want to look at is through there." He pointed to a stand of birch trees. "Looks like someone else has been this way recently."

Liss's spirits lifted. That would make things easier. It might also mean she'd been right about smugglers using this route.

Navigating carefully, she eased the snowmobile onto an even icier and more deeply rutted surface, the track left by one machine breaking its own trail. It was impossible to tell how often it had been used or when, but that it existed at all seemed to confirm her theory.

Behind her, Liss could sense Gordon's increased wariness. He must have guessed by now that she was up to something. She was surprised he didn't simply reach around her and hit the "kill switch."

She refused to feel guilty about her ruse. He'd agreed to come with her. If he'd needed the break she offered and had been looking forward to getting away from the case for a few hours, well they'd had a relaxing drive to get this far. She did owe him an apology, along with an explanation. He'd get both, but not until they reached their destination.

The trail suddenly became much rougher and the day seemed colder, too. Liss shivered in spite of her warm clothing. She wished she'd opted for mittens rather than gloves.

Gradually, the trees through which they'd been traveling began to thin out. A few minutes later, she pulled into a clearing. At the center was a small shake-shingle house—the "rustic cabin" Jason Graye had described.

Rustic was right. Not only were no phone or power lines in sight, but off to one side was a phone-booth-sized structure that could only be an outhouse. The quarter moon cut into the door confirmed Liss's guess.

She stopped the snowmobile, dismounted, and removed her helmet. Then she took a quick peek at the compass attached to the zipper of one of the many pockets on the outside of her hot pink snowmobile suit and turned so she faced due north.

The border with Canada was plainly distinguishable from the surrounding countryside—no fence or signs, but the trees had been clear-cut in a wide swath on both sides. She also saw evidence that the rough snowmobile trail they'd been following continued on across the gap in the pines and spruces, straight into the country next door.

Gordon's gaze followed hers. His face hardened. His voice was deceptively mellow. "Something you'd like to share, Liss?"

"It was a hunch. You've heard my theory about smuggling Tiny Teddies."

"All too often." He removed his helmet and ran his hand over his short-cropped hair. "You know I don't have jurisdiction over smuggling cases, right? There are channels I have to go through, rules to follow. Officers from the border patrol and customs are the ones who—"

Liss put her gloved fingers to his lips to stop the lecture.

"We're here now, Gordon. You can see for yourself that someone's been using this route to get into Canada. Shouldn't we at least look around?"

"Stay here." He headed for the cabin.

"No way." She caught up with him as he started to circle it.

There were no footprints showing in the snow except their own. Liss took that as a good sign. Scanning the ground, she almost ran into Gordon when he stopped abruptly right in front of her.

"Well, well," he said.

A shed was attached to the back of the cabin, little more than a lean-to to keep the weather off what was stored there.

"An ATV," Liss breathed, delighted at their discovery. She punched Gordon in the shoulder. "Maybe my theory wasn't so far-fetched, after all."

"Who owns this land?"

"Someone from out of state now, but he bought it from Jason Graye, and Gray got it from Felicity and Gavin—"

"Thorne!"

She winced at the sharp edge to his voice. Gordon was not happy.

"How do you know that?" he demanded.

"I asked."

"Why?"

"Oh, well, that's kind of a long story."

"I have time."

She stared at her boots. "I, uh, went to check on Eric Moss. I mean, no one had seen him for days. He might have been lying there in his house, injured, right?"

"Go on." Stone-faced, he waited.

Wrapping her arms about herself, Liss stamped her feet, glad she'd taken Stu's advice and worn mukluks. "Well, like most folks around here, Moss left his spare key over the door, so I went in," she ignored the sound of teeth grinding together, "and I checked around for him. He wasn't there, but he'd left behind a road atlas with this property circled in red. That made me curious."

Deciding he didn't need to know about the other visitor to Moss's house that night, Liss sent Gordon a sunny smile and shut up.

"So much for you staying out of police business."

"But Moss wasn't police business. You weren't interested in him. In fact, it's all your fault, really, that I went to his place. I never would have if you hadn't dismissed my suggestion out of hand."

He closed his eyes briefly. "Damn it, Liss! You withheld information germane to a murder investigation."

"I did not! You've been telling me for days there's no connection between Thorne's death and Moss's disappearance."

Gordon looked as if he wanted to throttle her. "Give me a minute," he growled. "Don't move a muscle."

While he stalked off around the cabin, Liss stared at the wooded landscape that surrounded it. It was quiet in the clearing. Too quiet. Liss was a small town girl, but that didn't mean she liked total solitude. She'd be terrified if she was stranded out here alone.

Nervously, she glanced in the direction Gordon had gone. He wouldn't go off and leave her here. He couldn't be that ticked off.

Just to be on the safe side, she retraced her steps to the snowmobile, casting wary glances at the line of trees as she went. Bears hibernated. She didn't have to worry about running into one of them. And moose were big and stupid but usually not a threat unless they were protecting their young.

The only danger she was in came from the man walking toward her. She knew at once that he was no longer Gordon. This was Detective Tandy. She expected him to produce his little spiral-bound notebook at any moment.

"All right, Liss. Let's hear your theory."

"There's a link between the Tiny Teddies and Thorne's death." She'd thought so all along but he hadn't wanted to listen. Well, he'd have to listen now. "Look at that!" She gestured toward the snowmobile trail. "That proves it. Someone has been crossing the border illegally."

"That doesn't mean they were smuggling, let alone bringing in contraband toys."

"It doesn't mean they *weren't*, either!" She pointed to the trail beneath her feet. "Can't you tell anything from looking at this?"

"Such as?"

"Whether or not the snowmobile was dragging a sled. How many times this trail has been used and in which direction. I don't know! Something."

"I'm a state trooper, not a Maine guide. When we get back to town, I'll inform the game wardens and the border patrol and customs and anyone else this might concern and they'll take over."

"That's it? That's all you're going to do?"

He gestured at the pristine . . . and empty . . . landscape. "Do you see anyone I can arrest?"

"This was Thorne's land."

"And if Gavin Thorne was the one who was smuggling, I can hardly arrest him, can I?"

She took a deep breath. "My theory, since you *did* ask, is that Thorne was in cahoots with Eric Moss. Moss knew about this property. That proves he was involved somehow. And he's the one who sold those bears to Marcia after Thorne's murder."

"Why are you so fixated on Eric Moss?"

"Because he *disappeared!*" Gordon could be so thick sometimes.

"Does Moss own a snowmobile?"

"I . . . don't know." Best to keep Sherri out of trouble. "He *could*. And it wouldn't necessarily have to be registered, either."

Gordon wasn't buying it.

Gritting her teeth, she shifted tactics. If he thought Felicity Thorne had murdered her husband, so be it. The important thing was that smuggling had to have played a role in Thorne's death. This clue—that trail leading into Canada—was important!

"Say it wasn't Moss. Felicity could be the smuggler, and the murderer. She owns two snowmobiles and Cabot Katz has another."

"And how is it that you know that?" His voice was dangerously quiet.

Liss was still groping for an answer when she heard the distant hum of an engine. She froze. Gordon frowned.

There was no doubt about it. The sound was that of another snowmobile and it was approaching at a good clip from the opposite side of the border.

There was no time to mount up and ride off. It was too late to go hide in the trees or inside the cabin.

"Stay behind me," Gordon ordered.

"No problem." For once, Liss had no objection to being protected. She couldn't be certain they were about to come fact to face with a killer, but it was a distinct possibility.

The other machine appeared in the distance. At any moment, the driver would spot them standing beside Stu's snowmobile. Out in the open. Exposed. Sitting ducks. Nervously, Liss edged a little closer to Gordon.

"I don't suppose you brought your gun with you."

"I was expecting a pleasant afternoon outing with a lady friend, remember?"

Gordon's sarcasm stung, but Liss could hardly blame him for being a little peeved at her. She'd brought him here under false pretenses. It was all her fault if she'd put them both in the path of danger.

Liss shaded her eyes and squinted at the approaching vehicle. As it crossed into Carrabassett County from Canada she saw that there were two people aboard. She couldn't tell much about either one of them, except that they were both heavily bundled up in snowmobile suits, one dark green and one navy blue. Helmets with full face masks further hid their identities, but it was easy to tell when the driver spotted them. Slushy snow slewed up in an arc as the approaching snowmobile skidded to a stop. The engine sputtered and died.

Since Stu's machine was blocking the newcomer's way to the groomed trail, Liss tried to convince herself that they'd had to stop. They'd have run right into it otherwise. Surely there was no reason to think there was anything sinister in the fact that the two riders were just sitting there, staring at them.

Gordon lifted a hand in a friendly wave. He ambled toward the other sled, a smile on his face. "Hey, there. Can you help us? We seem to be lost."

Neither the driver nor the passenger answered.

Gordon had told Liss to stay behind him, but she wasn't sure if that meant she should follow him or remain with the snowmobile. Keeping a wary eye on the two snowmobilers, Liss stuck close to Gordon.

If one of the riders was Felicity Thorne, she'd already have recognized both of them. Liss had removed her helmet, just as Gordon had, freeing her hair and exposing her face. If it was Eric Moss, he might not know Gordon on sight, but he'd surely have heard that Liss was keeping company with a state trooper. Residents of small towns like Moosetookalook thrived on gossip about the love lives of their neighbors. Odds were good that no one was buying the "we seem to be lost" ploy.

Gordon stopped a few feet away from the other sled. Liss still couldn't identify either the driver or the passenger, but she saw Gordon tense as the driver reached into one of those many convenient outside zipper pockets.

"Get down!" he shouted, throwing himself to one side and taking Liss with him.

They dodged just as an explosion of sound shattered the December stillness. The last thing Liss saw before she landed facedown in a snowbank was the barrel of a gun pointed right at her.

# Chapter Seventeen

Close to two hundred pounds of solid male crushed Liss deeper into the cold, wet ground just as a second bullet whizzed by. It came so close to hitting her that she felt a breeze as it passed.

Stunned and terrified, she made no attempt to move even though jagged shards of icy snow bit into her arm, her stomach, and her thigh. This was not the soft, fluffy variety. In spite of the layers of insulated padding she wore, she could feel every irregularity in the hard, uneven crust beneath her.

Her right hand had landed in a puddle. A trickle of frigid, half-melted sludge crept slowly under the cuff of her glove. In the catalogue of discomfort Liss was mentally compiling, that scarcely made the list. At the top was the fact that the entire left side of her face stung like the devil. It had struck a patch of snow that had refrozen solid as rock.

An engine roared to life. Stu's machine? The killer's? The sled sounded as if it were coming straight at them. Liss threw both arms over her head and squeezed her eyes shut, but at the last moment the oncoming vehicle veered aside.

Gordon's weight pinned Liss's legs, preventing her from rolling over. Her ears rang from the close-range gunshots.

Her heart raced so fast she was convinced it was about to leap out of her chest. Still, she managed to lift her face out of the snow an inch or two, far enough to see that the other machine was breaking a new trail to circle around Stu's sled.

Safely past that blockade, the snowmobile stopped again. The driver twisted around on the seat and once more lifted the gun. Unable to look away, Liss braced herself for the impact of a bullet. It never came. At the last second, the passenger knocked the weapon out of the driver's hand. It sailed high into the air, landed hard enough to penetrate the icy surface of the snow, and disappeared into a deep patch.

The two on the snowmobile began to argue. Liss cocked her head, straining to catch a word or two. It was hopeless. Her ears were still ringing. She couldn't hear what they were saying, but she had a feeling that the shooter wanted to go after the gun, or maybe turn the snowmobile around and try to run right over Liss and Gordon.

Gordon. Was he okay? He hadn't moved since he'd fallen on top of her. She tried to tell herself he was playing possum, but a sinking feeling in the pit of her stomach warned her that something was wrong with him. Had he been hit?

She'd just managed to prop herself up on her elbows when the engine revved again. As she watched, the snowmobile left the clearing, speeding off along the trail she and Gordon had come in on.

Once again Liss tried to roll over. "Gordon! Get up!" She shoved at his big, immovable body. "Gordon?"

Twisting at her waist, she finally managed to get a good look at him. His upper body was partially hidden from view by the angle of his fall, but she could hardly miss seeing that a spray of bright red drops had spattered across the white snow. He'd been hit by that first bullet and been bleeding as he fell.

Liss felt her face drain of color. Her breath caught and for a moment her heart seemed to stop beating. Her cry of distress seemed unnaturally loud in the stillness of the clearing.

Squirming, trying to free herself so that she could help him, she was once again horribly aware that he hadn't moved since he'd landed on top of her. Unconsciousness was not a good sign.

"You can't be dead," she whispered. "Oh, God! Oh, God. Don't be dead, Gordon. Please tell me I didn't get you killed!"

One of her legs came free, then the other. On hands and knees Liss crawled along Gordon's ominously still form until she reached his head.

He lay on his side in the snow, facing away from her. There was more blood on the whiteness pillowing his head. Afraid to touch him, afraid not to, Liss carefully rolled him over. The last thing she wanted was to do more damage, but she had to see where that blood was coming from.

A shallow graze, still oozing, scored Gordon's forehead. Liss let out the breath she hadn't realized she was holding. This was good. At least according to the mystery novels she'd read, dead bodies didn't bleed. If he was bleeding, that meant his heart was still pumping.

Belatedly, she gathered her wits sufficiently to bend down and place her ear on his chest. At first her own heart kept her from hearing his, but then she felt it beating strong and steady. Lifting her head, she touched his fingers to the pulse at his neck. That was even easier to find, and if anything was a little fast.

But he was still unconscious. Concussion? Shock? Brain damage? The wound didn't *look* very deep, but what did she know?

The low groaning sound he made was the sweetest music she'd ever heard.

"Gordon! Wake up! They're gone. We're safe."

Slowly, he opened his eyes. He blinked, as if he couldn't quite bring the anxious face bending over him into focus.

"Gordon, are you okay?"

Stupid question! Liss could have kicked herself. She continued to kneel beside him, reluctant to encourage him to move in case there was more to his injury than she could see. There seemed to be quite a bit of blood, but head wounds always bled a lot. She'd read that somewhere, too.

"I'll live." The shaky note in Gordon's voice was not re-assuring. He sounded weak as a kitten. Weaker.

"You've been shot."

"I got that." He lifted one trembling hand to his forehead. Using his fingertips, he gently probed the groove. "You okay?"

"We got lucky. The passenger hit the driver's hand and knocked the gun into the snow." She shuddered, remembering. "It was aimed at me. We'd be dead right now if—"

"Think you can find it?"

It took Liss a minute to understand what he meant. The gun. He wanted her to look for the fallen gun. "I . . . I think so."

"Get it."

"Shouldn't I dig out the first-aid kit first?" Berating herself for not remembering sooner that they carried one as standard equipment, Liss started to go after it. It might have been Gordon who'd been clipped on the head, but she was the one acting like she'd had her brain rattled.

Gordon caught her arm in a surprisingly firm grip. "Gun first. They might come back."

That possibility was enough to send Liss crunching her way across the surface of the snow. It was icy on top but gave under her weight, sending a foot plunging downward with every step she took.

She expected to have to dig for the gun, but it proved

easy to locate. It had fallen with the barrel pointing straight down. The handle stuck out at a right angle, as if waiting for Liss to reach down and wrap her hand around it.

Once she'd collected the weapon, Liss carried it carefully pointed away from herself. By the time she made her way back to Gordon, he was sitting up and had retrieved his helmet, which had landed a few feet away from him when he fell.

He took charge of the gun, tucking it carefully inside one of his zippered pockets. "Which way did they go?"

"Back toward the main trail."

"How long was I out?"

"It seemed like eons. Where do you think you're going?" In spite of her squawk of protest, Gordon levered himself to his feet.

"After them."

"Are you crazy?"

"Don't worry. I'm not planning on the gunfight at the OK Corral. I just want to see if we can get close enough to identify them."

"We'll never catch up. They've got too much of a head start."

Doggedly, Gordon made his way toward the snowmobile. He staggered the first couple of steps and his progress remained noticeably unsteady.

"Dizzy?" she inquired, catching up to him.

"A little. Good thing you're driving."

"Yes, isn't it." She was not about to go chasing after that other snowmobile, no matter what Gordon wanted. She'd take him back to his truck and drive him to the hospital. He could like it or lump it.

While he fished in a pocket and produced a cell phone, Liss retrieved the first-aid kit.

"No signal."

"And you're surprised?" They were nowhere near a tower and deep in a valley, besides.

Liss cleaned the wound as best she could and applied a bandage. Gordon still looked dazed, but she felt more confident. His injury didn't seem to be serious. Still, she intended to get him back home as quickly as possible.

She climbed onto the snowmobile. When they both had their helmets securely fastened and he'd wrapped his arms tightly around her waist, she started the engine.

She wouldn't bother loading the snowmobile onto the trailer, Liss decided. They could pick it up later, once she was sure Gordon was really all right.

Proceeding slowly, they reached the groomed trail. They hadn't gone far along it when Liss caught sight of the back end of another snowmobile. Gordon saw it, too. He let go of her waist with his right hand and reached for the throttle. She slapped his fingers away. Speed up when the driver of that sled had tried to kill them? No way!

"Get closer," he shouted in her ear.

Maybe it wasn't the same snowmobile, Liss thought. That one should be much farther ahead by this time.

But it was. The markings on the machine, the colors of the snowmobile suits the two passengers wore—everything matched. For whatever reason, they had delayed their getaway. Liss wondered if they'd stopped to argue over going back to the clearing to finish off inconvenient witnesses.

The driver glanced around and spotted Liss and Gordon. The sled sped up.

Gordon reached forward a second time.

Liss swiveled far enough to see his face. His eyes looked clear and they were fixed on the machine ahead. His determined expression convinced Liss that if she didn't cooperate and let him get to the throttle, he'd probably hit the kill switch, dump her off, and continue the pursuit on his own. Once again she slapped his hand away, but this time she followed orders and increased her speed.

"Hold on," she yelled over the noise of the engine.

They had nothing to worry about, she told herself. The bad guys no longer had a gun. But a wave of relief washed over her when they didn't open fire.

Stu's snowmobile hit a rough patch and slewed sideways. Her heart in her throat, Liss righted it and kept going. Nope. No danger of being shot at. Falling off the sled, however, was still a possibility.

Once again, Gordon shouted something into her ear, but she lost whatever he said to the roar of the engine.

The ride to the clearing had given Liss enough practice to feel comfortable on the snowmobile, even now when they were going faster than she liked. Figuratively, she shrugged her shoulders. She could do this, get close enough to the other sled to see the faces of the two riders.

Liss didn't allow herself think beyond that goal. The coordination she'd acquired from her years as a professional dancer stood her in good stead as she leaned way, way out on a turn. Gordon's grip on her waist tightened. He stopped trying to talk to her.

On the flat, she increased her speed yet again, in tandem with the snowmobile ahead of them. Concentration fixed on the spot of navy blue that was the passenger's back, her vision narrowed to the width of a tunnel. She saw nothing but her quarry, heard nothing but the rush of the wind past her helmet.

Coming in, Liss had reduced her speed when she went over icy patches, but this time around there was no slowing down. When the killer threw caution aside and veered off the trail onto virgin snow, Liss did the same without a moment's hesitation. Grimly determined not to lose sight of the other sled, she pushed Stu's snowmobile to its limits, following every zig and zag of the hair-raising cross-country course the other driver set.

There was potential for disaster here. Liss knew it, but she shoved the possibility ruthlessly aside. She didn't allow herself to think about the rugged terrain or the wretched condition of the snow or her own inexperience. She couldn't afford doubts. She had to believe she could control and maneuver the sled. With absolute faith in her ability to respond to the constantly changing demands of their situation, she trusted her instincts and kept going.

Liss barely felt the jolts when they went airborne and landed hard. The cold meant nothing to her, nor the snow flying in every direction as she barreled along. A certain curious detachment had descended, making her feel as if she were outside the action, watching herself chase across the countryside.

At the same time, exhilaration filled her. She let her body flow with the movement of the powerful machine beneath her. Following the other sled's lead was like improvising a dance with a partner.

On another level, she was aware that what she was doing was dangerous. Dangerous? It was just plain crazy. But she was on an adrenaline high and loving every moment of it. She couldn't stop now, especially since, at long last, she was gaining on the other sled!

A fine mist struck Liss full in the face mask. Momentarily blinded, she felt her stomach clench in panic but even that didn't slow her down. She swiped at the visor with one gloved hand and kept going.

Behind her, Gordon was molded to her back. His body shadowed hers as she leaned out on turns or bent low over the handlebars. His grip on her waist remained firm and he made no move toward the kill switch.

As Liss drew closer to the other machine, the driver

looked back. Liss stared hard at the face mask. She couldn't make out a single feature, but there was something. . . .

Abruptly, the sled swerved into a heavily wooded area. Liss followed, automatically decreasing her speed. She had no interest in colliding with a pine tree at fifty miles an hour.

Thirty was still fast enough to feel the pull of gravity on turns. The ground came frighteningly close when she leaned a little too far into one of them. It was Gordon who pulled them upright again before they both tumbled off.

Liss almost lost her seat a second time when she followed the other sled off snow-covered ground onto a dirt road. The impact of dropping a foot from snow bank to hard-packed ground rattled every bone in her body.

Their quarry was getting desperate, taking wild risks. Snowmobiles had not been designed to do more than cross the occasional street or railroad track. Liss felt as if her teeth were being jarred loose as they raced along the rutted surface.

Gravel and rocks tossed up by the sled ahead dinged off the front of Stu's snowmobile. From beneath the treads, Liss heard a grinding noise. Much more of that and the chase would be over.

They were on a hilly road full of twists and turns as well as ruts and soft shoulders. Liss slowed a little more, common sense asserting itself even as every other instinct she possessed urged her to continue her pursuit. Gaining more of a lead, the fleeing sled careened around a hairpin curve at breakneck speed.

Momentarily on higher ground, Liss could see what was obscured from the other driver's view by the blind corner. There was a stand of trees dead ahead.

Liss let up on the throttle. Her snowmobile skidded sideways and came a bone-jarring halt. The engine sputtered and stalled.

The crash of metal against timber was terrifyingly loud in the sudden quiet.

Liss's insides twisted and she squeezed her eyes shut.

It wasn't until she felt Gordon release her and slide off the sled that she could force herself to look.

As he ran toward the scene, she dismounted on trembling legs. With clumsy fingers she fished the first-aid kit out of its storage space and stumbled after him.

Both riders had been thrown. Gordon had already reached the driver, who had landed in the road. Glancing back at Liss, he gestured for her to go to the passenger. The figure in navy blue lay supine on the snow a few yards away.

Kneeling beside the fallen body, her heart in her throat, Liss opened the face mask. The features she revealed did not belong to anyone she'd ever seen before. A stranger stared up at Liss with a dazed look in her eyes.

Definitely a woman. Definitely alive. The snow had been deep enough and soft enough to cushion her fall.

"Can you speak?" Liss asked. "Don't move yet. You might have broken something."

"Just . . . winded . . . I . . . think."

"Good. That's good." Liss looked for blood. She didn't see any.

The woman wiggled her hands and feet experimentally. She winced when she tried to move her right leg, but didn't seem to be in severe pain. "What . . . what happened?"

"You hit a tree."

Liss turned her head to look at the driver of the crashed sled. All she could see were feet.

They weren't moving. Gordon had climbed the bank on the opposite side of the dirt road and had his cell phone to his ear.

It was cold out in the open. Bitterly cold. Blowing snow stung Liss's cheeks when she removed her helmet. She started to shake, but not from the chill in the air. Now that the chase was over, she realized just how close they had all come to disaster.

"Will you be okay alone for a minute?" Liss's voice wasn't steady, either.

"I'm not going anywhere. I think I did something to my knee." The woman managed a wry smile, but it cost her.

"Knees can be fixed," Liss said. How well she knew it! Promising she'd be right back, she went straight to Gordon, reaching his side just as he finished his phone call.

Dark eyes filled with sorrow, he turned to her. "She's dead, Liss." His voice sounded strained. "She was thrown into the same tree her snowmobile hit. The impact broke her neck."

"She? So, it's not Eric Moss?"

"No. And not Felicity Thorne, either."

She blinked at him in confusion. She'd been so certain they were chasing one or the other. "The passenger is a stranger," she whispered. "The driver, too?"

But Gordon shook his head. "The dead woman is someone we know, all right. It's Marcia Milliken Katz."

# Chapter Eighteen

"**G**ood thing Jim Uxbridge likes to check on his camp in winter," Pete Campbell muttered as they jounced over the ruts in the narrow dirt road. "If he hadn't plowed out after the storm, we'd never be able to get through."

"There they are!" Sherri tightened her grip on the Crown Vic's dashboard as Pete hit the brakes.

They were the first responders at the accident scene. Sherri was out of her jurisdiction and off duty besides, but she'd been riding with Pete when the call came in over the police radio. Knowing Liss's plans for the afternoon, she expected to find her friend with Gordon Tandy. What she couldn't predict was whether or not Liss was the one requiring medical attention.

She spotted the bandage on Gordon's forehead first. Then she caught sight of the body, half concealed by two trees with ugly slashes across their bark. Her heart stuttered and for a moment she forgot how to breathe.

Then Pete said, "There's Liss, sitting on that log."

"Thank God!" Sherri fumbled with her seat belt and scrambled out of the sheriff's department cruiser.

Taking the most direct route, Sherri cut across unbroken snow. Liss looked relatively undamaged, but her face was paler than the icy ground beneath Sherri's feet and she had a spectacular bruise coming up on one cheek. The silver space blanket wrapped around her shimmered in the setting sun every time Liss shivered.

A woman sat next to her, a middle-aged blonde cocooned in a second blanket, this one blaze orange. Sherri had never seen her before.

"There's an ambulance en route." Sherri's voice came out as a squeak. She had to clear her throat before she could go on. "You okay?"

"I'll survive. Did you know these space emergency blankets only weigh three ounces and will fit into a first aid kit? Stu had two of them. Isn't that lucky?" The hand that held the blanket closed trembled violently. "Why can't I get warm?"

A bitter wind soughed through the trees. Even bundled up, Sherri felt the cold slice through her. She could only imagine how much more strongly it would affect someone who'd just been in an accident. Neither woman looked as if she was about to go into shock, but they both needed shelter from the elements.

"Come on." Sherri helped the stranger, who she now saw had an Ace bandage wrapped around one knee, get to her feet. "We can sit in the cruiser and run the heater. That'll help."

It was a slow trek to the car. Sherri assisted the blonde. Liss managed on her own, but she was wobbly on her pins, and she insisted on carrying the backpack that had been sitting in the snow beside the log.

As she walked, Sherri listened for a siren, but there was no sign yet of the ambulance. It had to come all the way from Fallstown, much farther than Pete had traveled.

After Sherri installed Liss in the front seat and turned the heat on full blast, she helped the blonde settle into the back seat. Pete always carried a thermos of coffee. Sherri poured a few ounces of the hot liquid into one of the disposable cups he kept in the trunk. For the moment, she ignored the six-pack of bottled water and other assorted emergency gear.

Strictly speaking, she supposed she shouldn't give the woman anything to drink before the EMTs saw her, but there was no way of telling when they'd show up. In the meantime, the cold was a known danger. It was beginning to get dark, too. If the wreck had occurred any farther out in the wilderness, problems with hypothermia would have been inevitable.

"Here." She thrust the cup toward the stranger.

"Thanks." The woman's voice was low and throaty. "But I don't think I can hold that, even half full, without spilling it." Like Liss, she was shivering, shaking so hard that she was having difficulty keeping the blanket in place around her shoulders.

Sherri slid into the backseat beside the blonde and closed the door. She helped her to drink the coffee. After the first few sips, the tremors subsided to a manageable level. Before long, the stranger snaked one hand out from beneath the orange blanket and took the cup for herself. Only then did Sherri have the opportunity to sneak a peek at Liss.

On the other side of the clear, shatterproof barrier, she sat slumped and unresponsive, still huddled in her silver blanket. She was staring through the windshield at Gordon, who stood talking to Pete. Her view also encompassed the scarred trees, the wreck of the snowmobile, and the body.

Sherri swallowed convulsively. She'd been trying not to think too much about that motionless form. Gordon hadn't identified the victim over the radio, but whoever it was, that person would never be warm again.

She turned back to the stranger. "You got a name?" The question came out too sharply, but she didn't apologize.

"Donna. Donna Conroy."

"Okay, Donna. Try to sip a little more of this. We need to warm you up." Sherri poured another half cup of coffee and watched the other woman polish it off. The hot drink seemed to revive her. She had a little color in her cheeks and the shakes seemed to be a thing of the past.

Sherri was about to get out of the car and take the remaining coffee up front to Liss when the ambulance, sirens silent, pulled in behind the cruiser. Sherri helped transfer Donna to the care of the two EMTs before sliding in behind the wheel.

Instantly, hot air engulfed her. With the heater going full blast the car was way too warm, but Sherri didn't touch the controls. She pulled off her hat and gloves and unzipped her coat as she gave Liss a hard stare. Like Donna, Liss had stopped shivering, but she was still pale as a ghost and hollow-eyed with it. Her gaze never left the crash site.

Between the fogged windshield and the gathering dusk, there wasn't much left to see. Gordon appeared as a vague outline. The body was no longer visible.

"Do you need to be checked out for injuries?"

"No."

"Are you warmed up yet?"

"I'm too numb to tell."

"Frostbite?" Sherri poured coffee into a second disposable cup and handed it over.

"Brain dead." Liss automatically drank the dark brew but she continued to track Gordon's movements with her eyes. "We were chasing them, and then everything happened so fast." Her voice hitched.

Sherri could fill in some of the blanks for herself. Liss and Gordon must have encountered the other snowmobile at that cabin the Thornes had once owned. It had crashed while they were in pursuit and the driver had been killed. Being Liss, she probably felt responsible for the death. Add a dollop of guilt to the shock of witnessing a violent accident and sudden death and it was no wonder she was having trouble dealing.

"Would it help to talk about it?"

Liss shrugged.

"It would help *me*."

That got a faint smile out of her.

"Call it morbid curiosity, but I'd like to know what went down here."

Liss and Gordon wouldn't have been chasing just anybody. They'd made this trip by snowmobile specifically to check out a potential border crossing. At least Liss had.

Sherri sent a doubtful glance in Gordon's direction. Was it her imagination, or did he look even more stiff and unapproachable than usual?

Liss drank more coffee. Sherri surreptitiously lowered the driver's side window an inch. Her friend might still be freezing, but for anyone who hadn't just had a shock, the Crown Vic was an oven.

Liss's haunted expression kept Sherri silent when what she really wanted to do was pepper her with questions. Liss needed time . . . but not too much.

Sherri was torn. Was she just rationalizing when she told herself Liss mustn't be allowed to brood? That telling her story would help her cope? Sherri had questions—so many questions—but she held back. Liss would talk when she was ready. Hopefully *before* Sherri burst from trying to contain her curiosity.

"I had all the pieces," Liss said at last. Tears welled up in her eyes. "But I put them together in the wrong order."

"Someone *was* smuggling, then?"

Liss nodded.

"Who?" She expected to hear Eric Moss's name. Or maybe Felicity Thorne's. She was not at all prepared for what Liss actually said.

"Marcia."

"Mar—? No!"

That made no sense at all. Sherri peered through the windshield at the body. One of the EMTs had gone to have a look at it. By the illumination from his flashlight she could see him shake his head. There was nothing anyone could do for her.

"*That's* Marcia?"

Again, Liss nodded.

Sherri felt as if the bottom had dropped out of her stomach. Marcia hadn't been a close friend, but she'd known the woman in a casual way for years. She'd never suspected . . .

"You and Gordon actually caught Marcia crossing the border?"

Liss nodded. "We didn't know it was Marcia, but she recognized us. She shot at us. She tried to kill us. She probably would have succeeded if Donna hadn't knocked the gun out of her hand."

She'd had a gun? Marcia? Sherri tried to picture it. Sure Marcia had a temper, but . . . "Ohmigod! She killed Gavin Thorne!"

"I think so, yes."

"Where's the gun now?"

"Gordon has it. God, Sherri, I'm just sick. If only I'd been quicker on the uptake. Aunt Margaret told me, just this morning after you left, that Marcia and her husband were friends with the Thornes. They used to go on snowmobile trips together. Marcia knew all about the land they owned along the border. She knew how easy it was to cross into Canada. I don't think she bought those Tiny Teddies from Eric Moss. I think she went to Quebec and picked them up herself. Look!"

Liss hauled out the backpack she'd brought with her into the cruiser. As soon as she unzipped the top, Tiny Teddies spilled out over her lap. It was jammed full of the little bears.

"Whoa!"

"And if that gun was Thorne's, that means she killed him in cold blood, just as she meant to kill us."

"That's not what happened."

Sherri and Liss turned to stare at Donna. She had acquired a pair of crutches and been able to hobble from the ambulance to the side of the cruiser without Sherri noticing. She'd obviously overheard at least part of their conversation through that inch of window Sherri had opened.

"Do you know what did happen?" Sherri asked.

"I think so."

Sherri held up a hand to forestall a confession. "I'm Officer Sherri Willett with the Moosetookalook Police Department." She got out of the cruiser.

"You mean I should be careful what I say to you?" Donna managed a faint smile. She looked terrified but determined. "That's okay, Officer Willett. Go ahead and read me my rights. I knew I was breaking the law. I knew I was taking the risk of getting caught."

Sherri obligingly recited the Miranda Warning, then gestured for Donna to resume her earlier place in the cruiser. Liss left the front seat to slide in beside her in the back.

"Do you need to go to the hospital?" Liss asked.

"Eventually. They want to x-ray my knee. But I'm okay for now."

Sherri looked around for Gordon before she climbed in on Donna's other side. One of the EMTs was checking out the gash on the detective's forehead while Pete kept watch on Marcia's body. It would have to stay where it was until the medical examiner had a look at the accident scene. Sherri figured he'd be showing up any minute now, along with the rest of the state team.

"Okay, Donna. Tell us what you think happened." Sherri left the door half open so she could monitor events outside the cruiser.

"I don't suppose Marcia would have said anything to me if I hadn't seen the gun when we were loading up the sled. It gave me a turn. I asked her what she thought she needed a weapon for, and I told her I didn't want to ride with her if she was armed. She said it was just a souvenir, that she'd taken it from someone who'd used it to try to make a citizen's arrest. She laughed when she said it, and then she told me he thought he'd be a hero, but it didn't work out that way for him. That he suffered a tragic accident when his own gun went off. That it was poetic justice."

Donna's stricken expression convinced Sherri that she wasn't lying about what Marcia had said. She just wasn't certain that Marcia had told Donna the truth.

"Thorne must have found out she was smuggling Tiny Teddies," Liss said.

But Donna shook her head. "That was a new wrinkle. I think he must have caught on to her other . . . activities." She stared at the hands clasped tightly in her lap and blurted out the rest in a rush. "Marcia has been transporting illegal aliens into this country from Canada for a couple of years now. I'm just her latest cargo."

Sherri had heard the expression "you could have knocked me over with a feather," all her life, but she'd never experienced that level of astonishment . . . till now.

"I'm a Canadian citizen married to an American," Donna continued. "Fourteen months ago, we paid a visit to my parents in Quebec. Afterward, my husband and children were allowed back into the U.S., but I was told I couldn't cross the border with them. I still don't know why, but the bureaucratic nonsense and red tape have kept me out of this country ever since. Then I heard about Marcia."

"You heard what about Marcia?" Sherri asked.

Liss had an odd look on her face, as if she had an inkling of what was to come, but Sherri was clueless. She'd assumed Donna was involved in nothing more serious than smuggling Tiny Teddies. This was a whole new ball game.

"Marcia helps . . . helped other people like me get home."

"By snowmobile?"

"There's an ATV at the cabin," Liss murmured.

"What do you know about this?" Sherri's eyes narrowed suspiciously as she leaned in front of Donna to focus on Liss.

"Only that Marcia had a friend in the same situation who got fed up with waiting and came back to the U.S. illegally." Liss's voice was flat and toneless, but her face worked as if she fought to hold back tears. "Marcia didn't tell me she was the one who helped her. Maybe she wasn't. But she was quite . . . passionate about how unfair it was to keep people like Donna separated from their families."

"So she ferried them over the border out of the goodness of her heart?" Sherri didn't bother to hide her skepticism.

"Hardly." Donna looked chagrined. "Maybe it started out as helping a friend, but I had to pay her twenty-five thousand dollars for the ride."

Sherri gave a low whistle. With that much money at stake, it was hard to imagine Gavin Thorne taking the high road. More likely, he'd tried to get Marcia to cut him in on the action. Sherri could almost visualize the scene. Thorne producing a gun, threatening to turn Marcia in if she didn't agree to split the profits. Then Marcia losing that hair-trigger temper of hers and bang! No more threat of exposure.

"Marcia was supposed to drop me at a rendezvous point. My husband is waiting there." Donna sighed. "I have a feeling he's going to have a long wait."

Sherri fished in her coat pocket for her cell phone and handed it over. "Go ahead. Call him." She almost laughed at Donna's look of astonishment. "Traditional, isn't it? One phone call. Tell him you'll be at the Emergency Room at Fallstown Community Hospital. The ambulance will take you there."

"You're not arresting me?"

"I'm not, no, but I make no guarantees about what the state police or the border patrol will do. You're going to have to repeat what you told me to them."

Sherri exited the cruiser, letting Donna out so she'd have privacy for her conversation with her husband. She felt sorry for the woman as she watched her balance on the crutches while she punched in numbers. Even if she were allowed to stay, she'd probably be looking at jail time. Homeland security took this sort of thing seriously, even when there were extenuating circumstances.

"Gordon can't arrest her," Liss protested from inside the car.

"He may not have any choice." Sherri watched Pete approach, suddenly very glad that they'd worked out most of their differences in the course of that afternoon's long, no-holds-barred conversation. "She did break the law."

"It's a stupid law if it keeps families separated."

"There are lots of stupid laws around. That doesn't mean people get to pick and choose which ones to obey."

"I can't believe this! I can't believe any of this!" As if pulled by a chain, Liss's gaze returned back to the stand of trees. Full dark had fallen. There was nothing to see now but the pale glow of a couple of emergency flares Pete had set up.

"Believe it." One glance at her fiancé's grim expression convinced Sherri that she was glad to have been spared viewing the body.

"It was Marcia?" she asked him.

"No doubt about it."

"And Thorne's gun?"

"Probably. It's the right caliber. Gordon will have to wait for a ballistics report, but I'm betting it's a match for the murder weapon." Pete frowned. "But why would Marcia shoot Thorne?"

"I wonder if we'll ever know for certain," Sherri answered. "The only people who might have told us the whole story are dead."

Dan broke every speed limit driving north toward the Canadian border. He knew Liss was all right. She'd been the one who'd called him and asked him to pick her up.

That didn't stop him worrying about her.

She'd given him a brief and somewhat garbled account of what had happened over the phone. Smugglers. Murder. Attempted Murder. Death. He didn't like the sound of any of that.

He wasn't real happy to hear she'd been in the thick of things in the company of Gordon Tandy, either.

But she was alive. He had to remember that. And when she'd needed someone to pick her up, since she didn't qualify for an ambulance ride and everyone else was tied up with "police business," she'd called him. Not Margaret. Not Angie or Patsy. Him.

He slowed to a crawl on the logging road and eased off the gas even more at the sight of flashing lights ahead. It was full dark. The strobes sent eerie shadows into the woods.

A uniformed state trooper showed him where to turn his truck around and pointed him in the right direction to find Liss. He stopped at the first glimpse of her, sitting in Pete's cruiser with shoulders slumped and head down.

Every harsh word he'd thought on the endless drive to get there flew out of his mind at the sight. She didn't need recriminations, or lectures. He went straight to her, pulled her out of the car and into his arms.

Ten minutes later they were on the road. He didn't ask any questions. He had no idea what to say. But when she eased closer, as close as their seat belts would allow, and rested her head on his shoulder, he slid that arm around her and didn't let go until they were both safely home.

Liss had been watching the police search Marcia's house for hours. What a way to spend the day before Christmas! She'd seen Gordon go in, but he hadn't so much as looked her way. Sherri had been in and out a couple of times. So had other officers she recognized.

It did no good to brood because she'd been left out of the loop, she told herself. Unfortunately, knowing a thing and accepting it were not the same.

Liss couldn't settle enough to read or watch television. She hadn't slept well the night before but she wasn't able to nap. She'd tried more than once and failed every time. The only thing she'd accomplished all day was to phone the vet and make an appointment to have the kitten, who still remained nameless, examined and vaccinated.

When Sherri showed up at her back door, carrying a box gaily wrapped in Christmas paper and sporting a big red bow, Liss welcomed her with open arms.

"Merry You-Know-What!" Sherri shoved the present into her arms and hurried into the kitchen, brushing snow off her coat. Big puffy flakes had started to fall around noon.

"Your gift is under the tree," Liss told her.

"I'd kill for a hot chocolate. And while you're fixing it you can tell me why you're home and not at the Emporium."

"I opened up as usual this morning. I had a couple of last minute mail orders to send out by express mail. Then I closed again." Liss busied herself at the kitchen counter, clamping down on the urge to demand that Sherri tell her what the police had found at Marcia's.

"No customers? I'd have thought you'd at least get a couple of ghouls." Divesting herself of hat, gloves, muffler, and coat, Sherri stood next to the heat vent rubbing her hands together to warm them.

"Oh, I did. That's *why* I locked the door. One of them was that obnoxious newspaper reporter from the Fallstown paper. He wouldn't stop badgering me even when I told him 'no comment.' And then, when he finally accepted that I meant it, he had the nerve to suggest I'd make a bundle if I sold souvenir sweatshirts. He even suggested what they should say." Liss made quotation marks in the air. "Moosetookalook: Murder Capitol of Maine."

Sherri groaned.

"I told him he had Moosetookalook confused with Cabot Cove."

"And we're nowhere *near* the coast," Sherri quipped.

Liss sighed and handed Sherri her drink. "How come there are still cops at Marcia's?"

Sherri met her eyes over the rim of the mug. She sipped, swallowed, and sipped some more. "Probably better you ask Gordon. I really just came over to see how you were doing."

"I doubt Gordon will tell me anything about the case. He's pretty ticked off at me. He thinks I lured him to that cabin under false pretenses."

"Uh, Liss—you did."

Liss shrugged. She really didn't want to talk about Gordon or what had happened yesterday. Not right now.

"Well, with Marcia dead, there won't be a trial, so I suppose there's no reason I can't tell you what we found. Nothing. No computer. No ledgers. No Tiny Teddies other than the ones in that backpack."

Liss frowned. That didn't seem right. Marcia had known all about online auctions. She must have had a computer.

In a flash, the explanation came to her. She reached across the table and took Sherri's mug away from her. "Time to go back to work," she told her friend. "You have a root cellar, aka panic room, to locate."

# Chapter Nineteen

A short time after Sherri left by the back way, Eric Moss showed up at Liss's front door. He jumped when she opened it, as if he was more surprised to find himself there than she was.

"You're back!" she exclaimed. "Where have you been?"

He didn't answer her question, but rather asked one of his own. "Is it true? Is Thorne dead? Marcia, too?"

"I'm afraid so."

Although he must have expected her response, it seemed to shake his composure. Spry no longer, he slumped. His sun-browned and weathered face took on such a curious pallor that for a moment Liss thought he might be about to keel over.

"She killed him?" The words came out as a hoarse croak.

Liss hesitated. "Maybe you should take your questions to the police."

A shudder passed through him, racking his lean frame. "Can't do that. No police. Not yet. Please. I have to know what's been happening here while I've been gone."

Taking pity on him, Liss stepped back and waved him into the foyer. "You'd better come in out of the cold."

Once they were in her living room, she helped him off with his coat, an old-style plaid hunting jacket, and told him to sit on the sofa. He looked harmless enough, but she was taking no chances. No more of this TSTL stuff!

Automatically, she punched in Dan Ruskin's cell phone number. Even as it rang, she wondered why she wasn't calling Gordon, or at least Sherri. The pathetic figure on her couch was not an innocent bystander. He might well prove dangerous.

Dan answered on the third ring.

"Can you come over for a few minutes?" Liss hoped her voice sounded calm. The last thing she wanted to do was alarm Dan. Or spook her visitor. "Eric Moss is here at the house."

Alarm flashed in Moss's eyes. "Who're you talking to? I told you—no cops!"

"Just Dan Ruskin, Mr. Moss. You don't mind if he joins us, do you?"

Moss frowned. His eyebrows nearly knit together with the effort. "Guess not. The Ruskins are good folk."

As soon as Liss hung up, she crossed to the bay window, from which she could both see and be seen, and stood next to the glass. Dan had said he could make the drive from his current work site to town in less than ten minutes. From this vantage point she'd see his truck as soon as he made the turn onto Birch Street.

She also had a clear view of Second Time Around and the police cruisers parked out front. That was reassuring. If she screamed for help, someone would probably come running.

Moss's eyes bored into her back. His tension was palpable and before Liss could think what to say to him, he broke. "Tell me! She did kill him, didn't she?"

Liss turned to face him. "It looks that way. But I'm not a cop, Mr. Moss. Why did you come to me for information?"

"This Tiny Teddies thing." Moss scowled at her. "That was *your* doing."

A flicker of fear flashed through her at his confrontational tone, but her own irritation quickly trumped it. She'd had enough of feeling guilty. "Now hold on just a darned minute! The *pageant* was my idea. Bringing business to Moosetookalook was my idea. But I didn't create the Tiny Teddies craze and I certainly didn't force anybody to break the law."

Moss's belligerence evaporated as if she'd popped it with a pin. "Things ain't been going so well for me lately," he muttered.

As an apology, it left a lot to be desired, but Liss was inclined to accept it anyway. Remembering her impressions of Moss's house, she thought she had him pegged. Poor but proud. Cantankerous, but a good man at heart. Law-abiding? About that, she wasn't so sure.

"How is it that you didn't already know about Gavin Thorne?" she asked. "He was shot the night of the snowstorm."

"I left town before that. Been away for over a week."

"Away where?"

He seemed to shrink into himself. Embarrassment? Shame? Liss couldn't tell and she had to strain to hear his answer: "Canada."

Liss felt her eyebrows rise, although she supposed she shouldn't be surprised. Their neighbor to the north seemed to be the destination of choice these days. "How did you get there?"

"Drove."

In spite of her intention to remain visible, Liss could not help but be moved by the utter dejection in his voice. She took a few steps closer to him. He had come back to Moosetookalook. He'd scarcely have done that if he'd committed a crime. He'd be on the run. Wouldn't he?

"Talk to me, Mr. Moss. Did you know that Marcia was smuggling Tiny Teddies into the U.S.?"

The look of misery on his craggy face was answer enough, but he pulled himself together and confirmed it aloud. "I do now. Should have suspected it from the first, when she paid me to front for her." He dropped his gaze to his clasped hands. "I needed the money, so I didn't ask questions."

"So the Tiny Teddies you offered to me, the ones that finally went to Gavin Thorne after Thorne's last bear was destroyed, came from Marcia?"

"She gave me two hundred dollars just to offer them to you first, then him."

"She wanted to keep suspicion away from herself while still making a profit," Liss murmured. "So, how did you figure out that Marcia had smuggled them in? They might have come from a legitimate source. In fact, you were insisting that they had the last time we talked."

"That's where Thorne came in. He wanted the bears, but he was suspicious about where they'd come from. Just like you were, only he insisted on knowing. I wouldn't have told, 'cept he offered me money, too. More money than Marcia paid me."

He looked thoroughly ashamed of himself, but Liss couldn't find it in her heart to condemn him. It wasn't easy to make ends meet with nothing but a social security check and your own wits.

"What happened when you told him you were selling the bears for Marcia?"

"Thorne got real excited. He reasoned it all out right while I was standing there, listening—what she'd been up to, even the route she must have used to bring Tiny Teddies into this country without getting caught."

"And you went home and took a look at the atlas and marked the spot."

Moss goggled at her. "Now how in tarnation did you know that?"

"Never mind. Did you use her route?"

He looked at her like she was crazy. "And mess up my truck?"

"Snowmobile? ATV?"

"Don't own either. Besides, what would I do for transportation on the other side? I just took off in old reliable. Spent a couple of days hunting up bears. Filled the back of the truck right up to the top of the cap. Thought I had it made."

"What happened?"

"Got stopped at Coburn Gore crossing. Border cops confiscated all the Tiny Teddies. Destroyed 'em!" He looked appalled at the waste. "And the worst part is that I've got to pay me a stiff fine."

"You're lucky you didn't end up in jail."

"I guess." He conceded the point with ill grace.

Liss wanted to pat him consolingly on the shoulder, but she didn't suppose he'd appreciate the gesture.

The squeal of brakes heralded Dan's arrival. Footsteps pounded up her walk and onto her porch. The door, which she'd deliberately left unlocked, crashed open.

"Liss! Where are you?"

"Here, Dan."

He burst into the living room.

"Relax. We're just talking."

Ignoring the thunderous look on Dan's face, she kept her focus on Eric Moss. He rose and dipped his head.

"'lo Ruskin. I was just leaving."

"Excellent plan." Scooping up Moss's jacket, Dan handed it to him.

"Wait a minute! Just one last question, Mr. Moss. What did Jason Graye pay you for the night of the last selectmen's meeting?"

Moss goggled at her. "You know about that, too?"

"Not as much as I'd like to. What did you do for him?"

"Nothing illegal," Moss insisted, all the while backing toward the foyer. "Just passed on some gossip I heard when I was picking over to West Fallstown."

"Translation: Graye made a killing in a real estate deal thanks to your insider information."

Dan winced at her choice of words, but Moss just got prickly. "Man's got to make a living. Ain't easy these days."

"How true." Liss had continued to keep an eye on Marcia's shop with periodic glances out her window. Now she saw Gordon Tandy emerge from the building. "Here's the deal, Mr. Moss. All you have to do to keep me quiet about your dealings with Graye is to tell that state police detective standing in front of Second Time Around everything you know about Marcia, Thorne, and the Tiny Teddies. You'll have to hurry if you want to catch him before he takes off."

Moss looked from Liss to Dan, crushing his wool watch cap in both hands. "Guess I gotta, huh?"

"It would be best." Dan gave the older man an encouraging smile.

Even before the front door clicked shut behind Eric Moss, Dan and Liss had crossed to the bay window. Together they watched Moss intercept Gordon, saw Gordon glance toward Liss's house and then, very deliberately, turn to face away from her.

Liss's sigh turned into a grimace. She'd been sighing entirely too much lately. Feeling sorry for herself accomplished nothing. Action—that was the ticket.

"You need me anymore?" Just a hint of irony tinged Dan's question. He didn't look angry with her, but he wasn't pleased, either.

Liss went up on her toes to brush her lips against his mouth. "Thank you. He wouldn't go to the police till he'd talked to me and I didn't want to take any chances by being alone with him."

Only slightly mollified, Dan turned the light kiss into something more. When he'd rendered her breathless, he stepped away. "I have to get back to work."

"I know. Later?"

"Later," he promised.

As soon as his footsteps died away on the front walk, Liss grabbed the phone and punched in the number of Sherri's cell. Trailing the extra-long cord behind her, she returned to the window.

"So? Did you find it?" Liss asked when Sherri picked up. She waved when she saw her friend, phone to ear, step out onto the porch at Second Time Around.

"Paydirt. Whoa! Is that Eric Moss talking to Gordon?"

"Yes. Exchange of info?"

"Give me five. I'll come to your back door."

Ten minutes later, Liss and Sherri were once more seated at Liss's kitchen table, this time with hot coffee and a plateful of Patsy's homemade doughnuts in front of them. Liss had already recapped what she'd learned from Eric Moss.

Liss bit into a cruller. "Your turn to spill."

"Well, first of all, we found Moss's atlas at Marcia's place. Had his name in the front and everything."

"So she was the one who broke in and searched his house while I was there."

Liss thought back. She'd mentioned something about Moss when she'd talked to Marcia earlier that evening. It had been right after she'd tried and failed to convince Gordon to get a search warrant. Had she told Marcia he hadn't cooperated? She rather thought she'd left the other woman with the impression that the police would be checking Moss's place out very soon. That must have spooked Marcia into going to his house to make sure he hadn't left any incriminating evidence lying around.

"One mystery solved. Did you find anything else?"

"Everything." Sherri looked quietly pleased with herself. "And I earned major points thanks to you. The panic room door was well hidden. Looked like a solid wall. But once we knew it was the old root cellar, it wasn't hard to find the way in."

"And?" Liss seethed with impatience while Sherri took another bite of a doughnut.

"Marcia had all her records stored there, and her computer. That last batch of Tiny Teddies, the ones she was bringing in yesterday? They'd been presold online. She would have shipped them out by express mail so they'd arrive just in time for Christmas."

"Her buyers must have been willing to pay through the nose for that service! Did she sell the bears she took from Thorne's shop online, too?"

"Yes. That's why no one spotted any of them in her shop. She listed them all, with the date. Each one was labeled 'liberated from The Toy Box.'"

Liss shook her head, half in sorrow, half in disbelief. Had they known Marcia at all?

Sherri snagged a jelly doughnut. "Also, ballistics matched the gun Marcia fired at you and Gordon with the bullet that killed Thorne. She was the murderer all right. Assuming Donna Conroy's testimony is accurate, it looks as if Thorne threatened to turn Marcia over to the police and got shot for his trouble."

"What about Donna? What will happen to her?"

"She's looking at more red tape and a lot of uncomfortable interviews, but given the publicity attached to this case, I wouldn't be surprised if she got permission to go home to her husband and kids when it's over."

"Maybe Gordon will put in a good word for her."

Sherri considered the notion. "She did save your lives and help him wrap up the case, but it might not occur to him to give her a hand. Why don't you mention it to him the next time you see him?"

"You'd better do it. Gordon isn't too happy with me right now."

"Let me guess—you told him you broke into Moss's house?"

"That's the least of it." Liss hesitated. She'd been brooding about what had happened, keeping her gloomy thoughts to herself. Maybe it was time to talk things through with someone who would understand and sympathize.

"After the snowmobile crash, Gordon would barely speak to me. He gave me the space blankets and told me to wait with Donna and literally turned his back." Just as he had a few minutes ago when he was talking with Eric Moss. "I think he blames me for what happened."

"Nonsense. You ought to get a medal."

"I blame me, too, Sherri. Oh, not because of my part in promoting Moosetookalook and the Tiny Teddies and the pageant. I've worked my way through that guilt trip. But if I hadn't chased after Marcia, she'd still be alive."

"You weren't alone on that sled."

"I was the one driving, *and* the one getting a rush out of the whole thing."

The thrill of speeding through the wilds, the challenge of overtaking another driver—what had she thought she was doing, drag racing? Her impulsive behavior had been just about as stupid. It appalled her to remember how energized she'd felt, how invincible.

Sherri had a peculiar look on her face. She toyed with a loose yellow curl and said nothing.

"What?"

"I repeat. You weren't alone on that sled."

"Gordon *tried* to stop me. I realize that now. It wasn't his fault that the engine noise was so loud that I couldn't hear him tell me to slow down."

Sherri gave a derisive snort. "I don't know a lot about snowmobiles, but I do know he could have put an end to the chase at any time by reaching around you and hitting the kill switch. Or he could have employed the even simpler means of letting go and falling off the sled. You know you wouldn't have left him there."

Liss opened her mouth to deny Sherri's logic but it was irrefutable.

"I'll bet that's why he's in such a testy mood," Sherri continued. "He's beating himself up because he let you keep going. From his point of view, he put *you* at risk."

"If that's true, then he has all the more reason to reexamine our personal relationship. Why would he want to be involved with someone who not only deceives him but brings out the worst in him?"

Sherri rolled her eyes. "I give up. Believe what you like. I still think you're going to get at least one marriage proposal tomorrow, all wrapped up in Santa Claus paper. So, did you open your present from me yet?"

Liss blinked, tried to change gears to keep up with Sherri, and ended up blurting, "But it's not Christmas yet."

"Close enough. Besides, it's a gag gift—sort of—and you look like you need a grin." Dragging Liss into the living room, Sherri located the package she'd brought over earlier and hauled it out from underneath the tree. She pushed it into Liss's unresisting grasp. "Open it!"

Lumpkin and Nameless appeared at the first rustle of paper. Liss tossed them the ribbon and worked the tape loose at one end of the wrapping. It was pretty paper, silver snowflakes on a blue background, and only when she'd salvaged it did she look at the logo on the box.

Sherri's grin widened, as did Liss's eyes when she recognized the design. It belonged to a shop in Fallstown that handled a very special type of intimate apparel.

"You didn't!"

Sherri smirked.

Liss opened the box and peeked cautiously inside. Nestled in bordello-red tissue paper was a scrap of black silk.

"I couldn't resist," Sherri confessed. "I bought you your very own tiny teddy."

On Christmas morning, Liss came blearily awake to the familiar sound of bagpipes.

Very loud bagpipes.

Bagpipes being played directly underneath her bedroom window.

She stumbled out of bed and across the room. The window stuck, half frozen in place, but finally yielded to her efforts. She jerked on the tabs that held the screen in place, removed it, and stuck her head out into the crisp December air.

Gordon Tandy stood below in full piper's regalia. He didn't stop playing when he saw her. He went on to complete the tune, one she didn't recognize. That might have been because she wasn't familiar with it . . . or because Gordon was playing so badly. It didn't matter. She understood the gesture.

Grinning ear to ear, Liss gave him a thumbs up. She couldn't have asked for a better Christmas present. The bagpipe serenade beneath her window meant he'd forgiven her for tricking him into that snowmobile trip. It also meant he'd resolved to find time to practice the hobby he'd neglected for so long, just as she'd told him she hoped he would.

"Be right down," she called when he lowered his pipes.

Her words were nearly drowned out by Stu Burroughs's irate bellow. "Stop that racket!" he yelled. "People are trying to sleep!"

Liss laughed aloud. Families with children, like the Hogencamps, had probably been up for hours. And Aunt

Margaret, her nearest neighbor, would be the last person in the world to complain about bagpipe music, even badly played.

Of its own volition, her gaze darted across the corner of the town square to Dan's house. There was no sign of activity there. If he had heard the early morning concert, he was ignoring it.

"Later," he'd said yesterday. But he hadn't come back, nor had he called.

Liss delayed only long enough to run a brush through her hair and slip into underwear and the wool slacks and off-white cashmere sweater—imported from Scotland—that she'd laid out the night before. A bright green scarf with holly and ivy embroidered along the edges dressed up the square neckline.

She was halfway down the stairs before it struck her that Gordon might have meant the musical performance to be a romantic gesture. He'd come out at the crack of dawn after working nonstop to wrap up a murder case, and after he'd been wounded, too. He still wore a bandage on his forehead.

The smile on her face felt a trifle forced as she unlocked her front door and invited Gordon in.

"Thanks. My knees were about to turn to ice."

She glanced at the knees in question. Very nice knees. The back view wasn't bad either as he preceded her into the living room. The swaying tartan fabric of the kilt had a mesmerizing effect.

Or maybe she just needed coffee.

"Do you actually have Christmas Day off?" she blurted, unable to think of anything more clever to say.

"All day. Knock wood." He rapped on the oak table by the sofa as he passed it.

"I'll put the coffee on."

She bolted. She'd gotten a kick out of being awakened

by a bagpipe serenade, but she had no idea what to expect next. The only thing she knew for certain was that it was definitely Gordon in her living room, not Officer Tandy.

"What an inventive Christmas present," she said when she returned a short time later carrying two steaming mugs.

She'd intended to sit next to him but both cats were already on the sofa, Lumpkin on the back and the kitten beside Gordon. He was absently stroking her thick, black fur, eliciting a purr of sheer delight. Liss took the chair opposite.

"I'm glad you liked it. I'm still pretty rusty."

Liss hid her smile. "You'll get better with more practice." He'd won piping competitions years ago. She was certain it wouldn't take him long to regain his former skill.

Liss set her coffee aside and went to the Christmas tree. "I have a gift for you, too."

She'd selected an Aran sweater from the Emporium's stock. Gordon seemed pleased with her choice, even a little relieved. So much for Sherri's theory that he planned to propose marriage!

They finished their coffee in companionable silence. Gordon put down his empty mug and glanced at his watch. "I'd better get a move on. It's a long drive back to Waycross Springs."

Liss rose when he did, a little surprised he was leaving so soon. She walked him to the door. "Drive safe. The weather forecast is for more snow."

He turned to her in the foyer. She expected him to kiss her. When he didn't, she frowned.

"Is something . . . bothering you, Gordon?"

He didn't meet her eyes. "Looks like I've got to leave the area for a while. I've been selected for special training out of state. I just found out yesterday. I'll be on my way next week and be gone for three months."

Liss had no idea what to say to that. "Congratulations?"

He gave a snort of laughter and the tension broke. "Yeah. Well. I guess we'll see what we'll see when I get back. Take care of yourself in the meantime."

"If you say 'stay out of trouble,' I'll have to hurt you."

"Then I won't." He didn't kiss her good-bye, either. He just gave her a long, steady look, as if he were memorizing her features, and walked out her door.

Liss wandered back into the living room, wondering why she didn't feel more bereft. Instead she was in a mellow mood. She turned the tree lights on and began to hum "White Christmas." She was way off-key, but the cats didn't care.

Gordon wasn't angry with her. That was what she'd focus on. She suspected now that they'd never been destined for romance, at least not on her end, but she was glad they were friends again.

No more than forty-five minutes after Gordon left, someone knocked at Liss's front door. She'd had time to scramble eggs and make toast and consume them together with more coffee and a large glass of orange juice. Thus fortified, she let Dan Ruskin in.

"Merry Christmas." He pulled her directly into his arms for a smoldering kiss.

"Well! Merry Christmas to you, too."

"I'm here to drive you to the hotel for Christmas dinner."

"Okay." She and Margaret had been invited to The Spruces as Joe Ruskin's guests.

"And to give you your present."

Belatedly, she realized that he'd left a large, gaily wrapped parcel sitting on the porch. A *very* large parcel. Definitely *not* an engagement ring. Not unless he was doing one of those little boxes inside larger boxes tricks, and that didn't strike her as something Dan would do.

She passed him his present—a sweater similar to the one

she'd selected for Gordon—and set to work on the tape holding the paper over the oddly shaped gift. When the wrapping was off, she still wasn't sure what it was.

"It's a back-of-the-door bookcase. You said the other day that you didn't have enough space for all your books, so I built this for you."

Imagine him remembering that! "It's wonderful. Thank you."

The kitten clambered up the shelves to perch on top. Lumpkin eyed Dan's ankle. Liss scooped him up before he could bite.

"I have something to ask you," Dan said as he finished unwrapping his sweater. "Hey, this is nice. Thanks."

Liss felt her breath back up in her throat. She held Lumpkin tighter, turning him into a shield. Had Sherri been right, after all?

"Seems the local Scottish heritage society's Burns Night Supper in January is going to be held at The Spruces," Dan said.

Liss blinked at him, confused. That didn't sound like the opening line of a marriage proposal.

"Margaret has her hands full with all the other new things she's planning for the hotel, so we were wondering, Dad and I, if you'd be willing to do us a favor and help with some of the preparations. You can bring all that Scottish stuff from the Emporium out to the hotel to sell to the dinner guests."

"Burns Night? The annual celebration to honor poet Robert Burns? The night when all Scots pretend they actually like the taste of haggis?"

"That's the one."

Relief had her chuckling to herself. "Well, sure. Glad to. Why not?"

Dan gave her an odd look, making her wonder what he'd heard in her voice. "Great. Thanks."

He got her coat out of the closet and helped her into it, his fingers lingering on her neck as he lifted her hair out of the way.

Burns night, Liss thought, leaning against him for just a moment and savoring the closeness. *That* she had no problem saying yes to. As to anything else? Only time would tell.

# A Wee Bit More on the Daft Days

## (A Note from Kaitlyn Dunnett)

I've always loved the song "The Twelve Days of Christmas." Mixing the entertainments based on each day's gifts with some of the holiday traditions drawn from Liss MacCrimmon's Scottish heritage seemed to me a good way to give *A Wee Christmas Homicide* more holiday flavor.

Among the other titles I considered for this book were *Homicide at Hogmanay* and *Death in the Daft Days*, but there were two difficulties with both. One was that most people wouldn't know what Hogmanay or the Daft Days are. The other was that neither Hogmanay nor the Daft Days are celebrated on Christmas.

The Daft Days are the entire period from Christmas to Twelfth Night—the twelve days of Christmas—and were once (before the Reformation) a time of revelry celebrated with festivities similar to those in England.

Hogmanay refers to New Year's Eve. No one knows for certain where the name came from, but from the time of John Knox until the 1950s, nearly 400 years, celebrating Christmas was illegal in Scotland, banned by order of the

Reformed Church. Instead, gifts were exchanged to celebrate the beginning of the new year. In today's Edinburgh and Glasgow, huge street parties are held on Hogmanay.

Other Scottish traditions, too, have long associations with the date. December 31st was the day to clean house and settle debts—before midnight. After midnight, homeowners still hope that the first person to set foot in the house will be a dark-haired man, as that brings good luck for the coming year. This "first footer" traditionally brings gifts—coal, shortbread, salt, black bun, and whiskey. In some areas of Scotland, ceilidhs (dances) and torchlight processions are held. Among more recent traditions is the singing of "Auld Lang Syne" at midnight. The song was made famous by poet Robert Burns in 1788 but had been around in earlier versions for at least eighty years before that. "Auld lang syne" means "times gone by."

Black bun, one of the gifts brought by first footers, is also associated with Twelfth Night (January 6, the end of the Yuletide season). Most Americans would call this a fruitcake. Shortbread and venison stew are also traditional Hogmanay foods.

For all that Liss MacCrimmon's family originally came from Scotland, however, Liss is not Scottish. She's a Scottish-American woman living in Maine who has no qualms about combining New England Christmas customs with those of Hogmanay and the Daft Days. Her Christmas includes a tree in the parlor, stockings filled with treats for each of the cats, turkey on the table, with perhaps a choice of ham or roast beef, and mashed potatoes, fresh-baked dinner rolls, and an assortment of vegetables. There are pies for dessert, both apple and pumpkin, and Christmas cookies shaped like stars, snowflakes, snowmen, Christmas trees, and Santa Claus. Since Liss is a native Mainer, there is likely to be one other treat, as well—homemade whoopie pies.